Novel

CW00326319

SOUND OF THE SEA

Leo Walmsley by Selina Walmsley Craze.

Sound of the Sea

Leo Walmsley

Foreword by Stephanie Walmsley

First published in 1959 by Collins.

This edition published in 1996 by
Smith Settle Ltd
Ilkley Road
Otley
West Yorkshire
LS21 3JP

ISBN   1 85825 074 9
1 85825 075 7

British Library Cataloguing-in-Publication data:
A catalogue record for this book is available from the British Library.

Printed and bound by
SMITH SETTLE
Ilkley Road, Otley, West Yorkshire LS21 3JP

Foreword

The action and characters in this story are told through the eyes of a small boy. This adds greatly to the charm of the book, set in the village of Robin Hood's Bay between Scarborough and Whitby, on the Yorkshire coast.

The boy lives with his parents in a cottage on the edge of the North Cliff, where, years previously, part of the road had fallen into the sea. During a North East gale he wonders if their cottage will also fall into the sea. Brave and endearing, the little boy struggles to be part of the village gang, the 'Bramblewick Bumpers'. He is up against conflict. His mother is a good, church-going woman, anxious to protect her son against the rough village lads. But he wants to join them, banging his drum and waving his flag as they march up the hill on Mafeking Night. He wants to do dangerous things; climb cliffs for birds' eggs, go fishing far out on the scars when the tide is coming in fast.

These are the days when the village doctor rode on his horse to his patients, where the local vicar would give a boy a thrashing for throwing stones, and the policeman carried a truncheon and a pair of cufflinks. Days when there was great loyalty to the queen and her family, and people shared each others' troubles.

Life in this village called 'Bramblewick', with its delightful red-roofed cottages and cobbled alleyways, is dominated by the sound of the sea, the sound of great waves breaking on the cliffs like thunder, waves rushing up the slipway into the dock. There is so much atmosphere; the fishermen sitting by their firesides listening to the roar of the wind and sea, the village lads playing tip cat and marbles, the girls dancing round the maypole. There is great excitement during a terrible storm when the rocket goes off and the lifeboat crew have to pull with all their strength to reach the ship in distress.

The boy has his own adventures, out hunting for crabs and lobsters and nearly meeting disaster.

The vicar, a stalwart, noble character, is greatly respected in the village and regarded almost like a king. He too has his adventures, with strange, frightening things going on at the vicarage one night.

The characters are real, and vividly described in this story, set at the turn of the century. You feel for the boy's struggling artist father and hope he will sell enough paintings to make a living. You admire his tender-hearted mother and her high principles, and when the boy finds a stray dog you long for him to be allowed to keep it.

There is not a dull moment in this book, and the reader may feel he has stepped back in time to those days, so far off now, in this captivating village by the sea.

Stephanie Walmsley
Deal, Kent
October 1996

For

STEPHANIE, SELINA
AND SHAWN

I HAVE a photograph, very faded, taken in Bramblewick Dock from the slipway top showing in a space between the hauled-up fishing cobles and stacks of lobster pots, a group of boys of various ages.

They are a rough-looking lot. Most of them are wearing jerseys and short trousers with long black stockings. Some have home-made jackets over their jerseys. Some have only shirts, with their braces showing. Two boys are almost in rags with bare legs and feet. One boy (and he is the smallest in the group) is in knickerbockers with an incongruous Jack Tar jacket.

Each boy wears or carries something which shows that this is a special occasion: a paper billycock hat, a toy bandolier, a wooden sword, a wooden gun. One boy has a ship's bell, another an ox horn (one was always kept in each coble for use in fog) another a wooden rattle, like the ones the coconut-shy men had at Bramblewick Fair.

Several boys hold flags in their hands. On their jackets or jerseys, where soldiers wear their medal ribbons, are numbers of button-like discs. But the photograph is not clear enough to show that these discs are themselves photographic reproductions of the faces of heroes of the South African war : Lord Roberts, General Buller, General French, Lord Methuen, Sir George White, Gatacre, Kelly-Kenny, Baden-Powell, and of course Lord Kitchener.

All the boys save one are staring frozenly at the camera. It would have been a time exposure, and they have been warned by the photographer to keep still. The exception is the little boy with the Jack Tar jacket. He has moved slightly but you can see that he is smiling. He has a chubby puckish face. He has no hat. His hair is fair, and a tuft of it grows up straight at one side of his forehead, like a brush with half of its bristles gone. He has a sturdy body.

Tied with a piece of string to his waist is a sword made of two laths. He has a tin can supported by another piece of string for a drum, a drum stick in one hand, a small Union Jack in the other.

To me that photograph is like a scene from a movie when the projector has stopped. I have only to look at it, close my eyes, and the projector starts again, everything becomes alive, the characters move, speak, shout, wave their flags. I hear the sound of the sea, the cries of the gulls wheeling over the house tops, and I am that little boy, banging my tin can drum, waving my flag, shouting :

" Long live the Queen ! Down with Kruger ! Hooray— hooray ! "

This was Mafeking Day, May 1900.

I

It was a wonderful day. Although the war wasn't over, the wicked old Kruger and the cruel Boers had been licked again. And serve them right for daring to twist the British lion's tail! The soldiers of the Queen had won, as they always would, for they were the bravest soldiers in the world. They had beaten the Russians in the Crimean War, and the Indians in the Indian mutiny, and the natives in the Soudan who had murdered General Gordon, as well as many fierce savage tribes who had dared to dispute British rule.

One day I was going to be a soldier, wear a scarlet tunic, carry a real sword, a rifle with a bayonet, a revolver and a bandolier of ammunition and fight for the Queen, perhaps win the Victoria Cross, like Lord Roberts's son had done for trying to save the guns at Colenso; but I hoped that unlike him I would live to have the Cross pinned on my breast by the Queen herself.

I was not the only one to think like this, although most of the Bramblewick lads would go to sea when they left school, like their fathers. We were all proud that on the large map of the world which hung in our school-room so many countries and parts of countries were coloured red, showing that they either belonged to or were ruled over by Queen Victoria, Empress of India.

If it hadn't been for the Boston Tea Party, and that was before Queen Victoria's reign, the whole of the United States as well as Canada would have been coloured red too. And anyway the Americans were British really. They still spoke the English language.

9

The boy who carried the ship's bell was Ikey Harris. Although he wasn't the oldest or biggest among us, he was the boss.

Mother thought that Ikey was a very bad character. He was always fighting or egging other boys on to fight. He was cheeky and used bad language. He was always getting into mischief, and leading others into mischief.

But she was very sorry for his mother who was a widow. Her husband and three other sons had been sailors, and all of them had been drowned or died in foreign parts. She was afraid that Ikey would want to go to sea when he left school and that the same thing would happen to him.

Ikey was clever at the game of pin-and-button. This had to be played after dark. Very stealthily, one end of a reel of cotton was pinned to the top of the frame of somebody's living-room window. To the cotton, a foot or so down from the pin, was tied a heavy button, and the other end of the cotton was led away to a hiding-place.

When everything was fixed the cotton was pulled to and fro so that the button rattled on the pane. When the victim, usually some old person living alone, opened the door to see what it was, the boys stopped pulling, and started again when the door was shut.

Mother didn't like me to have anything to do with Ikey Harris, but I thought he was wonderful.

He had a freckly face, big white teeth and fierce eyes. He wasn't afraid of anyone, excepting perhaps the Vicar and everyone was afraid of him. He could fight and beat any of the village boys. He would climb the steepest and most dangerous cliff for seagull eggs. I had once seen him run along the causeway under the coastguard station wall when there was a rough sea breaking over it. He chose a moment when a big wave had broken and was sweeping back to meet another incoming one that was even bigger, and that wave would certainly have washed him away if he had faltered or slipped.

Ikey would call me rude names, and often clout me, but I was very happy if he allowed me to join in any of the games he got up, like football, with a sheep's bladder for ball, or cricket, with home-made bats, and stones or an old lobster pot for wickets, or shinny ower, which was a sort of hockey in which our sticks were made from the thick stems of tangles with their nobbly ends shorn of fronds so that they were like clubs. It was called shinny ower, because if a player got on the wrong side of the ball you were allowed to whack him on the shins with your stick. You didn't do this if your opponent was Ikey himself, or another big boy.

As I had to be home soon after dusk in winter-time I hadn't much chance of joining in Ikey's games like pin-and-button. But this was Mafeking Day, and this was going to be Mafeking Night. There was going to be a torchlight procession, round the village and Up-bank to the new houses, and to Thorpe. The brass band would be playing. There was going to be a bon-fire on the beach. An old coble was going to be set on fire with a barrel of tar from the gas-works, and Doctor Whittle, who had been in the Navy and served with Lord Charles Beresford on the *Condor* in the bombardment of Alexandria (this had been in another war which we had won) was getting a lot of fireworks to let off.

I wasn't going to miss any of this if I could help it !

Our gathering in the dock was only a start. It was Ikey's idea that we should have a procession of our own round the village. He went first of course, ringing his bell and striking up " Soldiers of the Queen." We followed in a mob. But there were songs just as popular as " Soldiers of the Queen," like " Good-bye Dolly Gray," and " Won't you Come Home Bill Bailey," and every boy sang the song he liked or knew best, or just shouted or whistled.

The dock was the only open space in the village itself. From it the slipway slanted down to the beach between the coastguard station and the Bay Inn.

The lifeboat house stood on the left side of the dock, facing the slipway top. Above the lifeboat house were rows of houses, each row higher than the other, for they had been built on the slopes of a ravine, and it was the same on the other side of the dock, only here the ground was steeper, for it rose to the edge of the North Cliff, and the houses were packed close together, with only narrow cobbled alleys running between the rows except for one called Chapel Street, which had been a cart road until a part of it had fallen into the sea.

Including the Bay Inn, there were three pubs in the dock. There was The Fisherman's Arms, opposite to the lifeboat house and The Robin Hood Tavern where the dock narrowed and the road began. The road followed the course of a covered-in beck to where a tunnel opened into the ravine, which it crossed by a stone bridge. On the same side as The Robin Hood Tavern was the fried-fish shop, and Neddy Peacock's coal warehouse, and on the other side the bakehouse, where many of the villagers took their joints to be cooked on a Sunday.

Like the Bay Inn and The Fisherman's Arms, The Robin Hood was open and full of customers. Most of them were sailors, having a holiday from their ships, and with plenty of money to spend. They were making too much noise themselves to take any notice of us. A lot of them would be drunk already, and there was sure to be some fighting in the dock after closing-time, another exciting thing to look forward to. Perhaps the police sergeant would have to lock someone up !

Neddy Peacock was supposed to be one of the richest men in the village, but he was also the meanest. He was a real miser. He'd do anything to make money. He had a big garden up on the cliff, and he'd sell vegetables from a stall in front of the coal-house, and he'd always charge top prices for everything. He'd always try to be " first-on " along the beach after a storm, picking up driftwood, which he would saw and chop into sticks, and sell in little bundles.

Although he wasn't a real fisherman he went salmon-fishing in the summer months.

Neddy was in his warehouse now, shovelling coal on to a weighing machine. He was an ugly man. He reminded me of a picture I had seen of a gorilla for he was very broad, with bent shoulders, and very long arms and bow legs. He was black with coal dust, which made the whites of his eyes, and his few big front teeth look whiter than ever. He didn't take any notice of us, and Ikey made us stop marching, and he cheekily shouted at Neddy :

" Eh—Neddy, haven't you heard the news ? England's cap-
tured Mafeking. We've beaten Mr. Kruger. Haven't you got
a flag to hang out ? "

Neddy glared at him :

" You cheeky young beggar. You want your backside braying ! "

" Listen to him ! " Ikey mocked, imitating Neddy's voice.
" You want your backside braying. You want your backside
braying. Come on, lads, give him a shout, all together, *awd
Neddy Peacock—awd Neddy Peacock !* "

We all shouted, but I was careful to keep well out of Neddy's
way, and I hoped that he hadn't noticed that I was shouting, for
I was very much afraid of him. He looked angry but he just
went on shovelling his coal, and then Ikey rang his bell again,
and started singing " Soldiers of the Queen," and the procession went on.

We reached the bridge. Just on the other side an alley branched
off the road to the right, leading up some steps and then back
along the edge of the ravine, past the Wesleyan Chapel and our
school, and then into Chapel Street which ran down into the dock
again. In Chapel Street was Dad's shop, and our cottage, whose
back was almost on the edge of the North Cliff which fell straight
down to the sea.

At the bottom of Chapel Street, near the dock, was the
post office stores, kept by Mr. Thompson who like Neddy
Peacock was a Wesleyan and a teetotaller and very stingy.

I thought that Ikey would be leading along this alley, and I
had decided that when we got to the top of Chapel Street, I
would turn back and join the procession in the dock again in
case Mother should see me with Ikey, and call me in. But Ikey
halted us, and made a speech :

" Eh, lads," he said. " What about marching up to Thorpe,
and knocking hell out of some of them Thorpe cloggers. There's
bound to be a few of them about, with their school on holiday
too. They're always cheeking us. Let's go and knock hell out
of them ! What do you say ? "

There was a standing quarrel between the boys of Bramble-

wick and the boys of Thorpe. Nearly all the boys of Bramblewick
were the sons of either fishermen or sailors. Those of Thorpe
were mostly farmers' sons. They didn't wear jerseys, but cor-
duroys which stank, and they wore clogs in winter. We called
them Thorpe cloggers, and they called us Bay bumpers. If ever
a boy from Bramblewick went to Thorpe and a clogger saw him
there'd be a fight straight away, and the same thing happened if a
clogger ventured into our village, unless his father happened to
be with him, in which case we'd just call after him, " Thorpe
clogger, Thorpe clogger."

I had never dared to go to Thorpe by myself, but I shouted
now as loudly as any of our gang :

" Aye—aye. Let's go ! "

" All right," cried Ikey. " But no stone throwing remember,
unless they start first, and no kicking. Only fists. If we see Joe
Pickering, I'll have a go at him. He put his fingers to his nose
at me last time I saw him, but only because he was in his father's
horse and trap ! "

We moved on, passing Barff's shop where you could buy the
pin-on buttons of war generals for a ha'penny each, and fish
hooks, and marbles and tops, penny lucky-bags, aniseed balls,
liquorice bootlaces and a sticky sweet called lasting stripes, and on
the opposite side, the Laurel Inn which was also full of customers.

Next, on the same side as the Inn, was the blacksmith's shop,
but it was closed, for Jack Martin the smith who played the trombone in the brass band would be in the pub. Here the road
turned to the left and then to the right again and became very
steep. This was Bramblewick Bank, which had stone steps on
one side of it, with a long wooden seat at the top for old people
to rest when they got out of breath, through climbing the steps.

When you got to the top you had a wonderful view. You
could look down and see the whole village, but you couldn't see
any of the alleys, or even the road because the houses on each
side of the ravine were too close together. You could just see the
red roofs and the chimney pots, and parts of the stone walls of
the houses, except on the edge of the North Cliff where there
were no other houses to hide them. Many of the houses here,

like the end of Chapel Street had already fallen down the cliff into the sea, and when there was a bad storm and great waves were breaking against the cliff I would be frightened that ours would go too.

But what you could see best from the bank top was the bay itself. The shore and the cliff made a big curve, with the cliffs getting higher and higher to High Batts, which made one end of the bay. If the tide was down you could see the scars running out a long way from the shore and curving like the bay itself.

Two of these scars reached straight out from the village and made the Fishermen's Landing, and they had long posts fixed to them to mark them when the tide was up. In rough weather all the cobles would be hauled up into the dock for the whole bay would be white with breakers, which roared like a great waterfall.

From High Batts's top the land rose even higher into rounded hills which were covered with heather, to a hill called Stoupe Brow.

The land between the hills and the lower cliffs was nearly level and this was where most of the farms were, although there were woods too in the valleys of two becks.

You couldn't see the village of Thorpe from the bank top because the new houses and the new church and the railway station were in the way. The lane that led to it went past the new church and the vicarage where the vicar lived.

Although Dad was a sidesman and went to church twice every Sunday, and had to take round one of the collection bags while the organ was playing, I didn't go very often, and I was glad, for I didn't like it. It was too solemn. I was always terrified of the vicar. Whenever I saw him in the village, I used to run away, and he looked more terrifying still in church with his robes on, especially when he stood at the lectern, which was made of brass in the shape of an eagle with its wings outstretched and its claws seeming to be tearing at some poor animal.

I didn't like the way the congregation kept on bobbing up and down, and repeating things after the vicar from the prayer book, and singing things that weren't hymns, in a solemn voice. They did sing hymns of course, but never ones I knew, like the

ones sung in the Wesleyan chapel, or they were sung in such a
way that you didn't recognise the tune.

I didn't like going to chapel very much and was glad that
Mother only took me to the evening service. But it was never
so solemn there, and neither the preacher nor the choir wore
surplices, and the preacher read the lessons or prayed or gave his
sermon from an ordinary pulpit. In church all the pews were on
the same level, and you could only see the people who were in
front of you. In chapel the rows of pews were arranged one above
the other, so that you could see everyone who was there and watch
them and think about them, and sometimes laugh to yourself
if you thought they looked funny, like Neddy Peacock, or a girl
called Fanny Stevens who had St. Vitus's Dance, and used to
keep on twitching her nose as though a fly was tickling it.

We turned into Church Lane. I wasn't frightened about
going to Thorpe and having a fight with the Thorpe cloggers.
Thorpe was only a small village, and even if all the boys were there
there wouldn't be as many as us. Besides I knew that Ikey would
be a match for anyone.

But we had a surprise. The new church was on the right-hand
side of the lane. Almost opposite on the left-hand side was the
vicarage, but beyond the church the lane curved round to pass
under the railway. Just before we reached the vicarage, some
boys, waving flags, came round the corner. One of them was
leading a donkey, and, tied to the donkey's back was a dummy
made of a stuffed sack with clothes on it. It had legs and arms
and a head, with an old hat. The face was made of white cloth,
and eyes and nose were painted on it. Round the chin was some
frayed rope to make it look like a beard. It was meant to be
President Kruger.

Ikey stopped us. There were more boys behind the donkey.
Like us they were dressed up, and they were carrying wooden
swords and guns, and they had tin cans for drums, and they were
singing and shouting. The boy leading the donkey was Joe
Pickering. He had in his hand a brass hunter's horn which must
have belonged to his father, who was huntsman of the foxhound
pack.

Joe blew the horn as the procession drew near, and he shouted at the top of his voice :

" Tally-ho ! "

They were only about the length of a cricket pitch away from us. I knew that if I had been by myself, I would have turned and run as fast as I could go. But Ikey didn't look a bit frightened. He said :

" Eh—it's the Thorpe cloggers ! It's saved us the trouble of going up to meet them. We're not going to let 'em pass. That's meant to be awd Kruger they've got on the donkey. We ought to have had one for the bonfire to-night, like Guy Fawkes. I reckon we'll bag that one. Come on lads. Let's give 'em hell, but leave Joe Pickering to me ! " and he started singing again, " Its the soldiers of the Queen my boys, the Queen my boys, the Queen my boys."

We marched on, and the Thorpe cloggers marched on too, until there was only a short space between Ikey and Joe and the donkey, and we were then at the vicarage gate. The vicarage stood back from the lane.

Both sides halted, and the noise stopped. Ikey and Joe faced each other. Gow Pickering, Joe's father, was a farmer of course, and he was the tallest man I had ever seen. He was almost a giant, and Joe, although he was younger than Ikey, was very tall and strong. And he was brave too. He didn't look frightened, although he must have known there was going to be a fight. He had plenty of other boys with him, and they all looked strong, but there was nearly twice as many in our procession. He just smiled at Ikey, but Ikey was sneering, and he said :

" Where do you think *you* b——s are off to ? "

" That's our business," Joe answered. " We're not asking you where you're off to ! "

" Less of your lip," said Ikey. " You're not coming any farther along this lane. You're not coming down Bramblewick Bank."

" Who wants to ? Bramblewick stinks of fish. We're going round the new houses, and we're going to have a bonfire to-night on Thorpe Green and burn old Kruger."

B

" If Bramblewick stinks of fish, that's not so bad as stinking
of cow muck like you Thorpe cloggers do. Cow muck and cor-
duroys ! You pulled a face at me, last time I saw you but you
had your father with you. Will you pull a face at me now ? Spit
ower, if you want a fight and then get your coat off."

" Spitting ower " was always the first thing you did when
you were going to have a proper fight. You put your left hand
under your chin and spat on the ground in front of the other boy.
Then you had to say, very quickly :

" *Here's yan on thi' lug, and yan on thi' mug, and there's yan to
start with*," and the fight would begin.

Ikey spat over. Joe called to one of the cloggers to hold the
donkey's halter, then he took off his jacket, rolled up his sleeves,
and spat over, but neither of them waited to say the rhyme.
They just went for each other. We all gathered round them in a
sort of ring, but giving them plenty of space, and we all shouted,
the cloggers for Joe, and we for Ikey, egging them on.

We had no rules, like real boxers have, except that there must
be no biting, or hitting below the belt. There were no rounds.
You just went on fighting until one boy was beaten, and it looked
as though this fight was going to go on a long time, for although
Joe was slower than Ikey, he was bigger and stronger and he
actually made Ikey's nose bleed a bit with one blow. But I knew
that Ikey would win in the end, and I shouted as loud as any
boy :

" Go on, Ike. Hit him. Hit him ! "

And then one of the cloggers without spitting ower suddenly
turned on me, pulled off my drum and gave me a smack across
the face. I hit him back of course and we started to fight, and
other boys started fighting too, so we couldn't tell what was
happening between Ikey and Joe. It was a real battle, with some
boys shouting and some boys crying, because they were hurt
and beaten.

It must have been one of the beaten boys who started throwing
stones. I don't think it was one from our side, because of what
Ikey had said. And I certainly didn't throw any. I was fighting
with my fists, and although I wasn't winning I was giving the

clogger who had smacked my face as good as he was giving me, and I also punched another clogger who joined in.

But someone was throwing stones. There were plenty of loose ones in the lane. Whoever it was he must have been a bad shot. For a stone hit one of the windows of the vicarage, and there was a loud crash of broken glass. And at that moment, the door of the vicarage opened, and there was the vicar himself, with a big stick in his hand.

I was lucky not to be by the door, for he seized the nearest boy by the scruff of the neck and whacked his backside, and then caught another. There was no more fighting. We were like a flock of terrified sheep attacked by a savage dog. We ran, every boy for himself, the Thorpe cloggers with their donkey galloping back to Thorpe and we back for our own village. Not until we had turned the corner of the lane did we stop. And it was only then that I saw that Ikey, with his nose still bleeding a bit, and one of his eyes swelled up, was holding Mr. Kruger in his arms.

2

ALTHOUGH MY face was sore with the smack the clogger boy had given me, and I had one or two bruises on my body, I wasn't bleeding, and my clothes weren't dirty, or torn, and Mother didn't ask me any awkward questions when I got home for tea. I was afraid that if she had found out that I had been with Ikey, and that we'd been fighting the cloggers actually outside the vicarage, she would have been upset, and would not let me go to the bonfire.

In spite of her never going to church, she respected the vicar, and thought that he was a very kind man. Once, when she had been ill, he called at our house and brought her a basket full of invalid foods, like calves'-foot jelly, and grapes from his own greenhouse, and a big bunch of roses from his garden.

There had also been a bottle of port wine, but mother had told Dad that he must take this back to the vicar, unopened, for she thought it was sinful enough for men to touch strong drink, and just terrible for a woman to do so, even if she were dying.

But what made her think more kindly about the vicar than anything else was that he had a son fighting in the South African war, and it was his only living son. The other one had gone to Australia many years before and died in the desert of thirst and starvation.

The one who was still living was a major. I had never seen him, but if he wasn't killed he would be coming home when the war was over. There was no one else in Bramblewick or the district who had relations in the war, and everyone knew that when the Major did come home his father would be very happy, and there would be a big " do " for although he hadn't won the Victoria Cross, he must be a hero to be in the war at all.

The vicar always said a special prayer for the soldiers during the service at church. Although he never mentioned his son's name, everyone knew who he was thinking of when he asked God to bless all the soldiers, and keep them from being killed or wounded or catching fever, and bring them all safely home after victory.

It bothered me that Dad and Mother started talking about the vicar at tea-time. The news about Mafeking being relieved had come first very early in the morning to the coastguard station, which had a telegraph line. The chief officer, Mr. Beecham, was a great friend of Dad, because they both came from Liverpool. He had knocked on our door, waking us up, and he had asked Dad to go and let the vicar know, so that the church bells could be rung.

Dad had been frightened at doing this, knowing that the vicar would be in bed and that he might be cross at being wakened, but he had done it, and instead of the vicar being cross he had been very pleased indeed to hear the news, and had told Dad to go and wake up the bell ringers. But they all lived a long way from the church, and what had awakened them was the vicar ringing one bell by himself.

" But he can't feel really happy yet," Mother said. " He can't do that until the horrible war is over, and his son is safe home. And it seems wrong for anyone to go in for jollification, while the fighting is still going on, and our poor soldiers are being killed or wounded or suffering from sickness. And it's wicked for so many of the men to be drinking in the public houses to-day. The public houses should be closed and there should be special services in the chapel and church, to thank God that Mafeking is relieved."

Dad usually agreed with whatever Mother said, but I knew he liked a bit of jollification (so did Mother if there was nothing vulgar about it) and that he was looking forward to the torchlight procession and the bonfire. It was Dad who had made my sword and tin-can drum, only he had told me not to play the drum in the house. Mr. Beecham had lent him a big Union Jack and he had fixed this on a long stick out of the living-room window.

He said to mother :

" Well there'll be special services on Sunday I expect. And we mustn't forget that we *have* won a real victory. Think what the soldiers and other British people in Mafeking must be feeling like to-day after seven months of siege. You know they've had to feed on rats, they were so short of food. Good old Baden-Powell ! I asked the vicar if he thought that his son had been in the fighting there, but he didn't know. It's more than two months since he had a letter from him. The procession is going to begin in the dock at nine o'clock. The bonfire I expect will be round about dusk."

I saw Dad and Mother look at each other, and I guessed that they were thinking about me and my bedtime, and whether I should be allowed to see the bonfire or not. I thought it would be a good thing to ask her if she would like me to run any errands for her after tea. That made her smile in a nice way, and thank me for being so thoughtful, which I took to be a good sign about the bonfire.

There was a bit of an argument later between her and Dad about my going out again, but in the end it was agreed that I should go with Dad, who was to bring me straight home if the men got wild, and there was a lot of swearing. A friend of hers, Miss Bushell, who kept a cake shop up the street, and belonged to the Wesleyan chapel, would come and keep her company, and they would both get on with making bandages for the Red Cross. She would lock the street door as soon as we were gone.

The dock was crowded when we went down. There were plenty of women as well as men, but the women with their little children all kept together, and it looked as if they had only come to watch.

Nearly all the men, and the boys too, including Ikey, were by the lifeboat house. I could see Jack Martin, the blacksmith, blowing his trombone. Another man was blowing a trumpet and someone else beating a drum, but they weren't making a real tune. They were just making a noise, and it looked as though most of the bandsmen were drunk.

I was glad that Mother hadn't come. The pubs were still

open, and they were so full that men were standing outside them drinking their glasses of beer. Everyone was shouting, laughing or singing and some of the men were swearing too, and I was afraid that Dad would be horrified and take me home before the procession started. But although we kept well on the edge of the crowd, and he held me very tightly by the hand, he didn't seem to mind the swearing, or seeing so many men drunk, and he kept on shouting himself, and seemed as excited as anyone. There was no quarrelling or fighting. Everyone seemed jolly.

The man who played the drum in the band and was the leader of it was called Henry Newton. He was a butcher and his shop was next door to ours. Mother didn't like him, because he was often in the pubs, and made vulgar jokes with his customers. But I liked him. Although he hadn't any children of his own he was very fond of them, and at Bramblewick Fair, when there were sports on the beach, he was always the one to arrange the races, and to see that there was no cheating, like a boy of twelve trying to run in a race for *under* twelves.

He used the bladders from his oxen and sheep and pigs for filling up with lard, but he would always give you one for a football if you asked, and he would even blow it up for you, with the shank of a clay pipe and tie it with a bit of string.

He was a big, strong man with a loud voice, and he was shouting now, but beating his drum too :

" Come on everybody. Let's make a start. Form up. The band first. Get your torches lit, them who has 'em."

It wasn't dark yet. I could see that several of the men, and some of the boys too had sticks, with tarry rope tied to their ends, and now they began to light them. There were flames and clouds of smoke. Henry shouted for everyone to keep quiet for a moment. The bandsmen, although Jack Martin was so drunk he could hardly stand, got into position, and after Henry had shouted again he banged his drum three times, and the band began to play and marched off, with everybody shouting so that really you couldn't tell what tune the band was playing.

And close behind the bandsmen was Ikey Harris, carrying the

image of Kruger pig-a-back on his shoulder, and still ringing his bell.

It was more exciting than our procession, because of the band and the torches, and there was still the most exciting thing of all to look forward to, the bonfire on the beach and the fireworks.

We joined the procession at the end, well away from any of the drunken men. We marched up the road.

But just before the bridge and the turning for Chapel Street, Dad said to me :

" If the band is going round Chapel Street, I think we'd better go back to the dock, and then down to the beach, and find a good place to see the bonfire before the crowd comes down."

I knew he was thinking about Mother, just like I had done with Ikey's procession, and that she might want us to go in when she heard all the noise, and I thought it a good idea that we should go and find a place for seeing the bonfire.

We hurried back along the road, and got to the dock, which was now almost empty, although there were still plenty of men in the pubs. The police sergeant was standing alone at the top of the slipway. He was big a man with a dark face, and a thick black moustache. He always had a stern expression. I had never once seen him smile. He had a walking stick in his hand, and I knew that under his cape he carried a truncheon, and also a pair of handcuffs.

Dad said good night to him. He didn't take the slightest notice. He was looking at the pubs and I thought he was hoping that he'd have someone to lock up before long.

We walked down the slipway. There was a wooden seat under the coastguard wall where the old men of the village would sit and talk to each other on a fine day. It had to be moved up to the dock in rough weather, out of the way of the waves, but several men were sitting on it now, smoking their pipes.

None of them seemed a bit excited about it being Mafeking night.

Dad spoke to them as we passed. The only one who answered was Captain Allen, who said gruffly " Good neet."

The tide was down. It was fine weather, and the sea wasn't

making any sound, and after the noise of the procession it was very quiet. Yet as we got to the beach we heard voices and saw several men gathered round an old boat which must have been launched down the cliff.

This cliff wasn't steep or high like the one on which our house was built. It was made of clay, and it sloped gradually to the beach. The small salmon-cobles and summer pleasure-boats were kept here during the winter, turned keel upwards, well out of the way of the waves.

It wasn't quite dark yet. Most of the men were fishermen and seemed to be quite sober. Among them was the lifeboat coxswain who, although he wasn't a Wesleyan, never drank. He was a big gruff man, with a beard. I didn't like him, but he was very brave when it came to going out in the lifeboat, like all the fishermen were. It didn't matter how rough the sea was. If there was a signal of distress, the lifeboat would be launched.

The men had put a straw mattress and some old sails and coils of tarry rope and other rubbish into the coble, and they were pouring buckets of tar from a barrel into it too. It looked as though it was going to make a wonderful bonfire, better than I had seen on any Guy Fawkes night. Yet none of them seemed very excited, and I heard one of them say :

" Well, this will be good riddance to *The Providence*. She was an unlucky boat. She drowned five men altogether, and Matt Skelton, who had her last, lost all his salmon nets first time he fished in her, and nearly got drowned too when she was capsized, coming ashore. She had a great hole in her side after that do, and he patched her up, but he couldn't get anyone to go with him next salmon season, and he died anyway that winter. She ought to burn all right, all the tar that's been put on her bottom, but let's put plenty more on to make sure."

" Who's going to set it off ? " someone asked, and the other answered :

" I reckon it will be the Doctor Whittle if he hasn't got too tight."

Dad squeezed my hand.

" Come on," he said. " Let's find a good place on the cliff.

We mustn't be too near the bonfire, with all the tar they are putting on it. It might be dangerous."

We climbed up to a grassy ledge, and then we heard the sound of the band again, and there it was, coming down the slipway, with the men waving their torches, and the boys running ahead shouting like mad. The band stopped playing at the bottom of the slipway, but Henry Newton went on beating his drum, and most of the people (the women were coming too) were still behind him, and walking alongside Henry was Doctor Whittle, carrying a big grocer's basket. But the doctor wasn't walking steadily, and as he and Henry got near the boat, he staggered and almost fell. Henry had to help him with the basket.

The doctor was a jolly man, good natured, and everybody liked him. He was short and fat, with a red face. He was a good doctor, and if anyone was ill, no matter what time of night it was he would come to see them, and if it was someone out in the country he would ride to them on his horse. He never charged much for what he did, or the medicines he mixed, and if they were poor people he didn't charge at all.

Mother didn't like him of course because he was often in the pubs, and sometimes got drunk, but she had been pleased the way he had looked after me when I'd had measles.

I had already guessed that the basket the doctor was carrying was full of fireworks. He must have sent to Burnharbour for them, for Bramblewick shops only had them on sale at Gunpowder Plot time in November.

He put the basket down when he reached the boat, and everyone now crowded round him, but they were all shouting so much we couldn't hear what was being said, although it seemed clear that he was going to be the one who was to start the bonfire.

There was a big rock with a flat top near to the boat. The basket was now lifted on to it, and the men helped the doctor to get up on it too, so that he was high above all the people who were on the beach. He was swaying a bit, however, and Dad said to me :

" I'm afraid the doctor's very much the worse for drink. But look, he's going to make a speech."

The doctor was now standing with the basket at his feet.

He raised his hands as a sign to everyone to be quiet, and Henry gave a shout :

"Order, please. Order—Order. Quiet for Doctor Whittle ! "

There was quiet for a moment : but the first thing the doctor said was :

"Long live the Queen."

And at once everyone started to shout and cheer again, and some started to sing "God Save the Queen" but they didn't get far with it. Henry was shouting for order again, and when at last there was quiet the doctor began his speech. It wasn't a real speech. It was all muddled up.

"When I was on the bridge of the *Condor*," he began. "Lord Charles Beresford. Her Majesty's ship *Condor*. Remember, Her Majesty's ship. Enemy shells bursting all around us. Flash-bang, Lord Charles Beresford, Admiral of the Fleet. Bombardment of Alexandria. Shells bursting all around us. Lord Charles Beresford. Like Nelson on the *Victory* at the Battle of Trafalgar. England expects that every man. I said to Lord Charles Beresford, bravest man who ever lived, I said, shells bursting all around us, I said . . ."

He didn't get any further with his speech. The crowd were beginning to shout again, and then Henry Newton, taking a torch from someone, passed it up to the doctor and shouted :

"Come on, Doctor Whittle. Set the bonfire alight ! "

The doctor took the torch. He waved it in the air, and before anyone could stop him, he dropped it, still blazing, into the basket of fireworks.

Henry Newton certainly was a brave man. Most of the other men ran back when they saw what had happened. But Henry got hold of the doctor and pulled him off the rock, and then he took the basket and threw it into the boat among the tarry rope and the straw.

The straw caught fire, and began to blaze. A jumping cracker shot out of the basket, and then the burning balls of roman candles, and showers of sparks from squibs and rockets, which because they had no sticks on them just went sideways. Everyone was standing back, and I was glad that we were well out of the way up on the cliff, for although I was excited I was really frightened, and I think a lot of other boys were too. Some children who were standing near us with their parents were screaming.

But Ikey Harris wasn't frightened. I had seen him standing among the men, carrying the effigy of Mr. Kruger, and he was in front now as near to the bonfire as anyone. And he suddenly ran forward, quite close to the boat and threw Mr. Kruger into the middle of the flames and the exploding hissing fireworks and then ran back, with everyone shouting and cheering louder than ever. And I cheered too, for it was the bravest thing I had ever seen.

But the bonfire itself soon made me forget that. The flames rose higher and higher. There were huge clouds of smoke. In the light of the flames these too seemed to be on fire, and, with crackers still exploding, it was like a picture I had seen of Mount Vesuvius in eruption.

Mr. Kruger caught fire of course. Many of the fireworks must have gone off together, for there was a very loud bang, and he jumped up almost as though he was alive, and then disappeared altogether, and after that there were very few bangs. There was only the roar of the flames and the crackling of burning wood as *The Providence* really started to burn. It became so hot that we had to move farther up the cliff. The flames lit up the whole of the beach and the coastguard station and the slipway as bright as daylight.

" I think we ought to be going home now," Dad said to me. " Mother will be getting anxious."

But we didn't move, and I knew he was enjoying it as much as I was. And then another exciting thing happened. A tall man in farmer's clothes had pushed his way through the crowd. It was Gow Pickering, the father of Joe. Ikey didn't see him. Ikey was watching the bonfire, and Gow made a grab for him, and began to clout him. Ikey struggled to get free, and actually tried to fight him but of course he was too small.

I knew that Ikey had done wrong in stealing Kruger from the Thorpe cloggers, and that in a way it served him right that

Joe's father should take revenge and punish him, but Joe himself should have been the one to settle it, not a big man twice Ikey's size.

Yet Gow must have been brave too. He must have known that he wasn't going to be allowed to thrash a bumper in front of all the men of our village. Henry Newton was the first to interfere, but Gow just pushed him away, and gave Ikey another clout. And then it looked as there was going to be a real fight, for another man moved up to Gow, pulled Ikey away and then stood facing him, with his fists clenched.

The man was Jake Harris, and he was Ikey's uncle. He was an ordinary sailor, but he had once been in the Royal Navy, and had been taught the proper way to fight. He had been a champion boxer and had won several silver cups and medals. He wasn't as tall as Gow, but he was much broader, and he had huge fists, which looked as though they would knock anyone unconscious if he struck hard with them. He was wearing a reefer jacket, and I saw a bottle of beer sticking out of one pocket.

Everyone seemed to forget the bonfire, and all the shouting stopped, for everyone was looking at the two men facing each other and like two roosters all ready to start a fight, each waiting for the other to begin.

I had never seen a real fight between grown-ups, for they always happened at night, usually when the pubs closed at eleven o'clock, and although I was excited, I was frightened again, and I don't think I would have minded so very much if Dad had decided that we should go home. But he didn't say anything, he was watching, as though he couldn't help it.

Would they " spit ower " I wondered, and then say the same words as the boys did before starting? I couldn't see Gow's face properly because of the way he was standing, but I could see Jake all right. He had a fat face, without any moustache or whiskers, and usually he looked quite jolly. And he didn't look so very angry now, for although he was dark, the light of the fire made his cheeks rosy, like those of Father Christmas.

I was feeling more frightened than ever. I didn't want them to fight. I wished the police sergeant would come and stop them before they began, for I thought that one of them might kill the other, and that would be murder, and I said to Dad :

" I want to go home," and Dad said, " Yes, I think we'd better," but he didn't move. He was still watching the two men.

And then, when everyone was expecting the fight to begin, a funny thing happened. Jake said something to Gow, and actually smiled, and Gow smiled too. Then Jake pulled the bottle from his pocket, took a drink and offered it to Gow, who took it and had a drink. Everyone laughed, and suddenly Jake put his arms round Gow's waist, and hugged him and they started to dance round just like two performing bears.

No one seemed disappointed that there hadn't been a fight. Everyone was laughing or cheering. Even Ikey looked quite happy, and was ringing his bell, and shouting at the top of his voice. Doctor Whittle climbed up on the rock again. He had a bottle in his hand and he was waving it, and I think he wanted to go on with his speech about the Battle of Alexandria, but no one would listen, and he swayed, and would have fallen off the rock if some of the men hadn't helped him down.

And the bonfire was still blazing, although not quite so brightly as before.

" I think we'd better be starting for home now," said Dad. " It must be long past your bedtime."

This time he did move, and we climbed down the cliff on to the beach, keeping clear of the crowd. We stopped on the slipway for a last look at the bonfire. There was no one on the seat now. The old men must have gone to bed, perhaps without even bothering to look at it. The dock was as quiet as the shore had been when we had first gone down, although the pubs were still open.

The police sergeant was just where we had seen him last. He looked at us but he didn't speak, and we hurried up Chapel Street without seeing anyone.

Ours was a very small house. The living-room was over the shop, where Dad sold his pictures. Dad knocked gently at the front door. We heard Mother coming down the stairs, and then saying in a frightened voice :

" Who's that ? "

" It's only us," said Dad. She unlocked the door and let us in, and she asked Dad to lock it again, and also bolt it, and she held me very tightly by the hand as we went upstairs. I thought she was going to be vexed, but she was only frightened, for Miss Bushell hadn't come after all, and she had been by herself all the time. Apart from the procession, there had been several drunken men shouting in the street, and one of them had knocked on the door, and her heart had come into her mouth.

Dad said he was very sorry that she had been frightened and that he wouldn't have taken me to the bonfire if he had thought that Miss Bushell wouldn't come, and he did so want to give me a treat. He didn't say anything about Doctor Whittle being drunk, or mention Gow and Jake, and Mother just asked me if I had enjoyed myself. I said " yes " and then she said :

" Well you must get off to bed straight away. I hope that there won't be any more noise to-night. I expect that Miss Bushell was really too frightened to venture out. That's why she didn't come."

She had already lit my candle, and she went with me to the attic where my bed was. She watched me undress, and when I came to say my prayers, she asked me to say something about the war and our poor soldiers, and for their anxious wives and parents, and mention the vicar's son too, and ask God to bring him safe home.

She tucked me in and kissed me good night. But I was too excited to go to sleep, and if I had done so I would have awakened soon, for the people were coming up from the beach to the dock again. The men would be going into the pubs to get more drink before they closed at eleven o'clock. They were still singing and shouting, and I could hear Ikey's bell.

I could understand why Mother had been frightened. I was glad that I was home and in bed, and that the street door was locked. And yet I couldn't help wishing a bit that I was watching what was happening. I was sure that the policeman would be locking someone up before long.

I thought of all the exciting things that had happened during the day from the start of our procession, and of how Ikey had

started his fight with Joe, and the vicar rushing out with his
stick, and of how brave Ikey had been in throwing Kruger into
the bonfire. I wished that I could do something as brave as that.
Even when Gow had clouted him, he had tried to fight back,
and hadn't seemed a bit afraid.

Yet Ikey had run as fast as anyone when the vicar had appeared.
There was *someone* he was afraid of ! Ikey wouldn't dare to
play pin-and-button at the vicarage. That *would* be a daring thing
to do. I started to imagine myself doing it, perhaps with another
boy, as witness.

It would have to be done on one of the front windows of the
house. It was a back window that had been smashed with the
stone. There was a lawn at the front, with some bushes which
would be just right to hide in, and pull the cotton. I knew this
because once a year the vicar allowed people to have a look at his
garden, which reached from the lawn down a bank to the stream
that ran through the village.

It was a wonderful garden. There were gravelled paths
winding between the beds, with seats here and there, and wooden
archways, with flowering creepers growing on them, and a pond
with lilies and goldfish in it. The vicar was very proud of it, and
particularly of his roses, with which he had won many prizes
in London, and although he had a gardener he did a lot of the
work himself.

No one was allowed in the garden except on this one day,
and there was a high wall round it with bits of broken glass fixed
on the top. In one part of it there was an orchard with all sorts
of fruit, but this was never shown to anyone. I knew where it
was though.

I wondered if I would dare to do it ! It would be just as brave
a thing as running round the coastguard's wall when the sea was
rough. If I was caught the vicar would certainly thrash me,
and also tell Dad, and perhaps even the police sergeant, and I
might be sent to prison. Mother would be vexed if she knew that
I was even thinking of it, especially so soon after I had said my
prayers, so I tried to stop thinking about it, and just listened to
the noise from the dock, going on as loud as ever, although I

still didn't hear any quarrelling sounds. Everyone seemed jolly. Only the police sergeant must have been feeling disappointed.

I must have fallen asleep, for the next thing I heard was the men in the dock singing " God Save the Queen " with the band playing too, but very much out of tune, and that was followed by " Lead Kindly Light," which was always sung when the pubs closed and everyone went home. And after that all the noise gradually died away, and I really went to sleep. Mafeking Day was over.

3

ALTHOUGH SHE agreed with Dad that the village with its red roofs and winding alleys was very artistic, and the beach and cliffs and country around pretty, especially in spring and summer, Mother didn't like Bramblewick.

She and her two sisters, my Aunty Annie and Aunty Fanny, had been brought up in a good religious home in Liverpool, and although some parts of Liverpool, like those near the docks, and Scotland Road, which had a pub at every street corner, were rough and low and full of bad characters, the part where she had lived had more churches and chapels than pubs, and everyone was well behaved.

Her father and mother had been very strict. She and her sisters went to chapel twice every Sunday, and to prayer meetings during the week, and until she was nearly grown up she was never allowed to go into the city by herself, and yet sometimes she would tell me that she had done things which would have shocked her parents and her sisters too if they had found out. She had actually been to a theatre, not just once but many times.

Whenever she told me about this it was as though she still felt guilty about deceiving her parents, but she never pretended she hadn't enjoyed it. It was not a music hall or a theatre where they showed ordinary plays she had been to. Such places were usually vulgar and even wicked.

An Irish girl-friend of hers called Harriet Moore (I called her Aunty Harriet) had first persuaded her to go. Harriet's father was a shopkeeper who was given free tickets for showing advertisement bills. Mother was eighteen then and nearly grown up,

34

but it was an afternoon performance, and not in winter-time so that she was able to get home before it was dark.

What she had seen was a musical play called *H.M.S. Pinafore*. The words had been written by Gilbert and the music had been composed by Mr. Sullivan who composed religious music too, and had actually performed before Queen Victoria herself, who would never admire anything that was in the least vulgar.

Mother would get quite excited when she told me about the play itself. She would describe the scenery, and how the characters were dressed, and although she couldn't remember all the words, she would sing most of the songs like " I am the Captain of the Pinafore " and " Dear Little Buttercup."

She and Aunty Harriet had also seen other plays by Gilbert and Sullivan, *The Pirates of Penzance*, *The Gondoliers*, *Iolanthe* and *The Mikado*, but her favourite was *Pinafore*, and she sang or hummed those songs so often that I learned them too. She told me that if ever Dad made enough money for us all to have a holiday we would go to Liverpool, and perhaps I would see *H.M.S. Pinafore* for myself.

Yet tears would sometimes come into Mother's eyes when she talked about Liverpool, and I knew that she longed to go back. Both her parents were dead. Her sisters still lived there and one of them, my Aunty Annie, was married and had a family of her own. Her husband was a preacher.

She had once stayed with us for a few days. She was far more religious than Mother was, and when we went for a walk in the village she stopped everyone we met and offered them religious tracts from a black bag that she carried. It made me blush. She even offered one to Neddy Peacock, who wouldn't take it because he must have thought she wanted money for it.

Mother had told me that I must never say anything about the theatre to Aunty Annie, and I noticed once while she was staying with us that she started humming " Dear Little Buttercup " and quickly changed into a hymn, and I think it worried her a bit that if we went for a holiday to Liverpool we would have to stay at least some of the time with Aunty Annie, although Aunty

Harriet, who was also married, was always writing and asking her to come and stay.

Dad never seemed to long for Liverpool. Although he didn't approve of the drinking that went on, and agreed with Mother that there were several bad characters in the place, he liked Bramblewick. He thought that when he did make a lot of money either from his pictures, or from one of his inventions, we should go to Italy where he could study some of the world's greatest paintings as well as find good subjects for his own.

I wanted to go to Liverpool for a holiday of course, especially if we stayed with Aunty Harriet, who seemed to be so jolly, and it would be wonderful to go to the theatre. And I thought it would be nice to go to Italy, for that would mean going in a real ship, but I liked Bramblewick just as much as Dad did.

No matter what time of the year it was, there was always something exciting happening, or something exciting to see or do, or to look forward to, although it couldn't be expected that there would ever be anything like Mafeking Day again, unless it was the day the vicar's son came home.

It was exciting just to see the cobles landing with their catches of fish. In winter the fishermen used long lines with hundreds of hooks on them. They set off for the fishing grounds very early in the morning, long before daylight, and often I would be awakened by the sound of the cobles being launched from the dock.

They couldn't go if the sea was so rough that the waves were breaking across the mouth of the landing, and yet the rougher it was the better it was for fishing, and it had to be really rough to keep them ashore for they were all poor men, unlike the sailors of Bramblewick who were paid regular wages! Sometimes although the weather seemed all right when they set off a storm would come on, and they would have to rush for the landing.

When that happened there would be a crowd of people watching the cobles as they sailed or pulled towards the landing mouth. If it looked very bad the lifeboat gun would be fired, and the boat itself would be got ready to launch, although the crew would have to be made up from the old fishermen or coast-guards or sailors, as the regular crew (including the coxswain) were the ones who were in danger.

And always, and it didn't matter if it was snowing, the vicar, who was the secretary of the lifeboat, would be there, and once I saw him put a lifebelt on, ready to go as one of the crew.

But although in the past, cobles had been capsized and men drowned, I had never seen the lifeboat launched just for the fishermen. One by one the boats would get to the landing mouth, and pull about until they got a wave that was rushing straight in between the posts but not breaking, and the men would pull with all their might, and ride in with the wave into the calm water between the scars.

When the last boat was in, the doors of the lifeboat house would be shut, and the people, including the vicar, would go home. But the work of the fishermen wasn't over. The cobles would be aground in shallow water at the shore end of the landing, and the men wearing long leather sea-boots would get out, and start carrying their catch to the scar, where there were several pools. The fish would be tipped into them, gutted and washed and thrown into baskets.

The old retired fishermen, and boys too, would help with this, and while they worked there would be hundreds of sea-gulls flying about over their heads, and pouncing on the fish guts, and making a loud din, but never loud enough to drown the sound of the great waves breaking on the scar ends.

A rough sea didn't always mean that the catches were big. Sometimes a storm would come on so suddenly that the men would not have had time to haul their lines and that would mean no fish at all, and the lines, which cost a lot of money would be lost. I always felt sorry for them when this happened, yet the men themselves never got bad tempered about it or complained. They'd make up for it when they did get a big catch !

Most of the fish they caught were cod and ling and conger for which they were paid a penny a pound. If they were very lucky they'd catch haddock, which might bring as much as tuppence. You could tell haddock from cod because they had black marks on each side of them which were supposed to be the finger and thumb marks of Saint Peter.

I never missed seeing the boats come in if I could help it. As soon as the catch was carried up to the dock, the men would bring down the launching carriages, one for each coble. The cobles were very heavy. All the ballast would be thrown overboard, and the masts and sails and rudder carried ashore. The carriages were made of a strong oak beam with a small wagon wheel at each end. One would be pushed into the shallow water up to the bow of the first coble. Then, while several men on each side raised the bow, a man at each wheel would push the carriage under the keel, until the coble just balanced on it. It would be tied with thick ropes to the thole pins, and two long ropes would be taken ashore for those helpers who were not wearing sea-boots, and didn't want to get wet. Then one of the fishermen would shout " heave-o " and everyone would pull, and I would always get hold of the rope too and pull as hard as I could.

If it was a storm, with the tide flowing, I would feel very pleased when the last coble was pulled up into the dock, where they would be safe, no matter how bad the storm became, and I knew that the fishermen would feel happy too, especially when night came and they were sitting by their firesides, listening to the roaring of the wind and sea outside.

Although it could be so dangerous, and often frightened me, I loved the sea, and it was just as exciting when it was calm as when it was rough, especially when there were spring tides, in summer, and the weather was warm enough to paddle.

The lowest ebbs were in the morning or late evening (long past my bedtime) and if it wasn't the holidays, it had to be a Saturday, for on Sunday, no matter how warm the weather was, and how low the tide went down, I had to be in my best clothes and boots and wasn't allowed on the shore by myself.

Even with a neap tide ebb, there was always something of interest to find on the scars, or in the pools between them. The scars, because of the waves pounding on them in rough weather, had no weeds growing on them, but they were covered with millions of little barnacles whose pointed shells hurt your feet un-

less you wore sandshoes. But wherever there were cracks or little
gulleys in the rock, deep enough to hold water, there would be
bunches of short pink weed, that was like coral, and sea anemones
with tentacles like the petals of flowers, and tiny fish, which, if
you frightened them, would dart into the weed, being careful not
to touch one of the tentacles of the anemones as they did so or
they would be caught and eaten !   .

If you wanted to give an anemone a treat you could knock a
limpet from the rock, squeeze out its soft body, and drop this
on the anemone's tentacles. At once the tentacles would close
round it and draw it into its mouth.

There were bigger pools between the scars. Here the weed
could grow for the scars protected them from the pounding of
the waves. Some of them had sandy bottoms, and you could
catch shrimps in them and baby dabs and flounders. The flatfish were too small to eat, but they looked lovely if you put them in
a glass jam jar with water in it.

But these pools because they were shallow and safe usually
attracted visitor children in summer-time. There would be
little girls with their dresses tucked into their bloomers, with
penny shrimp-nets, and their parents sitting on the scars watching
them, sucking oranges or eating bananas, and the little girls
would scream whenever they caught a shrimp, or saw a little
shore crab. I hated them.

You'd never find anything big or valuable in the neap tide
pools, like real eating-crabs or lobsters or big flatfish. You
could only get these at low water of the spring tides, far out at
the scar ends where the visitor children never ventured with
their silly shrimp-nets.

Crabs and sometimes lobsters were found in the crevices
under the scars. Some of these crevices were just like caves,
reaching in a long way, with small entrances, and you couldn't
tell just by looking whether there was anything in them or not.
You had to use a crabhook.

My crabhook which I had swapped with one of the fishermen's
sons for a penknife, was a thin stiff iron rod with a small crook
at one end and a point at the other for spearing flatfish. You

pushed the crooked end into the cave and wiggled it about. You could tell by the sound it made if it was touching a shellfish or just the rock.

If it was a crab it might get hold of the hook with one of its claws, and then it would be quite easy to pull it out. If it didn't you had to wiggle the hook about until it caught on part of its shell and keep on jerking and pulling until it came in sight.

Lobsters were scarcer, and more valuable, and more difficult to catch. You got them in holes which had water in them. You'd know it was a lobster because as soon as you touched it with your hook it would start flapping its tail. Lobsters had more sense than crabs, and they moved quicker. They would fight you with their long big claws and try every trick to escape.

The flatfish were of course in the water. Between the scars were pools or creeks like those where you caught shrimps, with sandy bottoms, only they were much deeper and reaching to the actual sea. The flatfish would be lying on the sand with their bodies almost buried in it with only their eyes showing. You had to wade, with your feet bare, very very slowly.

If there was no wind to blur the surface of the water, you would see the eyes of the fish, and tell from that how its body was lying. You had to creep until you were just above it, and then, with all your strength jab the pointed end of the crabhook down on to the middle of its back, and if you had struck all right hold on with the hook while you bent down with your free hand and got your fingers into the fish's gills, lift it out of the water and rush for the scar and your bag.

The commonest flatfish was a flounder, but sometimes you got plaice and dabs.

It was no use trying for lobsters or crabs or flatfish except on a spring tide ebb, and the lower the tide went down the better your chances were of getting something good. The snag was that almost as soon as it was low tide, it would start flowing again so that you would only have a few minutes at the very best places and it was maddening if you had to spend a long time trying to get a crab out of a hole, especially, as often happened, if it turned out to be undersize, or a " softie," and then find that the tide was flowing, so that it was too late to try for flatfish.

And there were other things to look for. A sailing ship had been wrecked near Cowling Scar many years ago. There had been no proper lifeboat at Bramblewick then, so one of the cobles had been launched to try and save the ship's crew. The sea had been terribly rough. Before the coble reached the ship it was capsized and all the men in her were drowned.

The men in the ship had tried to escape in their own boat when the tide was low. This had capsized, and only the captain had managed to reach the shore. He'd had with him all the ship's money when he had got into the little boat. It was in an iron box, more than a hundred guineas, and this of course had sunk.

I'd heard an old fisherman say that once when fishing in his boat near Cowling Scar when the water had been very clear he had seen some gold coins on the bottom. The water had been too deep for him to touch them even with his boathook.

Cowling Scar reached out farther to sea than any of the other scars. Everyone knew that it was dangerous for the channel that separated it from the next scar was only shallow enough to wade at the very lowest ebb. When the tide turned the sea would rush into the channel like a flooded river and turn the scar into an island.

Mother had made me promise never to venture on to it, and I don't think I would have done if one Saturday in the summer that followed Mafeking Day there hadn't happened the lowest tide I had ever known.

4

I<small>T WAS</small> in June, before the summer holidays, and there were no visitors about. It was very hot, there wasn't any wind and not a cloud in the sky, I had never seen the sea so calm or the water so clear. The bay was like a great curved looking-glass.

I never wanted to have any other boy with me when I went hunting down the scars, in case there was an argument as to where we should go, and anyway most of the other boys, including Ikey, liked to play cricket on a Saturday.

But I wouldn't be the only one hunting. Many of the old fishermen had crabhooks, and so had Neddy Peacock, and if he thought he could make a bit of extra money, and not miss any customers for his coal and vegetables he'd shut up his warehouse and he'd try to be at the best places before anyone else had a chance. It was a good job there were plenty of places so that no one could hunt all of them in one tide.

The best thing was to start off when the tide was half-way down, and follow it as it ebbed, and that was what I did that morning, walking down one of the longest scars next to those which made the fishermen's landing.

All the fishermen (including Neddy Peacock) fished for salmon and salmon-trout at this time of the year. They went out at dusk, shot their nets close to the scar ends, and hauled them as soon as it was daylight and came ashore, and I was never up early enough to see them land. They didn't haul their boats but left them anchored in the landing if the weather was all right, and as they were not allowed by the law to fish for salmon on Sunday they'd go to bed on Saturday morning. There was not one of them in sight.

I walked down the scar to the water's edge. The other scars where I was going to hunt were already showing, but Cowling Scar was still under water, although it would have been easy to tell where it was if the sea had been rough, for even at high tide the waves would break on it.

Each scar was tilted, so that one edge made a little cliff, but the other slanted gradually to the cliff edge of the next one, and it was under the cliffs that you found the crab holes. I was very excited, for although I didn't know that it was going to be an extra low ebb I was certain by the way the scar was baring that it was going to be a good one. I was certain to get some crabs, and the water was so clear I was almost certain of getting a flatfish or two.

There were some holes that often held crabs on this very scar, and in a few minutes I would be able to try the first one. There was only about two feet of water over the scar edge, and I was looking down at it when I heard footsteps on the scar behind me. It was Neddy Peacock with a crabhook in one hand, a bag in the other, and he was walking very quickly.

I was frightened. I wondered if he remembered Mafeking Day, and the way we had shouted at him and mocked him, and if he had noticed that I had been with the other boys. I had always steered clear of him since then, and I would have moved off now if there hadn't been water on each side of me. He looked terrible. Although he must have been salmon fishing that night his face was black with coal dust. His shirt was dirty. He was wearing a pair of old ragged trousers, and boots without stockings.

I pretended I hadn't seen him, and went on looking down into the water, but he came right up to me and shouted :

" Eh—what are you up to ? "

" I'm only looking for crabs," I said.

" It's no use looking for crabs here. Gan somewheres else. There's plenty of other spots."

" The tide isn't low enough yet."

He glared at me like a savage animal.

" It will be soon. This scar's for me, all the way down to low water, and the next one too, so be off with you."

I was angry. No one had a right to claim any of the scars. The rule was, first on—first served. But I was too frightened to tell him so. I backed away from him and began to move back along the scar, and almost at once he stepped into the water by the hole that I was going to try first, and started work with his hook.

I stopped, within a safe distance, watching him. In less than a minute I saw him pull out quite a nice crab. He put it in his bag and started to work again. I nearly cried with anger then. That crab should have been mine. Oh if only God would send a flash of lightning down and kill him !

But he didn't get another crab from that hole. He got up on the scar, ready to go to the next one, and then as he picked up his bag I shouted at the top of my voice :

" *Awd Neddy Peacock ! Awd Neddy Peacock !* "

And I stuck my tongue out at him, and put my fingers to my nose.

I was not certain whether he heard and saw me or not, for I ran, and didn't look back until I was nearly half-way up the scar. Then I stopped and turned. He was working at the next hole, almost up to his knees in water.

I was still too vexed to be worried about having called after Neddy, and pulled a face at him. But I wasn't going to let him beat me and stop me hunting. He was right in saying that there were plenty of other spots. It just happened that this scar was the first one with holes that you could get at before the tide was really low, and by now all the scars, including a bit of Cowling Scar were almost bare, and at the ends of them the tangles were showing, the real sign of spring low water.

Tangles were seaweed, with tough stems sometimes eight feet long and broad leaves that were like those of palm trees, and they made a sort of forest along the scar ends. It was supposed that if anyone fell into the water where the tangles grew he would be drowned for certain, no matter whether he could swim or not, for they would wrap round him like the arms of an octopus, and drag him down.

There were five scars between the one I was on and Cowling. I thought I wouldn't bother about the first one of these as Neddy had claimed it, but I just hoped, as I walked across it, that every hole in it would be empty for him, and that would serve him right for being so greedy. I even thought that it would be a good thing if he fell into the water among the tangles, and that if he wasn't drowned he'd get a fright.

But I forgot about Neddy as soon as I started on the first hole and heard a flapping sound inside it. It was a " wet " hole. I was certain at first that it was a lobster, but I couldn't feel any shell, and after a while I found that it was only a fish called a bearded rockling, something like an eel, and not worth bothering with, for it was only about six inches long. I went on to the next hole and the next, and there was nothing in either of them.

I was still a long way from low water. Neddy was still on the first scar, but he was a long way out from the place where he had got the crab, which was now dry. I thought I had best hurry along my scar as far as I could go, where I was far more likely to get something good and leave the near-holes until the tide flowed, and I ran, keeping my eye on Neddy as I did so.

It was when I reached the end of the scar that I realised that already the tide was lower than I had ever seen it before. And it was still ebbing. Every bit of scar had weed growing on it, but not the weed that you found in the pools near the shore. Some of it was very short and crumpled, so that it was just like walking on a soft carpet. Some of it was like thin leather boot-laces, yards long. I thought that this sort of weed must be more dangerous than tangles for anyone who fell among it when the rock where it grew was covered by the tide.

It was all so fascinating that I almost forgot that I was after crabs and lobsters. Stranded by the ebb were dozens of big prickly sea urchins, and starfish, some like the ones you could find under stones on a neap tide, with five arms, only much bigger, and some coloured like ripe strawberries, that had thirteen arms and were as big as dinner plates. In the crevices among the weed which still contained water were huge anemones, the ones that the fishermen sometimes used as bait for winter cod-fishings and called scar cocks. They were more beautiful than any flowers.

It was wonderful to think that really I was walking on the sea-bed, that I was seeing things that only a diver could see as a rule and I imagined what it would be like when the tide was up again with the sea urchins and starfish crawling among the weed, and real fish, like big cod and conger eels, and lobsters and crabs, swimming or crawling about, not hiding in their holes. But it would be horrible to feel that weed twining round my limbs I thought, and I was glad that the tide was still ebbing.

I hadn't forgotten about the crabs, and the flatfish I hoped to spear, and I started hunting again. I couldn't find any likely holes however. At the " cliff " edge of the scar, the water was quite deep and it was so thick with tangles I couldn't see the bottom at all. I'd have to move back along the scar, to where the water was shallow enough to wade, and I did so and found one very likely looking hole.

But all I got from it was one small crab, and two more holes that were near had nothing at all. I wondered if Neddy was getting any. I hoped he wasn't. I would have loved to have seen him fall into the water.

He was now on the third scar, near to the end of it. As soon as he tried one hole he would actually run to the next so as not to waste time and I knew it wouldn't be long before he came to where I was hunting especially if he thought that I was being lucky. I decided to move to the next one, which was very near to Cowling Scar.

I went to the end of it first. There were no tangles on the edge of it, where the water was deep, and the bottom was clean sand, just the place for a flatfish.

And sure enough there *was* a flatfish, bigger than any I had ever seen except those landed by the fishermen from their boats !

It was lying half buried in the sand quite close to the scar. I could see its head, and its eyes on their little stalks and the shape of its gill opening, for this was quivering as it breathed, and I could just make out the shape of its tail a long way from the head, and I knew that it was a sole, for which the fishermen always got a bigger price than for any other fish except salmon.

I was so vexed that I nearly cried, for I knew that I could not possibly catch it where it was lying. The water would have come over my head. I might be able to touch it with my crabhook, but only just, and touching it would be no good. That would just frighten it and make it swim away.

Would the tide ebb any farther, so that I could wade to it? It didn't seem possible. It must be nearly low tide by now, and before long it would start to flow again, and I still hadn't got one good crab. If only I had a rod and a line with me, instead of my crabhook! I could have lowered the bait just in front of the fish's mouth and it would have been certain to bite. It seemed to be looking at me with its funny little eyes, and I imagined that it was smiling at me, mocking me.

I looked round and saw that Neddy had come a little nearer. Well, I thought, I wasn't going to let him get it. I'd frighten it, and, if I was lucky, it might swim into shallow water, and give me a chance.

I reached down my crabhook towards it. Before the end was near the fish, it gave a flip of its tail, and then at full speed it swam out to deeper water and out of sight, leaving behind it a cloud of swirling sand.

I had to bite my lip to stop myself crying with disappointment. If I'd caught it, it wouldn't have mattered if I hadn't caught anything else, and I'd have walked past old Neddy, and let him see it, just to annoy him and have my revenge. I would never see a fish like that again. Even a big lobster wouldn't make up for it.

But it had gone. I had to try for a crab before the tide turned, and I set off up the scar again. And then I thought of the captain's money-box. I was only one scar away from the one next to the Cowling, and I ran for the channel where at ordinary spring tides you could just wade across.

The channel, and I had never seen it like this before, was dry. The tangles were lying flat, just like a cornfield that has been beaten down in a heavy rainstorm. I was soon on the scar itself.

Although it was tilted, with a high edge and a low one (where the channel was) it was different from the other scars. It was short, and not very wide. There was no weed on the high part of it, only barnacles, but below the edge of it which made another cliff the tangles began again, only as in the channel they were lying flat for quite a long way seawards.

I climbed down the cliff. I was terribly excited. I was sure that the tide had never ebbed as far out as this before. I should be able to reach the very place where the fishermen had seen the gold coins. I must walk out as far as I could go.

It wasn't easy, for the tangles were so slippery, and so thick that they covered the rock. I kept poking with my crabhook as I went. There were hundreds of sea urchins and starfish among them, and huge anemones.

I got to the water's edge and started to wade, and I went on until I was knee-deep among the tangles, which were now half floating.

I was beginning to feel a bit frightened. The tangles were so thick I could only see bits of the bottom. I stopped when the water was over my knees. The tangles were all round me. It would be dangerous to go any farther. And it was lucky I did stop, for when I poked the tangles in front of me to one side, I saw that another step would have taken me over a ledge, and I would have fallen over it for certain.

I peered down over the ledge, still pressing the tangles to one side. It wasn't so deep as the place where I had seen the sole. The bottom was rock, without any sand. But there was something there that wasn't rock. It was a piece of worm-eaten wood with what looked like some rusted iron bolts sticking out of it, part of a wrecked ship, and close to it, on the rock, was something that glittered and was yellow, like gold.

I only saw it for a moment. The stems of the tangles were like indiarubber and they bounced back as I pressed them, hiding the bottom. I tried using my left hand as well as the crabhook, and again I got just a glimpse of the piece of wood and the glittering yellow thing near it, but only a glimpse, and I couldn't be certain what it was for the tangles sprang back, and now I saw that the tangles all around me were moving, swaying. *The tide had started to flow.*

I wasn't going to give up yet, for only gold could shine like that. It couldn't be anything else but the guineas from the captain's money-box that had fallen out of the box when it had rusted away.

I leaned forward as far as I dared, and pulled the tangles aside with all my strength, and for another moment I got a clear view of the bottom, and I saw that all over it there were little yellow shining patches that did *look* like gold coins, but were only the reflection of the sun shining down between the tangles.

I knew it was wicked to swear. But I did swear. I shouted every wicked word I could think of. I'd been tricked! I was so angry that I seized my crabhook in both hands and whacked at the tangles about me. But the next moment I was only frightened. The water had risen well above my knees. I could feel the tangles moving, and as fast as I could go I started back for the edge of Cowling Scar. The tide would be flowing up the channel on its shoreward side.

I was glad to get out of the tangles, to be on " dry " ground again, just below the edge of the scar. I was safe now for although the tide would be flowing up the channel on the shoreward side it would be some time before it got too deep to stop me getting across it.

I was still feeling very vexed and disappointed. This had been just about the unluckiest day I had ever known, in spite of it being the lowest of all tides, and such perfect weather. It was awful to think that I had got only one small crab.

I moved to climb on to the scar. Just at the foot of it was a pool almost covered with tangles. Among the tangles was something that made me forget everything else, including the channel and the flowing tide. It was the tip of one of the feelers of a lobster. There was only about an inch of it showing. It was moving very gently from side to side.

The pool didn't look deep. It reached to the foot of the scar. Because of the tangles I couldn't tell if there was a hole there or not. My crabhook would be of no use at present. I would have to use just my hands.

I crouched down over the pool and gently started to move the tangle leaves near where the tip of the feeler was showing. I saw the other feeler, then the point of the lobster's head, and one of the big claws. I couldn't see its tail yet, but I knew by the size of the claw that it was a beauty, worth a dozen crabs, worth almost as much as the sole.

To catch a lobster (or a crab) with your hands you must seize it from behind, just where the big claws join on to the body. I had to wait until I could see the second claw. Then I grabbed. As I did so, it gave a terrific kick with its tail, broke loose and shot away to the other end of the pool near the scar, and under the weed again.

I rushed after it, tore back the weeds, and saw that there was a hole, only a small one and that it had got inside it, tail first, with its two big claws and its feelers waving angrily. The nippers of the claws were open, ready for a fight. I daren't touch it now with my hands. I poked at it with the crabhook, and it did seize the end, but it must have known what I was trying to do for it let go as soon as I pulled.

I tried again, and this time I got the hook in between its claws. It slipped out when I pulled. And then although I was not standing in the pool I felt water round my feet. The tide was lapping the foot of the scar. I remembered the channel.

But I wasn't going to lose that lobster, even if it nipped me. I bent down close to it, poked at it with the hook until again it grabbed the end in one of its claws. And then with my hand I grabbed at the claw itself, pulled with all my might, drew it out of the hole, and with its tail flapping like mad and its other claw trying to nip me, I leapt up on to the top of the scar, and threw it down on to the bare rock. And I couldn't help giving a shout of joy. It was a beauty !

It was still trying to fight, but I got it into my bag without it nipping me, and then I ran for the place where I had crossed. Before I reached it I began to fear that the worst had happened. The tide had already covered it, and the current was racing in, with the long brown fronds of the tangles waving and twisting in it as though they were alive.

Almost opposite to me on the scar next to the one that made the channel was Neddy, with his back towards me working at a hole.

I was frightened, but I thought I could just do it. I was wearing only short trousers and a shirt and as they were already wet it wouldn't matter if I went up to my waist. I waded in, the water getting deeper with every step, but what was worse the current stronger. I wouldn't have minded that though but for the tangles. I couldn't see the bottom for them. They were twining round my legs, and before I was half-way to the other scar, the water was up to my waist, and I could hardly stand against the current.

I couldn't do it. I shouted, " Help—help ! " I was really terrified. And Neddy heard me. I saw him stand up, and look at me. I knew then that it would have served me right if he had just gone on crab-hunting and left me to drown, the way I had cheeked him, and wished that he would fall in among the tangles, but I shouted again, very politely :

" Please, Mr. Peacock, will you help me ? Please, *please !* "

He put his crabhook down, and then, not very quickly, he walked to the edge of the channel just opposite me and stopped, glaring at me in the most awful way :

" What's up with you ? " he shouted. " What have you been doing on Cowling Scar you young beggar ? "

" I've only been crab-hunting, Mr. Peacock," I said. " Help me across. The water's too deep. I'm going to be drowned if you don't help me. I'm sorry I shouted after you. I'll never do it again."

He went on glaring at me, and then he said :

" Sarve you right if you were drowned. Stay where you are."

And then he stepped into the water, and came towards me, pushing the tangles on one side with his thick legs. He was nearly up to his waist when he reached me, and the water was nearly up to my armpits. Another minute and I would have been

washed away for certain.   He put his arm round me, lifted me up
and held me under his arm so that I felt his muscles squeezing
me like bands of iron.   He carried me to the scar, and then he
set me down as though I had been a bag of coal.

I was shaking with fright, not because of what I thought he
was going to do to me, but because I'd had such a narrow escape.
I didn't care if he did give me a hiding.   He'd saved my life,
and I felt I had to do something to show how thankful I was to
him, and I said :

" Thank you, Mr. Peacock.   Thank you, thank you ! "   And
then I said, very politely, " I've got a lobster, Mr. Peacock.
Would you like it ? "

I opened my bag.   He looked greedily at my lobster.

" Where did tha get that ? " he growled.

" Just on the other side of Cowling Scar.   It wasn't in a hole.
It was in a pool.   I got it with my hands."

" Thoo did, did tha ?   Thoo's done better than I've done all
morning.   I've only got five small crabs."

" You can have it if you like, Mr. Peacock," I said.

He stared at it.   I was sure that he did want it.   But instead of
grabbing it, he got hold of my arm, shook me, and then let me go.

" Be off with tha," he growled.   " I don't want thy lobster.
But thoo keep a civil tongue in thy head in future, or I'll bray
thy backside until thoo can't sit doon.   And don't thoo start
looking in them holes I was working at when thoo shouted for
help."

" No, I won't, Mr. Peacock," I said.   " And I hope you find a
lobster or two in them.   Thank you very much."

And then I ran as fast as I could for home.

5

I THOUGHT that Dad was very clever. As well as being able to paint pictures, he could make things like cupboards and book-cases and furniture, although he hadn't many proper tools, and he had to use boxes and packing-cases he got from the grocers for wood. He had to take these to pieces first, keeping all the nails, and straightening those that were bent.

He often went to auction sales, and bought things that were going very cheap as no one else would bid for them. He had bought a tricycle with a broken frame and only two wheels for sixpence. Also an old pedal sewing-machine with many of its parts missing, a knife cleaning machine, and a clockwork meat-roasting jack with a broken spring.

Mother thought that these things were junk and she wouldn't have them in the house, so Dad kept them in his studio. This was on the south cliff, above the coastguard station. It had once been a fisherman's warehouse. Dad had taken off one side of the tiled roof, and made this all glass, like a green house, which gave him what he called a " north light."

If it was a wet day, and there was no school, Dad would let me play in the studio sometimes. I loved watching him working at a picture, especially if it was one of something I knew, like the view of the village from the north cliff, showing the beach and the bay and High Batts point.

He would have the canvas on his easel if it was an oil painting, and stand with his palette in his left hand. Now and again he would move back from the easel, and look at the picture with his eyes half closed to " get the effect " as he called it. He would be very pleased if I said the picture was nice, but he didn't like it if I said there was something wrong, like the colour of the fields above High Batts cliff. They were grass fields and I knew they were green. But he made them grey, and he said if I really looked at them, from the place where he had composed the picture, they *were* grey, because of the distance, and if I said that grass couldn't be any other colour than green he would get really cross.

But he only painted pictures like these to sell to the summer visitors. What he liked best was painting portraits of people, and that meant they had to sit for him. He wanted to do a portrait of the vicar. One of the vicar's dearest friends was a real lord, the Marquis of Normanby, and the Marquis was a friend of Queen Victoria herself.

The marquis sometimes stayed at the vicarage. I was very disappointed when I had first seen him, for he didn't look very much different from any other man. Besides he was a clergyman and wore a round collar like the vicar. He had been a chaplain at Windsor Castle, and that was how he knew the Queen so well, and even yet sometimes went to see her.

Dad thought that if he did a good portrait of the vicar, the vicar would be bound to show it to the Marquis. That might lead to him doing a portrait of the Marquis, who *might* show it to the queen, and who knew what that might lead to ?

And then there was the major, the vicar's son. As soon as he came home from the war he *would* make a wonderful subject in his full-dress officer's uniform, full length, holding his plumed hat in one hand, touching the hilt of his sword with the other. Or perhaps seated on his charger, seeing that he was a cavalry officer.

But although the vicar had bought one or two of Dad's pictures to give away as presents to his friends, Dad hadn't yet dared to ask him to sit for his portrait. He was a very busy man, and Dad knew that he would need at least a dozen sittings of an hour each, if he was to make a good job of it.

Sometimes Dad practised on me. I'd have to pretend I was a fisherman's boy, and sit on an old lobster pot, holding a model coble in my hand, smiling at it with pleasure, but I just couldn't sit long looking at one thing when there were so many interesting things in the studio to look at, and I was always glad when he would say after perhaps only five minutes :

" Well that's enough for one day."

What I liked best was when Dad was working at one of his patents, or trying to fix up the tricycle. It would be a great help to him he said if he could get it to go, for he would be able to ride for miles into the country and find new subjects for pictures, and carry all his painting apparatus tied to the machine instead of carrying it on his back.

I was hoping that he would have room for me too !

He had mended the broken frame with splints, in the same way a doctor mends a broken leg, only using wire instead of bandages. The difficult job was to find a wheel to replace the one that was missing. It was one of the side wheels and these were a different size from the front one. He had tried wheels from perambulators, and from old bicycles, but there wasn't one that would fit, and what I was afraid of was that he might give it up, and use the two good wheels of the tricycle to go into his washing machine.

He had already used bits of the meat roasting jack and the sewing-machine for this. The idea was to save the work of washing clothes in a posh tub, beating them with a sort of heavy club, which was what Mother had to do on wash day.

Dad had a wooden barrel which he had sawn in half. It had paddles inside it, like the paddles of a steam-boat, only they were upright. You moved these backwards and forwards with a handle, and it worked well when there was just water in the barrel. But when he put any clothes in it, it took him all his strength to move the handle at all, but that, he said, was only because the paddles were too heavy. If they were made of light metal, with holes in them to let the water through, it would be easy, and he was certain that he would get some firm to take it up, and pay him a lot of money for the idea. What he was afraid of was that if he showed it to anyone before he had got it perfect, they might use the idea and not pay him anything at all.

Another of Dad's clever ideas was a lead pencil that would never need sharpening. He hadn't been able to make one, because he hadn't the proper tools, but his idea was that the pencil itself would be made of metal instead of wood. It would be a tube, and the lead part would be inside it as in an ordinary pencil, except that it wasn't stuck. The bottom end of the lead would be fixed to a small piece of metal which would slide up the tube when you wanted it to, and that would make the point of the lead show at the other end.

I thought that this was very clever indeed, for lead pencil points were always breaking, but one day the postman brought a big catalogue from Gamages in London, and among the things in it was a picture of a new sort of propelling pencil which was almost exactly like the thing that Dad had thought of. Dad was vexed, but although there were thousands of other things advertised in the catalogue, there wasn't a clothes washing machine, so he thought he was still all right about that, and he was always having new ideas for inventions.

In spite of Mafeking having been relieved, the South African War was still going on. The vicar had heard that his son had been in hospital. He had fallen off his horse while playing polo and hurt his ankle. But he was now with a force that was trying to capture a Boer general called De Wet, who had taken the place of Mr. Kruger. So far the major hadn't won any special medals, but I went on hoping that he would win the Victoria Cross, and the vicar went on praying every Sunday (although still without mentioning his son's name) that he would come back safe and sound.

I always imagined the major riding his charger, waving his sword, leading his men into battle against the Boers, not caring whether he was wounded or even killed so long as he beat the enemy. It would be awful though if he was killed, and when I was with Mother in chapel, and it came to what the preacher called " silent prayer," I always put in a special bit about him.

Mother too went on knitting and making bandages to be sent to the Red Cross for the sick and wounded soldiers and some people in the village were collecting money for a Comforts' Fund, to send parcels to our soldiers who wouldn't be home for Christmas. It was decided to have a special concert to raise money for this.

A committee was formed to arrange the concert, and Dad and his friend Mr. Beecham the coastguard were on it.

Mr. Beecham was a funny man, always joking, and he could sing comic songs too, especially when he had a drink or two. Not that he spent much time in the pubs or was ever drunk.

6

THE CONCERTS we had in the village, although I liked going to them, were never really funny. They were held in the Victoria Hall, a place as big as the Wesleyan Chapel, which stood next to the gas-works at the back of the village not far from the dock. It belonged to the church, and no one could use it unless the vicar agreed.

There was a platform at one end of the hall, with a piano and a table and chair for the chairman, who would begin with a speech before announcing the first item on the programme. There were chairs for the performers in front of the platform and steps for them to climb on to it when their turn came. There were chairs too for those who paid most to come in, but for those who paid only sixpence or less there were only forms, and if there was a big crowd those at the back had to stand.

The first item was always a piano solo and it was usually played by the mistress of the church girls' school, Miss Lawson, who was the one who arranged the concerts and decided who should take part in them. Miss Lawson was tall and straight. She had a pale severe face and wore black clothes. She was very strict with her scholars.

After her piano solo there would be songs, either by men or women singing alone or duets or quartets, with more piano solos or duets or someone giving a recitation in between.

One girl who sometimes took part had a very beautiful voice. Her name was Florence Taylor, and her father was a ship's captain who had plenty of money and lived in one of the new houses near the station. She was now in London having her voice trained and it was expected that one day she would become famous and perhaps sing at the Albert Hall. She was very pretty too.

But there was another girl, Bessie Binns, who had a voice that was much stronger than Miss Taylor's. Her favourite song was " Cherry Ripe." When she got to the top notes her voice was so loud that it almost made you deaf. It was like the whistle of a railway engine when you were standing near it on the railway platform. Although it wasn't meant to be funny I would always start giggling when Bessie sang and Mother would nudge me to stop.

A concert would remind Mother of her days in Liverpool, and going to the theatre and put her in a sad mood when we got home. Except for Miss Taylor's singing she never seemed to enjoy them much yet she said there was one good thing about them. There was never any vulgarity.

I don't think Dad thought much of them either, and Mr. Beecham, who hadn't been stationed at Bramblewick long and had only been to one of them, said that it had nearly sent him to sleep.

He had helped to get up concerts when he'd been in the Navy, either on board ship or in barracks at Portsmouth or Chatham. Singing was all right he said, but you needed other things to make people enjoy themselves, comic songs as well as serious ones, and sketches, and what were called " turns," like they had in a music hall.

The platform ought to be made to look like a theatre stage. There should be a curtain and scenery, and the performers should come on from the side instead of stepping up in sight of the audience.

Dad hadn't been to see any of Gilbert and Sullivan's plays in Liverpool, but he had been to a music hall and while he admitted to Mother that some of the things he had seen had been rather disgusting such as a comedian who had made vulgar jokes and a female contortionist who wore nothing but tights and twisted herself almost into knots, there were other things like Japanese jugglers and acrobats and a troupe of trick cyclists, and a lady who had sung Tosti's " Good-bye " so beautifully she had made many in the audience cry, including Dad himself.

The vicar wasn't on the committee, but Miss Lawson was, and Dad said she hadn't been a bit pleased with Mr. Beecham's idea about having comic songs and theatricals. The vicar would have to be chairman of course. She hoped that Miss Taylor would be able to come from London to take part. The audience would be disappointed if they didn't have their favourite performers and items, and these performers would be very hurt if they were not asked and their relatives would stay away.

She had agreed that it might be an improvement if the platform was made to look like a real stage. It could not be done unless the vicar agreed, and *she* wasn't going to ask him, so it was decided that Dad would do this after the next vestry meeting, and also ask if he would mind if Mr. Beecham got up a sketch for the concert.

Dad had spoken to the vicar, who had been quite pleased about it, as the concert was in such a good cause, and he had seemed in such a good mood that Dad had been tempted to ask him about sitting for his portrait, but decided he'd better wait for another time.

The concert was to take place in October, and for weeks before Dad could think of nothing else, for he and Mr. Beecham were to fix up the stage and the curtains, and Dad would paint scenery, and there were to be footlights too like a real theatre. But he was worried too. Although he was getting on well with the scenery Mr. Beecham was having a lot of trouble with Miss Lawson, who, he said, was nothing but an old stick-in-the-mud, and green with jealousy.

Mr. Beecham had nearly had a row with her about the piano. His idea was that this shouldn't be on the platform but on the floor like the orchestra of a theatre. Miss Lawson said she couldn't play her opening solo with the piano there. Mr. Beecham said that the concert shouldn't start off with an ordinary solo. That could come later in the programme. In a theatre the orchestra started playing before the curtain went up. She could do the same, only play tunes that everyone knew, like " Good-bye

Dolly Gray " and that might start the audience singing and put everyone in a good mood to start with.

Miss Lawson said that she had never heard of such a thing. She would never play such common tunes, and if the piano wasn't on the platform she wouldn't play at all, either solo or as accompanist to the other performers especially Miss Taylor.

But in the end she had agreed about the piano, although she was to have her own way about all the other items on the programme except the sketch, which would have to come at the very end, so that if anyone didn't care for it they could walk out, having already had their money's worth. After a lot of argument she had also agreed that another coastguard, Mr. Tims, could play what Mr. Beecham called popular ditties, while the people were taking their seats, so long as it was clear that *she* wasn't playing them.

Mr. Tims was an Irishman, and like Mr. Beecham he was always full of fun. He was rather fat, and Mr. Beecham called him Tubby, when they were not on duty. When the rocket brigade had a practice, which they did every three months Mr. Tims was always the man chosen to be rescued in the breeches buoy. There was a wooden post with steps on it fixed on a scar near to the shore. This imitated the mast of a wrecked ship. The rocket would be fired from the shore. The breeches buoy rope would be hauled out and fixed to the top of the post.

It was always done when the scar was almost surrounded by the tide, and there was deep water between the post and the shore. Mr. Tims would climb the post, get into the buoy, with his fat legs dangling through the breeches, and then those on shore would heave away, and he would be hauled through the water.

Even if it was winter, and the water icy cold, Mr. Tims always laughed and seemed to enjoy it. But when he got to the shore he had to pretend he was nearly drowned, and fall unconscious so that the rocket brigade company could practise artificial respiration on him. He would look just like a dead man, but after a while he would come to, and then he would be given a drink of rum, and he used to say that it was worth being nearly drowned for that.

The sketch was called *Darky Town*. Mr. Beecham and Mr. Tims, and Henry Newton, and two other men were to take part in it, but no ladies. They did the practising for it in Dad's studio at night, and Dad wouldn't tell us what it was about. That was a secret so that it would come as a surprise to everyone. All he would say was that it was very *very* funny, and that Mr. Beecham and Mr. Tims were real screams.

7

It was dark and stormy, the night of the concert, only there wasn't any rain. The sea was rough and the tide was high, and waves were rushing up the slipway into the dock when Mother and I walked down on our way to the hall. All the cobles had been hauled up close to the lifeboat house.

The shops were shut, for it was early closing day. But the street lamps were lit. They were gas lamps and their flames spluttered and flickered with the wind. The pubs were open of course. Mother held my hand very tightly as we passed by the door of The Fisherman's Arms. It wasn't crowded like it had been on Mafeking Day and there was no sound of singing, but there was a strong smell of beer.

There was a crowd of boys, including Ikey Harris, standing outside the entrance to the hall. They laughed and shouted at us as we passed, which I thought was because I was wearing a velvet suit with a white collar and tie that Mother always made me wear for special occasions. I blushed and pretended not to notice them.

Henry Newton was at the door to take the entrance money. He was in his best Sunday clothes. He must have been in the pubs though for his breath smelled strongly of beer. Close to him stood the police sergeant, who came to every concert or meeting in the hall, for he never had to pay, because it was his duty to keep order.

Although we were poor, Mother didn't like other people to think we were too poor to have good seats, and she paid a shilling for herself and sixpence for me. Dad wouldn't have to pay because he was going to work the curtain.

We were early, yet the hall was more than half full when we got inside. Before we got to our seats I noticed that things were different. For one thing all the walls were draped with flags, which Mr. Beecham must have borrowed from the coastguard station. And at the platform end, instead of there being just the platform, with a window behind it, it was closed in right up to the ceiling with painted canvas, stretched tight so that it looked solid. But there were curtains too, also made of canvas but loose and hanging in folds.

Behind the curtain, someone was playing the piano. It wasn't Miss Lawson, for she was standing up near to one of the front seats looking as severe as usual. Besides, the tune was " In the Shade of the old Apple Tree."

We sat down, and Mother whispered to me :

" It does look like a theatre. Oh, if only it was going to be *H.M.S. Pinafore* ! "

And just as she said that the tune of the piano changed to " Dear Little Buttercup," and Mother very softly started to hum it. No one else seemed to take much notice of the music, which soon changed to another tune, just like a barrel organ. All the time more people were coming in and taking their seats. As at other concerts those who were going to take part went to the front and I saw Miss Taylor, wearing a cloak made of fur, but showing that she had a white evening dress underneath it.

There was a big clock on the wall. The concert was to start at seven. By the time it got to five minutes to, the hall was packed. Most of the people were women. There were no drunkards or other bad characters. Some of the women had their children with them, but the boys who had been standing outside were at the back of the hall, and some of them had climbed on to the window sill. They were behaving well because the sergeant was near them. People were talking, but not loudly, and the piano was still playing. And then suddenly it stopped, and everyone was quiet, and looked towards the entrance door.

The vicar had arrived.

He stopped for a moment just inside, blinking a little at the light. He was wearing a long black overcoat, with a black fur collar, and he was holding his top hat in one hand, a silver-mounted stick in the other.

He was tall, but not so tall as Gow Pickering. Although he was very old, he held himself straight, like a soldier. Mother often said that he looked like the Duke of Wellington, because of his long hooked nose. Dad said that he had the noblest face he had ever seen, that with his silvery hair and proud expression he looked like a king or an emperor, and that was one reason why he longed to paint a picture of him. But the first time Dad had taken me to church I'd thought the vicar was God Himself, and I'd been almost too frightened to look at him.

I couldn't see whether he was paying to come in or not. Both Henry Newton and the policeman were looking at him respectfully. Then he began to walk down the aisle between the seats and everyone started to clap, and he smiled, looking from one side to the other.

But as he got near to the stage, he stopped, and looked puzzled at things being so different. There was no platform for him to step up on to.

And just then the curtains began to move. They were drawn back although you couldn't see who was moving them. And there was the platform with the piano on one side, a table and chair on the other. But at the back was a huge picture, painted on canvas, reaching the whole way from side to side.

It had been done by Dad of course. It was the view of Bramblewick Bay from the north cliff, with some red-roofed houses, and some cobles, and fishermen mending nets close up, and High Batts cliff in the distance, with its fields grey of course, and yet looking all right.

Everyone stared at it. There was no clapping, but everyone in the audience, including the boys at the back seemed to say " *Ooooo* " and I heard several voices saying " lovely," " pretty," " champion " and other words and sounds that showed how good they thought it was. I felt very proud that it was Dad who had done it.

The vicar must have thought it was good too, but as he stared at it, Mr. Beecham, who was wearing ordinary clothes

E

instead of his coastguard's uniform came out of a doorway at the side of the stage, and respectfully signed to the vicar to enter the doorway. There must have been some steps inside for in a moment the vicar appeared on the stage, near to his table and chair, and he sat down.

Mr. Beecham hadn't followed him though. He signed to Henry Newton at the back of the hall, and shouted :

" Lights down there." And he reached up to a gas bracket half way up the hall, and turned the jets low. Henry did the same with the one at the back, so that the hall itself was almost in darkness just like it was when there was a magic lantern lecture.

But there was plenty of light on the stage. There was a gas bracket hanging from the ceiling, and at the edge of the platform although you couldn't see the jets, there was a row of lights which shone on to the stage, lighting up Dad's picture better than ever. Mother squeezed my hand again :

" Footlights," she whispered. " It *is* like a real theatre."

No one was clapping now. Everyone was looking at the stage. The vicar wasn't smiling either. I thought that if he had been in church, and in his white robes, I'd have been just as frightened of him as before, for the light shining on his hair from the ceiling and on his face from the footlights gave him a queer extra-holy look.

He took out his spectacles, put them on, picked up a piece of paper that was on the table and started to read. The clock struck seven. He stood up with the paper in his hand, and the audience clapped again, but stopped as he started to speak.

He didn't make a long speech, and he was very solemn, perhaps because he was thinking about his son. He said that the concert had been got up so that parcels could be sent to our gallant soldiers who were still fighting for God and Queen and Country in South Africa. Many of our soldiers had already given their lives. Many had been wounded, or suffered from fever. Although we were all here to enjoy the programme that had been arranged for us, and to have a happy time, our thoughts must be with the soldiers too.

I heard Mother sniffing when he said this, as though she was crying, but she clapped loudly when the vicar ended his speech by saying that he would now call upon Miss Lawson to give the first item on the programme which was to be a piano solo by Mendelssohn.

The vicar sat down. Miss Lawson who had been sitting in one of the front chairs got up and walked to the stage door, out of sight. The clapping stopped. Everyone was waiting for her to appear on the stage. But instead of that there was a·loud clatter from where the steps must have been, and a frightened cry from Miss Lawson herself, and then the voice of Mr. Beecham :

" It's all right now. Step this way."

I started to giggle, but Mother squeezed my hand and whispered :

" Sssh ! "

Dad told us later that it had been rather dark inside the stage door and Miss Lawson had slipped on the first step, but Mr. Beecham had saved her from really falling.

She appeared now on the stage, but was looking very bewildered, and vexed too. The lights seemed to dazzle her. They made her face seem different too, all yellow like a Chinaman's. But the audience was clapping again, and she sat down at the piano, put her music on it, and as soon as the clapping stopped started to play her piece.

It didn't last long. Everyone clapped when she finished, but no one shouted " encore " and the vicar stood up to announce the next item which was a duet called " The Keys of Heaven." A man and a woman got up from the front seats and walked to the stage door, but Miss Lawson just stayed at the piano to play the accompaniment.

" The Keys of Heaven " was a humorous song about a young man offering all sorts of gifts to a young lady to persuade her to marry him. Everyone knew that the man and woman who were to sing it were married and had children, and as the same couple sang the same song at almost every concert, and everyone knew the music and the words by heart, it wasn't really funny.

Yet they did *look* funny when they got on to the stage, because the footlights not only made their faces yellow, like Miss Lawson's, but also very old and wrinkled, like Neddy Peacock's, and both of them kept on blinking as they sang, because the light dazzled them.

I was glad they didn't get an encore. Although I wanted to hear Miss Taylor sing, I was longing for this part of the concert to be over, so that we could get to Mr. Beecham's sketch.

A lady gave a humorous " Yorkshire " reading, but she seemed to be dazzled by the lights, and stuttered and kept on losing her place, and although the audience laughed and seemed to enjoy it she didn't get an encore either. Miss Lawson then played a duet with another lady, and the next item was a song by Bessie Binns, and I started to giggle before she got on to the stage.

She wasn't a pretty girl like Miss Taylor. She had ginger hair and a red freckly face, with a big mole on one cheek. Her father was a ship's cook, who spent most of his time at sea, but she had lots of sisters and cousins and aunts in the village, and they were proud of her and thought that if only she could have her voice trained it would be even better than Miss Taylor's because it was much more powerful.

The song she was to sing this time was " Drink to Me Only " and not " Cherry Ripe " as usual. As soon as she appeared on the stage there was an extra loud clap, because all her relations were in the audience. She was wearing a bright green dress with some green ribbon in her hair to match. Like the other performers she looked a bit dazzled and bewildered and when she came forward to the edge of the stage I saw that she was trembling from head to foot.

It was very hard for me to stop giggling, for I did think she looked funny, and a really funny thing happened next, for Miss Lawson instead of starting the music for " Drink to Me Only " began " Cherry Ripe " and had got almost to where Bessie was to join in before she found out her mistake.

Nobody laughed aloud. Miss Lawson started again with the right tune and soon Bessie began " Drink to Me Only " very softly at first but soon getting louder, and it was all right until she got to the top note. When she did something seemed to go wrong with her voice. Instead of a clear note, she just squawked like a frightened hen. I couldn't help laughing out loud, and the boys at the back of the hall laughed too, and I thought that Mother was almost laughing when she squeezed my hand again and whispered to me to " hush."

Bessie didn't stop singing, however. She went on to the next verse and this time before she reached the top note she seemed to take a deep breath, and the note was so loud and shrill it made me jump.

There was loud clapping when she had finished. For the first time someone shouted encore, although I expected it was one of her relations. But Bessie had come down off the stage, and although the clapping went on, and someone shouted " Cherry Ripe " she wouldn't sing again and the vicar announced the next item which was a part song by two ladies and two men called " Sweet and Low."

I liked this, but I was longing for the sketch, and I was glad when, after another piano solo and a recitation, the vicar announced that Miss Taylor was going to sing, for I guessed that this was going to be the last item before the sketch. I had noticed that between the items Henry Newton and one or two other men who were to take part in it, had gone through the stage door.

Of course there was loud clapping when the vicar announced Miss Taylor. Her song was to be " The Holy City " and it had to be her only song for her teacher had told her she had to be careful not to strain her voice. I saw her stand up and hand her fur cape to her mother, who was with her, and walk to the stage door.

Even the vicar clapped and smiled when she appeared on the stage, and she smiled at him, and walked to the front of the stage and smiled and bowed to the audience. None of the other performers had done this of course. She didn't seem a little bit nervous, and the footlights didn't seem to bother her, although they did make her face rather yellow.

She was wearing a lovely dress, and I thought that I had never seen such a lovely face as hers. The clapping stopped. Everyone in the audience seemed to hold their breath, and for the first time since the concert started, I could hear the roar of the sea coming from the dock.

Then Miss Lawson started to play the opening bars of the tune. She stopped a moment, began again and Miss Taylor joined in.

Although it was a religious song and very solemn, I thought it was the most wonderful song I had ever heard, with Miss Taylor singing it. I almost forgot about the sketch. She didn't sing half as loud as Bessie had done, but every note was smooth and clear, and every word was clear too, and when she came to the " Jerusalem, Jerusalem " bit I felt that I could really see the city of Jerusalem, with angels flying in the sky, all of them singing " Hozanna " softly and beautifully.

I clapped like mad when it was finished, and shouted " encore " and lots of other people did, even Bessie's relations. Although the vicar had said it was to be her only song, I hoped that she would at least sing one verse over again. But she only bowed and smiled, and then turned to Miss Lawson and smiled to her as though to thank her for playing the piano, and then moved behind the curtains out of sight. But the audience went on clapping even when she came out of the stage door again, to take her seat.

The vicar now stood up again. Except when Miss Taylor had walked on to the stage, he hadn't smiled once during the concert, but sat looking solemn and gloomy, and Miss Lawson had done the same, although I'd thought she looked vexed too.

The vicar said that we had now come almost to the end of the concert, which he was sure everyone had enjoyed. There was only one more item, a sketch, and he understood that this would need the whole space of the platform, and he would have to take his seat in the hall. He hoped that we were all going to enjoy the sketch which promised to be something unusual.

Miss Lawson had stood up and she was the first to move off the stage. The vicar followed, and as soon as he got to his chair in the front row the curtains were drawn again, hiding Dad's picture.

The vicar and Miss Lawson sat down. Someone, I guessed

it was Mr. Tims, started to play the piano. The tune was " Way down upon the Swanee River."

But after just one verse, the curtains opened again.

At first there wasn't a sound in the hall. Everyone seemed to be holding their breath in surprise.

Dad's picture had gone. Instead there was an imitation of a grocer's shop with a big printed sign, JOE MACKINTOSH— HIGH CLASS GROCER. There was a long counter with a set of scales on it : also packets of flour and jars and bottles, a soda water siphon, some mouse-traps, fly-papers, all marked with their price, and there were shelves with more groceries, and strings of sausages at the back.

Behind the counter was a black man with white curly hair and big red lips. He was scooping sugar from a big tin with the word SUGAR printed on it, into one pan of the scales.

I hadn't guessed yet that the man was Mr. Beecham himself, wearing a wig, and with his face blackened with burnt cork and his lips painted so that they looked enormous. There was a one-pound weight on the other pan of the scales. It didn't come up and balance with the sugar he put on it, but instead of putting more sugar he bent down behind the counter and lifted up another tin. On this tin was printed the word SAND.

Some of the audience were tittering a bit, but no one really laughed yet. He opened the tin and scooped some of the white sand out and put this on the pan with the sugar. The pan went down with a bang. He mixed the sand and sugar together with his hand, and poured the mixture into a paper bag and held it up and laughed, with his eyes rolling from side to side :

" Dat suh am good measure ! " he said. " None o' mah customers is going to guess that ain't pure sugar."

It was only when he spoke that I knew it *was* Mr. Beecham.

I had never seen or heard anything quite so funny. And everyone else seemed to think the same too, although I couldn't see the vicar and Miss Lawson. Everyone was laughing so loud that I could hardly hear what he said next.

He put the bag on a pile of other bags which had a card saying BEST PURE SUGAR, and then he looked towards what was meant to be the doorway into the shop, and quickly hid the tin with SAND on it under the counter.

He was just in time, for in came a fat darky woman, with a red scarf over her head, and carrying a shopping basket. She looked even funnier than Mr. Beecham, but this time I knew straight away that it was really Mr. Tims in disguise.

As she came in Mr. Beecham rolled his eyes, and then winked at the audience, and said in a cunning voice :

" Why here's one o' mah best customers, ole Mammy Jones! " and to her he said :

" Mornin' Mammy Jones. 'Ow is you this mornin' ? "

" I ain't s' good Mis' Mackintosh. Ise got a rumblin' in my cranium, an' rummaticks in mah legs, an' ah ain't got no appetite fer food—— "

" Ah'll fix yer good," Mr. Beecham interrupted. " You wants one o' mah special pills ! "

He took from a shelf behind the counter a big jar which had printed on it CURE ALL PILLS EXTRA STRONG. He took out one pill and held it up. It was bright red in colour, as big as a pigeon's egg. I laughed so much I nearly choked. Every-one else was laughing too, including Mother. I could feel her shaking.

But this was only the start. It went on getting funnier and funnier, although with everyone laughing so much I couldn't hear everything the characters said.

" Mammy Jones " bought a pill. And then she bought two pounds of sugar, and went out. Mr. Beecham winked at the audience as soon as she was out of sight and said :

" Mammy Jones won't guess there's sand in dat sugar if she eats dat pill ! Dat pill am pure soap," and then he gave a frightened look towards the door, and said :

" Oh ! My—oh my, here's Lijah Brown wi' dem sossiges dat ah sold him. Ah hope he ain't found out what ah put in dem."

Another darky came in. It was Henry Newton, with his face just as black as Mr. Beecham's. He was holding a string of imitation sausages. He started shouting angrily at Mr. Beecham, and although I couldn't hear properly what they were saying

I could see that Mr. Beecham was pretending to be sorry, and wanted " Elijah " to take some sugar in place of the sausages.

But " Elijah " was still angry, and he banged his hand on to the counter where the mouse-traps were. He gave a loud shout and held up his hand with a mouse-trap pinching his finger, and he walked up and down pretending it was hurting him and that he couldn't get it off. Mr. Beecham roared with laughter at him.

When that happened, Mother, although she was laughing herself, asked me in a whisper if I wanted " to do something." I did, but it would have meant going outside, and I didn't want to miss any of the fun, and I shook my head and went on laughing.

Two more darkies came in. One of them I could tell was Dicky Bedlington, a sailor, who sometimes got drunk. I couldn't tell who the other was. Dicky was playing a mouth-organ, the other one singing. They were rolling from side to side as though they were pretending to be drunk.

Mother stopped laughing.

" I hope there's going to be no vulgarity," she whispered. " Are you sure you don't want to go ? "

But she had to start laughing again, for Dicky pretended to fall against the counter, and *he* got caught with a mouse-trap, and while he was dancing about the other man picked up one of the fly-papers, which stuck first to one of his hands and then to his other one, and then on to his face.

Dad, as well as having to work the curtains, had to tell the characters what to say next if they couldn't remember. He told us later that Henry should have come off the stage before these two characters came on, and that none of them, even Mr. Beecham himself, could remember all the words they had to say. He had to admit too, to Mother, that before the sketch had started, and the men were blacking their faces behind the curtains, Mr. Tims had given every one of them a drink of rum.

Yet Mother, although she said that she had been shocked and ashamed by the vulgarity of it all, had laughed almost as much as I did, except at the very end. She had almost screamed when " Mammy Jones " had come on to the stage again with her face all covered with soap suds, from the pill, and carrying an enormous rolling pin and tried to give Mr. Beecham a whack with it, and Mr. Beecham to protect himself, had seized the soda-water siphon and squirted it over her head.

And Mother hadn't stopped laughing when, while this was going on, Miss Lawson had got up, and, looking as serious as if she had been at a funeral, walked right out of the hall. No one seemed to take any notice of her. Everyone was enjoying the sketch too much. And it got funnier still. All the characters seemed to have gone quite crazy, and they were laughing too, and seemed to be enjoying themselves as much as the audience.

Mr. Beecham and " Mammy " were the funniest, for Mr. Beecham kept on squirting the soda water, and she was whacking him with the rolling pin, although it couldn't have hurt him really for it was a bit of rubber tube. You could see it bend. The soda water washed some of the black from her face too. Henry, who had got the mouse-trap off his fingers, joined in the fight by trying to whack Mr. Beecham with the sausages, and then Dicky took a handful of fly-papers and stuck some of them on Mr. Beecham's face.

Mother said later that all of them must have been at least partly drunk with the rum, yet she must have seen Miss Lawson walk out, and if she had been disgusted herself, I don't think that she would have laughed so much. She would have walked out too and taken me with her, which would have meant missing the funniest thing of all.

It started with " Mammy " picking up one of the paper bags of flour from the counter and throwing it at Mr. Beecham. It hit him on the head and burst. He threw one back but it hit Henry instead of her and then they all started throwing the bags at each other. The grown-ups in the audience were laughing, but the lads at the back were shrieking, just like they did at a fight, egging them on, and the policeman didn't try to stop them. He must have been laughing too.

And yet the vicar couldn't have been laughing. I think that everyone must have forgotten about him until he suddenly stood up, lifted one hand, and shouted at the top of his voice :

" *Stop ! STOP !* "

As he did this a bag of flour, I couldn't see who had thrown it, and I don't think it was done on purpose, burst almost at his feet making a white cloud round him and making a white patch on his black coat.

He shouted again. Those on the stage stopped and stood still, and everyone in the hall stopped laughing and there was silence as though it had become a church service, and everyone was looking at the vicar who was looking terribly angry.

" This is disgraceful," he shouted. " I will have no more of it. The concert is ended. Draw the curtains whoever is in charge of them. And let us end it at least in a respectful way by singing the National Anthem. I call on Miss Taylor to begin ! "

Dad who had kept out of sight all the time must have been very frightened, for it was he who'd had to ask the vicar's permission to have the sketch. But he worked the curtains all right. Everyone stood up. And Miss Taylor whose fur cape was also patched with flour, started " God Save the Queen."

And that *was* the end.

8

ALTHOUGH everyone, except the vicar and Miss Lawson, seemed to think that the concert had been the best there had ever been in Bramblewick, and Dad himself heard a lot of praise for the picture he had painted for the stage, he was very worried about what had happened at the end, for he felt that it had dished his chances of ever persuading the vicar to sit for his portrait.

The vicar hadn't said anything to him about it, but he had been more than usually cool in his manner, and Dad was certain that he felt that he was to blame. He passed Miss Lawson several times in the village, and had touched his hat to her, but she had cut him dead. He and Mr. Beecham and Mr. Tims had taken down the stage front and the footlights and removed all the scenery, and it looked as though if there ever was another concert everything would be done in the old way.

And, although it was rather funny, an awful thing happened to Dad at evening service a few Sundays after the concert just when he was beginning to hope that the business of the sketch had blown over.

One of his jobs as sidesman was to help take the collection while the last hymn was being sung. He and another sidesman, Captain Redman, had to walk along the aisle and wait at the end of each of the pews while the collecting bag was passed along from one person to another and then back, when they went to the next pew. He took one side of the aisle, and Captain Redman the other.

I wasn't there of course, but Dad told us all about it when he got home. It was while he was waiting for the bag to be passed back to him, when he had done about half of the pews, that he suddenly began to think about *Darky Town* and the fight with the flour bags, and of how one bag had nearly hit the vicar, and he felt himself starting to giggle, just like I did when I looked at the girl with St. Vitus's Dance in chapel or heard Bessie Binns singing.

Everyone in the church was very solemn, and standing up singing the hymn, and Dad tried hard to stop thinking about the sketch, and he actually pinched himself and bit his lip.

I knew how hard it was to stop a giggling fit once you felt it coming over you. It was like wanting to sneeze or cough, or feeling sick, and the more you wanted to stop the worse it was. And that was how Dad felt. He knew it would be just terrible if he burst out laughing. When the nearest person in the pew handed the bag back to him, he lowered his head so that his face wouldn't be seen, and then he knew that he just couldn't hold it back much longer.

When the bags had been along the last pews, and the hymn was nearly finished, they had to be taken to the vicar who would be standing waiting with the silver chalice, by the altar rails.

Then the vicar would solemnly turn and place the chalice on the altar and ask a blessing on the money. Instead of going to the next pew, Dad, with the bag in his hand, started back along the aisle, where he had already collected, towards the entrance door.

He imagined that everyone must have been staring at him in surprise to see him walking towards the door with the collecting bag, as though he was going to steal the money instead of taking it to the altar, but that thought made him feel worse, and just as he got to the end of the aisle he really began to laugh out loud, only he managed by keeping one hand to his mouth to make it sound like a fit of coughing, as though he was really ill.

People were sometimes taken ill in church during the service. Women sometimes fainted, and once during the sermon, a young man who was in the choir had fallen in a real fit, foaming at the mouth. The vicar had stopped his sermon while the man was carried to the vestry by other members of the choir, but he had gone on with it as soon as everything was quiet, just as though nothing unusual had happened.

Dad couldn't pretend he was as ill as that. He knew that he would be all right once he got outside the church, and he thought the best thing then would be to wait in the porch, or go round to the side door, and hand the bag to the vicar as he came into the vestry when the service was ended.

It was a cold rainy night. The inner door, which led into the porch, was shut. The porch had stone benches on each side of it. It was here that the church notices like marriage banns were shown. The outer door of the porch was never shut, and people often used the porch as a shelter if they were caught near the church in a rainstorm.

Dad lifted the latch of the inner door as quietly as he could, then pulled the door open. And there, sitting on one of the benches, was the police sergeant, puffing away at his pipe, not thinking that anyone would see him while the service was going on.

Policemen were not allowed to smoke when they were in uniform. And smoking inside the church, even if it was only the porch, was sacrilege. Policemen were not allowed to sit down on duty either.

Dad didn't think of that just then, for the very sight of the sergeant gave him a fright, and he didn't see that he had given the sergeant a fright too. He had stood up, and quickly put his pipe away. Dad shut the door. He'd stopped laughing, but he made himself cough, putting his hand to his mouth, and then without another look at the sergeant, he rushed straight past him out into the churchyard and the pouring rain, without his hat or coat of course.

He knew now that the only thing he could do was to go to the side door, which led into the vestry where the men and boys of the choir put their surplices on, and took them off after the service. The vicar used this door to get in and out of the church.

It was very dark. He was in such a hurry to get out of the rain that he tripped over the kerb of a grave and fell full length on top of it, among the artificial flowers that were lying on it, and he dropped the bag, and thought he'd lost it. He found it all right, but when he got to the side door he found that it was bolted on the inside, and there was no porch to give him shelter. So he had to stand and wait in the rain for the service to be over.

It was a good thing for him that the collection was taken after the sermon and not before. He heard the last verse of the hymn. The vicar would now be holding the chalice for Captain Redman to put his bag on it. What would he be thinking about the other bag ? Dad said that he was just shaking with cold, and fright too.

There was a silence after the hymn. Then he heard the organ starting to play again which was the sign for the vicar to lead the choir back to the vestry, when the congregation would start to leave. At last he heard the bolt of the door being drawn and he stood back against the church wall while the men and boys, in their ordinary clothes, came out, hiding so that none of them would see him.

When the last of them had gone he went in and walked into the vestry. There was the vicar, and the organist, Mr. Conyers, an old man with a white beard. Mr. Conyers was helping the vicar on with his fur-collared coat.

Dad told us that he could not remember all that happened then, for the vicar just stared at him in the most dreadful way like a judge sentencing a murderer to be hanged. He didn't ask Dad any questions, and when Dad started to explain what had happened he stuttered. He couldn't tell the real truth of course. He had to say that he had been suddenly taken ill, and thought he was going to be sick, and as he was wet through and shaking it must have sounded as though he was speaking the truth. But the vicar just went on staring at him and at last he said :

" That will do. Such a thing has never happened in my church before, and I trust that it will never happen again. Be more careful in future about what you eat and drink before coming to service. Give me the bag and I will lay it on the altar. Now go and get your coat and hat before the verger has turned out all the lights. Good night to you ! "

Dad had to change all his clothes when he got home. They were his best Sunday ones too. Mother couldn't help laughing a bit when he was telling his story, and he giggled himself, especially when he mentioned the sergeant, who really might have arrested him on suspicion of trying to steal the collection bag. But when he told us what the vicar had said to him she was angry.

She said that if he had been a real Christian he would have been sympathetic, instead of scolding Dad. She was sure that a Wesleyan minister wouldn't have behaved like that. He didn't know that he hadn't really been ill. Instead of going for him, he should have said he was sorry, and asked him how he was feeling, and perhaps taken him to the vicarage and got his house-keeper to give him some hot tea before he set off for home.

Dad stuck up for the vicar then. Mother was wrong to blame him. It must have upset him very much when only one collection bag had been placed on the chalice to be blessed. Also he was very worried about his son. That would make him crotchety. We had to remember too that he was the richest, most influential person in the district and then Dad turned on me and said I must be very careful not to repeat anything he had said about his giggling, for if that reached the vicar's ears he would be finished for ever.

I promised, of course, but although I didn't say so, I took Mother's side in the argument. I thought she was right about the vicar and that I'd like to pay him back for being so unkind to Dad, and also for being so huffy about the concert. And I thought again about playing pin-and-button on him. I wondered if I would ever be brave enough to do it.

9

I WOULD have liked to have seen *Darky Town* all over again. Seeing Mr. Beecham and Mr. Tims and Henry Newton in their ordinary clothes it was hard to believe that they were the same persons who had acted on the stage and been so funny. It started a new craze among the lads, led on by Ikey of course. Although this was the season for football and shinny ower, and tip-cat, hoops, marbles, tin-in-the-ring and also pin-and-button, the craze now was to play " darkies," have " shops " like Joe Mackintosh's and have fights with anything that looked like flour, and the best thing for this, as flour was dear, was to use whitening, the powder mixed with water and used for painting ceilings.

Ikey had the best shop. He made the counter of fish boxes. He had some mouse-traps, and he had bits of old rope for sausages. He couldn't get a soda-water siphon, because they were expensive, so for squirting the water he had a big squirt which his father, before he had been drowned, used for cleaning the top windows of their house. It would drench anyone who got a full go with it, so Ikey saw that no one used it except himself. He played the part of Joe Mackintosh, and a boy called Fatty Welford, whose father was a baker, played Mammy, and Ikey had his special pals for the other parts. The rest of us were just the audience, although we did black our faces and pretend to be darkies, and we joined in the fight.

It wasn't very funny compared with the real thing. Mother didn't like me rubbing burnt cork on my face and hands, for it was difficult to wash off, and the mothers of the other boys, including Ikey's, got angry too, not only about the cork, but about the whitening which had to be washed off clothes, and it wasn't long before the craze ended, and we got on to other games.

One of the games I liked best was marbles. If the weather was dry our pitches could be anywhere where there was a patch of hard level ground, although the best places were on the flagstones in the middle of the cobbled alleys. The pitch would be about six feet long. There would be a little hole just big enough to take a marble. Any number of boys could take part in a game, but as a rule there weren't more than six.

New marbles were expensive. You only got six for a ha'penny, and I only got a ha'penny a week pocket money so I had to be careful not to play with boys who had got the knack of a pitch. I would never play with Ikey. He had so many marbles that he carried them in a cloth bag, and he had won them all from other boys chiefly at the gas-works pitch.

This was where we went when it was raining.

I loved the gas-works quite apart from playing marbles in it, particularly in winter-time. It was always beautifully warm.

The man who looked after it and emptied and filled the retorts twice a day was Mr. Birch. Although he was married he hadn't any children of his own. Perhaps that was why he liked to have boys playing in the gas works. They had to behave themselves however. He was particularly strict about bad language.

He wasn't such a big man, but he was strong with thick arms that were covered with tattoo patterns, including a Chinese dragon. He had ginger hair. He wasn't born in Bramblewick. He had once been a sailor and had travelled all round the world. The last ship he had sailed in had been wrecked on High Batts in a storm and although he and the other sailors had got ashore safely, he had decided not to go to sea again.

Mr. Birch was a Wesleyan and a local preacher. He had once preached a sermon about himself telling how he had been converted and he had surprised some of the congregation by the things he said. He actually admitted that he had sinned heavily as a young man and had broken many of the Commandments. He didn't say which ones he had broken, and I don't think that

anyone ever found out, but he said that he had fallen to most of
the temptations which Satan sets like a spider's web for sailors
in foreign sea ports. One of them of course was strong drink,
and he said that he had used profane language and had even been
blasphemous without a thought of the punishment that was in
store for those who did so in the Hereafter, the eternal fires of Hell.

And then at last he had heard the message of Salvation. This
had happened when he was in Cardiff waiting for a ship after he had
spent all the money from his last voyage on drink. He had
pawned his watch, and all his other possessions except the clothes
he was wearing. It was a Sunday night and he was cold and
hungry, and he was even tempted to steal to get money to buy
drink again. But he saw the door of a Mission open and a notice
saying HOT SOUP AND WELCOME TO ALL.

He had gone in and a woman with a kind face had given him a
bowl of hot soup and then tried to persuade him to go to a service
that was being held. He hadn't wanted to go a bit, for he had
always preferred pubs to churches or chapels. But he had gone,
and he had heard a sermon from a man who wasn't dressed like a
clergyman telling the Message of Salvation, and that had done it.
The man had talked to him after the service, and he had been
given some more soup, and he had been told where he could sleep
that night without paying, and from that night his whole life
had been changed.

If ever a boy used bad language in the gas-works Mr. Birch
would send him out straight away and he wouldn't be allowed
to play until he had said he was sorry and promised never to do
it again. He had sent Ikey out once. Ikey boasted he'd had his
revenge by playing pin-and-button on Mr. Birch the same night,
but I didn't believe it, for there was no place near to Mr. Birch's
cottage for anyone to hide. It was just swank, and Ikey did tell Mr.
Birch he was sorry a few days after, and if he did swear, as he
might do if he lost a lot of marbles in a game, he'd do it underneath
his breath, like I did sometimes if Dad or Mother vexed me.

There was no marble playing while the retorts were being
attended to. There were three retorts, made of thick iron.
They were like ovens, very long and wide enough for a man to

crawl into. But they were bricked in so that you could only see their doors and the pipes that led up from them to the washing tanks and purifiers through which the hot gas bubbled and passed on its way to the gasometer.

There were two retorts side by side, with the third one above, and below was the furnace with an ordinary iron door with hinges. The retort doors were iron plates without hinges and they were held on to the mouths of the retorts with big screw clamps. Each retort had a spare door, and the first thing Mr. Birch had to do was to get the spare doors ready. He had a bucket of lime mortar and a trowel and along the edge of each door where it would press on the edges of the oven he would spread a coating of mortar.

Even in daylight it was dark and gloomy in the place when the retorts and furnace were closed, for the windows were grimy and sooty, but a gas jet was always burning near to the retorts. When all was ready Mr. Birch would take off his jacket, roll up his shirt sleeves, take a piece of newspaper and twist it into a spill, light it at the gas jet and lay it on top of the door of the first retort.

This was when the first excitement began. He would unscrew the clamp slowly, and suddenly the door would come loose. There would be a loud pop, and flames would shoot out all round the door as the gas which was still in the retort caught fire from the paper.

The flames would soon go out. With a pair of tongs Mr. Birch would take off the hot door and drop it on the floor and you could look straight into the retort. The whole place would be lit up with a red glow, and even if you were as far back as you could go you could feel the heat of it.

But there were no flames inside the retort. The coal that had been shovelled in at the last filling had been changed into red-hot burning coke.

With a long rake Mr. Birch would now begin to pull this coke out on to the floor, which was covered with iron plates, and this was where some of the bigger boys would be allowed to help. There was a trough of water, and they would fill buckets from it and throw it on the coke which would hiss and send up clouds of steam which looked red from the glow of the retort.

Even when all the coke was out the retort was still red hot, and quivering, just like the scars and cliffs of Bramblewick quivered in the sun on a very hot summer's day.

The next thing was to fill it with fresh coal. There was a heap of this on the floor. It wasn't like the lumpy coal that Neddy Peacock sold for house fires. The bits were small, like gravel. Mr. Birch had a big shovel. He would fill this from the heap, hold it for a moment then take three strides towards the open retort and at the third stride swing the shovel and shoot the coal so that it went to the far end of the retort. At once the coal would catch fire and long flames and clouds of smoke would shoot out as he strode back for another shovelful, and this would go on until the retort was almost full.

Then with the flames still coming out, he would lift the spare door on to the iron rods that held the clamp, push it forward and start to turn the handle of the clamp until at last the door touched the retort mouth. The flames would suddenly go out, and the place would be almost dark again. He would tighten the clamp until the mortar began to squeeze out to make certain that no gas was escaping, and then he would mop the sweat from his face and get ready for the next retort.

When all three were filled and the coke quenched, Mr. Birch would open the furnace door. The furnace was bigger and even hotter than the retorts, although it had no flames, for it only burnt coke. First Mr. Birch would rake it to get out the ash and clinkers, and then he would shovel into it the coke from the retorts.

It was while he was doing this, and we were all (including Ikey) looking into the furnace, that Mr. Birch once said, in a most frightening way that the furnace was just like Hell on a small scale. That the wicked would be shovelled into it just like he was shovelling the coke, only that they would go on burning for ever. Although I was sure he meant this for Ikey it really did frighten me more than anything I had ever heard about Hell in chapel or Sunday school, for he sounded as though he would enjoy doing it. Yet he didn't often talk about religion, and he was a kind man the way he let us come into the gas-works and let us play marbles when it was too wet to play outside.

He would sometimes play himself too, but if he won he always shared his winnings with the boys who had lost. He knew the knack of the pitch of course. It was on the floor near to a wooden seat where he sat to put the mortar on the doors. It was smoother than any pitch in the village, for it was a sheet of iron, and the hole was a rivet hole. The sheet was bent a bit and to pitch or shove a marble you had to allow for this and aim to one side.

Next to Mr. Birch himself Ikey was the one who knew the knack best. I never won when I played a game in which he took part. I didn't hate him for this, but I had been glad when Mr. Birch punished him. I was certain he had lied about playing pin-and-button on Mr. Birch in revenge.

10

MOTHER WAS very smart at finding out what I was thinking about, especially if I had done anything wrong and it was preying on my mind so I had to be careful not to let her suspect that I was thinking about playing pin-and-button on the vicar, and I never did think about it when she was looking at me.

It wouldn't be a wicked thing to do anyway. It wouldn't mean breaking any of the ten commandments. The vicar wasn't God. The vicarage wasn't a sacred place like the church. I should only be playing a practical joke on him, and if it annoyed him that would just show that he couldn't take a joke, and everyone was supposed to be able to do that, although Neddy Peacock couldn't.

I *had* nearly made up my mind to do it. But although I had been with the other lads (including Ikey) when they'd been playing pin-and-button. I'd never done the actual thing myself, either fixing the pin or pulling on the cotton. It was the fixing of the pin that was the riskiest part. If the boy who was doing it made a noise, the victim might hear it and rush out and there was the risk too, that someone, perhaps the sergeant himself might come along the alley, and usually two boys had to keep watch on each side of the victim's house, and whistle if they heard anyone coming.

I had a perfect button. I had found it on the beach one day, and thought for a moment it was a sovereign or a guinea, for it was stuck with only its edge showing in a crack in the scar. It was made of brass and it had a little ring in the middle. I had wound some of Mother's black sewing cotton on to an old bobbin, and with one of Dad's drawing pins, which was much better than an ordinary pin, I had practised on the looking-glass in the attic, which was my bedroom.

The looking-glass was not quite like a window, but it worked quite well for practice and I was certain I would be able to do it just as easily on one of the windows at the front of the vicarage where the lawn and the garden began, although it would be no good unless it was the window of the room where he was sitting. I should know which room this was by the light in it.

Yet it was a daring and risky thing to do, and I kept on putting it off. For one thing I did need at least one more boy to go with me, to keep watch, and I couldn't think of a single boy that I could trust. If I asked one of them, he might say yes, just for swank, but he would be bound to split and if it reached Ikey's ears, Ikey although I was so sure he daren't do it himself would be jealous of my doing it and would be very angry.

I had one narrow escape too from letting Mother know. We had just finished supper one night when Dad said he thought he heard someone knocking at our street door. He went downstairs and we heard him opening the door, and then closing it again. He came upstairs and said :

" That's a very strange thing. I was certain I heard a definite knocking, but there was no one there. The street seemed quite empty too."

He sat down and the knocking came again. We all heard it, but it sounded to me as though it was a knocking on the shop window, " *Tap tap—tap tap.*" *I* knew what it was now, but I didn't say anything.

Again Dad went down, opened the door, waited, then shut it and came upstairs, looking rather vexed. It started again before he had time to sit down and he rushed downstairs and opened the door for the third time. And then we heard laughing and mocking cries and the sound of boys running away, and I thought that one of the voices was Ikey's.

Dad shut the door and came up again. He was still looking a little vexed but he *was* smiling.

" It was just some of the village boys having a lark," he said. " Boys will be boys I suppose."

And that was when then I got such a fright, for I was actually feeling the button in my pocket when Mother looked at me straight in the face and said :

" I hope that you will never play games like that, for it's a rude thing to do. Some people, particularly elderly people, might be really frightened, if they heard a knocking on their doors or windows late at night. It would be cruel as well as rude."

If she had asked me straight out then if I had ever played pin-and-button or that I was ever thinking about doing it, I would have had to say yes, but she didn't say another word, although she might have guessed from the way I was blushing that I had a guilty conscience.

*   *   *   *

Apart from practising with my pin-and-button, I had worked out how I was going to do it. Because she knew that Mr. Birch was such a good man, Mother didn't mind my going to the gas-works to play marbles and staying there after dark so long as I was home by half past six. In winter it got dark about five o'clock. Unless it was later than half past six she would never think of going there to look for me, or asking Dad to do so. There would be no need for me to tell her that I was going to the gas-works. I would let her see my marbles, and she would guess, but to be on the safe side I would go there first and watch the retorts being emptied and filled, and then quietly slink off.

I wouldn't go through the village and up the Bank and along Church Lane. I would be bound to pass someone going that way, who would notice me and might be called as witness, when it became known that someone had actually played pin-and-button on the vicar.

My plan was to keep to the fields all the way. The gas-works was at the back end of the village, and on the landward side of it there was an open place called the drying ground used by women for drying their washing, and by the fishermen for drying their nets in the salmon season.

Above this was a grassy hill, which on the other side sloped down into the valley of the beck before it got to the village.

There was a hedge here, and a pasture and a cow-house, owned by a farmer called Knaggs who sold milk, taking it round the village twice a day in two cans which he carried with a wooden yoke. It cost three ha'pence a pint.

He was a rather crusty man. Although his cows were allowed to graze on the hill, and even on the drying ground (once one of them had eaten quite a lot of washing from a line), he hated seeing anyone in the pasture that was fenced in, and he would shoutangrily at any lads who went up the beck bird nesting. He also kept a bull. I had never seen this for it was kept shut up, but I had heard it bellowing.

Mr. Knaggs also owned all the fields on the other side of the beck up to Church Lane, except the one next to the vicar's garden, which belonged to the vicar himself. I was afraid of cows and very much afraid of bulls, but even the cows were kept in in winter-time, so really there wasn't anything to be afraid of if I went this way, except the dark. If it was very dark I couldn't do it of course. The best time would be when it was moonlight, yet not full moonlight, when sometimes it was almost as bright as day.

I went on thinking about it, and making up my mind to do it, and then putting it off. It was just like having my first bathe in early summer when the water was still icy cold, I would first of all paddle, and then take my clothes off, and put them on again without going in even as far as I had been paddling.

Then one evening I really did make up my mind. Mother always had tea waiting for me when I got home from school just after four o'clock. I was sure she didn't guess anything during the meal. Although the sea hadn't been rough, the tide was ebbing. I told her truthfully that I was going down to the beach to see if I could find some firewood, and that I expected I would go along to the gas-works when it started to get dark.

I wasn't such a fool as to ask her if she wanted me to run any errands first for she knew how I hated running errands, and she would have suspected that either I had done something wrong, or was going to.

Acutally I did feel a bit guilty as I hurried out, for I loved her very much, and in spite of her having been vexed with the vicar about Dad I knew it would upset her terribly to know that I was going to take revenge. Besides it wasn't going to be just revenge. I wanted to do something that Ikey would be afraid of doing.

I did go to the beach. There were a few boys there playing tip-cat, but I supposed that was because they had lost all their marbles, for marbles was the chief craze just then. But tip-cat was a good game.

You had a piece of square wood about four inches long and pointed at each end. The sides were numbered one to four. A ring about three strides across was marked on the ground, and the first boy to play took the cat and spun it, like tossing a coin inside the ring. There was a stick called the striker, and he had as many strikes as the number that turned up on the cat.

He had to hit one of the pointed ends so that the cat sprang up into the air, and before it reached the ground he whacked it to make it go as far as possible from the ring. The other players would stand round like fielders at a game of cricket and if one of them caught it it would be his turn to play. If no one did the first player would strike again and again until he had used up all his " goes," and a mark would be made where the cat had fallen last. The next boy would play. The boy who got the farthest would be winner.

It was lovely when the cat sprang up just the right height, and you felt the stick strike it hard, and saw the cat sailing over the heads of the fielders.

I would have liked to have joined in now, for they were all small boys and I was certain that I could have beaten them. But I walked past them a little way along the beach and up to high-tide mark to see if anything had washed up. I didn't expect to find anything as the sea hadn't been rough, and it was a neap tide, and I didn't find anything, but I did feel that by doing this I was keeping my word to Mother.

And already it was starting to get dark, although I knew it wouldn't get quite dark, for there was a bit of moon already shining in the sky, just right for my going across the fields. It wouldn't be too dark, and it wouldn't be too light either.

I hurried back, up the slipway, and through the dock, and then to the gas-works. The doors were open, I peeped in. I saw that most of the boys were already there, playing marbles before Mr. Birch started on the retorts. I heard Ikey's voice.

I thought then how surprised everyone would have been if I'd walked in, and just said, quite calmly, with the same voice that Ikey used :

" Eh, lads. I'm just off to play pin-and-button on the old vicar. Do any of you want to come with me ? "

None of them would have believed me, but it made me feel important just to imagine saying it. Actually no one took any notice of me, and after that one peep I moved on past the gas-works and up towards the drying ground.

It must have been nearly five o'clock by now. If it hadn't been for the moon it would have been almost dark. There were lights in the houses that were nearest to the drying ground. I kept well away from these houses and I ran up the hill.

I stopped at the top, for I was a bit out of breath, but I wasn't frightened. I could see the whole village from here although the houses were blurred by the smoke coming up from their chimneys. It was rising straight up and making a sort of cloud for there wasn't a breath of wind. Most of them had lights in their downstairs windows, and some of the street lamps were already lit. I could see the lights of ships far out at sea too. The sea wasn't making any sound.

I looked down the field towards the beck, and I could just make out the vicarage on the other side of it, and beyond it the church and the railway station. I heard the whistle of an engine and saw the lighted carriages of a train coming along the line. It was the five-o'clock train. I would have to hurry if I was to get to the vicarage, play pin-and-button and be back home before half past six.

I started off again, down the field which sloped to the beck. I could see Mr. Knagg's cow-house with a tiny light showing from its door. He would be safe inside, milking his cows, but I thought I would best steer well away from it and the other farm buildings in one of which was the bull. He kept pigs and hens too,

I could hear the pigs grunting and also the mooing of the cows as I got to the hedge of his pasture. The gate through it was near to the farm so I had to find a gap to squirm through and that took me some time for it was a thick thorn fence with barbed wire in it and it was hard to see where the wire was.

I managed it all right though and I still wasn't feeling frightened although I did wish that I had another boy with me for I couldn't help feeling a little lonely. I wished in one way that Ikey was with me, although if he had been he would have been boss and wanted to take all the credit.

The pasture wasn't big. There was another hedge running alongside the beck, and it was even darker here because as well as thorn bushes there were some trees. To make things worse the ground was boggy and mixed up with smelly cow muck, and I knew I would have to wash my boots before I got home or Mother would know I hadn't just been to the gas-works playing marbles.

It was a good job the beck wasn't in flood. I had to climb one of the trees, go along a branch which hung over the hedge, and then drop, and there wasn't enough water for me to get my feet wet. I scrambled up the other side, and from the iron railings I knew that I had reached the vicar's field, which was next to his garden.

I had been in this field before. Although most of it was sloping, there was a nearly level patch half-way down to the beck, just like the drying ground. Here on May Day, the girls from Miss Lawson's school danced the Maypole, after one of the girls had been chosen as May Queen. There would be a big tent, and a tea party, paid for by the vicar, to which even Wesleyans were allowed to go.

The tea was all right, but I thought the Maypole dance a bit silly. The girls wore white cotton dresses, with wreaths of primroses and violets round their necks, and bunches stuck on their heads with ribbons. There was a wooden platform near to the maypole, with an armchair on it that was supposed to be a throne. The girl chosen as Queen would sit on this chair, with maids of honour on each side, and then some lady (a friend of the vicar's

or a relation of the Marquis or someone important) would put a
cardboard crown painted gold on the queen's head and say that
she was crowned Queen of May. Then Miss Lawson would start
playing a tune on a small harmonium and the girls would start
to sing. The first verse was :

> " I am May, blythe and gay,
> Listen to my pretty lay.
> I will sing, songs of Spring.
> Happy news I bring !
> Tra-la-la."

and the chorus went " tra-la-la-la," over and over again.

Then the dance began. The pole was as tall as a coble mast.
At the top of it were tied about twenty long ribbons of all sorts
of colours. The girls stood round in a ring, each holding the
end of a ribbon, and when the music began again they started to
move, some one way and some the opposite way, in and out. As
they went the ribbons were plaited round the pole, making a
pattern, and of course they got shorter and shorter until at last the
dancers were almost up to the pole. Then they stopped and waited
for Miss Lawson to give the word when they would dance the
other way round, unplaiting the ribbons until they were back
where they started.

Even on May Day Miss Lawson wore black clothes and looked
as severe as ever, and the girls never as much as smiled when they
were dancing, and I was always glad when the dancing was over
and we went into the tent for tea.

I could see the maypole now as I climbed over the iron fence
and I thought then how I hated girls. They never played games
like football or cricket or shinny ower, or tip-cat, or pin-and-
button, or did things that were brave or dangerous. Although
they made plenty of noise and quarrelled with one another,
they never used bad language. They played with soft rubber
balls, bouncing them up against a wall and catching them :
or hopscotch, or a game called checkers with little coloured
pot blocks, and they sat round door-steps to do this. Or they

played with skipping ropes, a thing any boy would be ashamed to do.

I couldn't imagine any girl doing what I was going now, all by myself and not really frightened. And I was sure there was no other boy who would have done it either.

I stopped on the other side of the railings. The wall of the garden was on my left. It reached from the top of the field down to the back itself, and I knew that it would go along the beck for the width of the garden and up the other side. I couldn't see any lights now except the moon and the stars. It was very still. The train had gone. The only sound I could hear was the low mooing of Mr. Knagg's cows until an owl hooted from one of the trees near the beck, and it was so sudden and loud that it did make me jump and I got hold of the railing again and was almost tempted to climb back on to the beck side.

But the next time it hooted I was ready for it, and it didn't frighten me, and I set off across the field to the wall and reached it. It was a very high wall, built of smooth stone blocks. The joints between them were cemented, without even a crack that I could get my fingers into let alone my toes for a foothold. But I remembered that half-way up the field there was a door in the wall which was opened on May Day for the vicar and his friends to come into the field.

I got to the door. It was big, and it fitted into an archway just like a church door but with its top almost hidden in ivy. There was the same sort of an iron ring handle on it to lift the inside latch and I moved this, but when I pressed against the door it didn't budge. The moon wasn't giving much light, and the wall and the door were in its shadow. Yet there was enough light for me to see that trailing down from the wall close to the door were some stems of ivy, some of them just in reach.

I got hold of them, bunched them together, and found they were strong enough to take my weight. I heaved myself up, and got one foot on to the ring of the latch, which stuck out just far enough, and then getting another grip on the ivy, whose branches were thicker and stronger here I heaved myself higher until I was on the wall top.

The ivy stems on the other side were like thick rope, as easy as a ladder. I climbed down. I was inside the vicar's garden, and I still wasn't frightened, and yet I had already done something that no other boy had dared to do.

I kept still for a while, and listened. But for the owl, everything was quiet. There was a lovely sweet smell in the air. I could hardly believe it, for it was nearly winter time, but there were white roses in full bloom on a big bush near to where I stood. I thought how nice it would be if I plucked some and took them back to Mother. She loved flowers of any sort.

But that would be stealing, just as bad as stealing apples or plums from the orchard which I knew was at the back end of the garden. I wasn't going to do anything like that. All I was going to do was to play a practical joke on the vicar. Besides there wouldn't been have any fruit in the orchard. It would have been picked long ago.

I felt in my pocket for the button and cotton reel with the drawing pin stuck into it, to make certain I hadn't lost them, and then I started off. There was a gravelled path leading upwards from the wall door through the flower bushes. I kept to the side of it so that my boots wouldn't crunch on the gravel.

I came to the lily pond. It had paving all round it. There weren't any lilies, and I couldn't see any goldfish, but that was perhaps because it was too dark. They'd be hiding at the bottom anyway. If I'd had a hook with me and a worm it would have been fun to try and catch one, although of course I would have put it back.

There were some stone steps leading up from the pond, and I knew that I couldn't be far from the house now. I trod very carefully keeping to the shadow of the bushes, some of which were evergreens, very thick. And they got thicker still when the ground became level. They were like a wall, and the path ran through an archway, actually cut out of the bushes which above the arch were trimmed in the shape of two big vases.

I peeped through the archway, and there was the lawn, and the front of the vicarage, with two big windows on the ground floor, on each side of the door, and only a few strides away from where I stood. There were some tall dark trees on the left, one of them a monkey puzzle and they made a shadow across the lawn, which was a good thing, as I would have to move over it.

At first I couldn't see a light in any of the windows. Perhaps the vicar wasn't in. It would be no good my fixing the button unless he was.

Then I did notice a chink of light in one of the windows on the right-hand side of the door. It was in the middle of it, and it seemed to be coming from between two curtains. I crept across the lawn. There was a flower bed just under the window which had the light with some tall plants in it, and when I got to it, I crouched down, and waited to make sure that I hadn't been seen or heard.

Then I stood up, and straight away I saw that it was going to be no good. The windows of the vicarage were not like the windows in the village houses. Although they came close to the ground, they were nearly twice as high, with only two large panes. The top of the wood frame, where the pin should be stuck was out of my reach. But what I *could* do and it might work better than pin-and-button, was to rap at the window with my knuckles and then run for it.

I must make certain first though that the vicar was in. I moved closer to the window, put my hands on the sill. I had been right about the curtains. There were two of them and there was a gap between them big enough for me to see clearly into the room. And there *was* the vicar sitting at a table in the middle of it. Hanging from the ceiling just above his head was a bright oil lamp.

It was a very nice room. It must have been the library, for there were book-cases full of books, and lots of other furniture and thick carpets on the floor with a rug in front of the fireplace. There were vases and other ornaments on the mantelshelf. The vases were filled with roses, and there was a big bowl of roses on the table too, red ones as well as white ones.

I saw all these things, but it was the vicar I looked at most. He was sitting with his back to the fire with his elbows on the table. In front of him was a big writing-pad and a silver ink-stand. Behind the inkstand, close to the rosebowl, were two silver

G

photo-frames standing upright. I couldn't see the photos clearly but I could tell that one of them was of a young man in soldier's uniform, and I guessed that it was the major, and that the other was of the vicar's other son who had died in Australia.

There was a sheet of writing-paper on the pad. The vicar was holding a pen in his hand, and it looked as though he had started to write a letter. He wasn't writing now. He was just staring at the photographs, and I thought that he looked quite different to what he usually looked. He looked holy with his long silvery hair, but he didn't look stern like he did in church, or angry as he had done at the end of the concert, and must have done when he had spoken to Dad in the vestry.

He just looked sad. And as he stared at the photographs, I saw his lips quivering, and tears running down his cheeks. He was really crying, a thing I had never seen a grown man do before, although tears often ran down from Dad's eyes when he had a bad giggling fit, not because he was unhappy.

And the vicar was unhappy. He was unhappy because his first son was dead, and his second son was still in South Africa fighting the Boers, and might be killed too before the war ended. He must have started to write a letter to him and the photos must have made him long more than ever for his living son to be home, and perhaps talking to him in this very room, telling him of his adventures.

I felt very sad myself, and sorry for him. If I hadn't known that really I was doing something wrong in being in the vicar's garden and felt a bit guilty, I think I would have said a special prayer to God just then, to bring the major safe back. I wasn't going to rap on the window anyway, or do anything else to annoy him.

I turned away from the window, crouched down, looked at the lawn and the archway through the bushes, and ran as fast as I could go for home.

I I

No ONE ever found out about my going to the vicarage. I had
got back across the fields all right, although I'd had one fright.
Just as I'd reached the iron rails at the bottom of the vicar's field,
the vicar's riding horse had come galloping down the hill, whinny-
ing loudly and with its hooves clomping, and it was as terrifying
as if it had been Mr. Knagg's bull.

I got over the rails just in time. It charged right up to me,
stopped, whinnied again and then galloped off.

Apart from this I didn't see any living thing, and didn't hear
any human voices until I got to the gas-house door. The retorts
had been filled. The lads were playing marbles again. I thought
it would be wonderful to have walked in, and waited for someone
to ask me where I had been, and for me to have told them, leaving
out about my having seen the vicar crying, telling them that I
had played pin-and-button on him.

I hadn't even gone inside. I had hurried down to the dock and
on to the shore and washed the mud and smelly cow muck from
my boots and then gone home as though nothing at all had
happened.

Yet without Mother asking me to, I had mentioned the vicar's
son in my prayers, and would have included the vicar too if I
hadn't thought that this might have made her curious. Besides,
it would have seemed a bit silly praying for a clergyman. God
was far more likely to listen to him than to me.

I went on feeling sorry for him though. I couldn't forget how
I had seen him crying like a baby, although the next time I saw
him he looked just as fierce as ever.

So far there hadn't been any real storms or wintry weather and

it must have been near the end of November before the first one
came. Usually storms got up during the night. First it would be
the wind that would wake me up, and I could always tell by the
way it rattled the tiles if it was blowing from the sea. Then I
would hear the sea itself making a deeper sound, and if the tide
was high with the waves breaking on the cliff it would be almost
like thunder, and my bed would shake.

This one started in the morning, and it was a Sunday morning
too, during church and chapel time.

It had been foggy for several days. This didn't make much
difference to the fishermen, for they never went far out to sea to
shoot their lines, and every coble had a compass, and also a
horn to blow if they heard a big ship coming nearer and there
was a danger of them being run down.

None of them fished on Sunday. All the cobles were safe in
the dock. Dad had gone off to church. I was in the living-room
with Mother, who had started to get the dinner ready, and I was
reading an adventure book. The fog was so thick outside that
Mother had lit the lamp.

The wind and the sea never sounded so loud in the living-room
as it did in the attic, because this part of the house was lower
than the cliff edge, and although now and again there was the
sound of a steamer blowing its horn, there was no sign of a storm
coming on.

And then there was a sudden *bang*.

We both jumped. Almost at once there was another bang, but
sounding a little farther off. It was the lifeboat gun. The first
bang was the gun itself, the second the shell bursting and throwing
a green star, like a rocket, not only to call the lifeboat crew and
launchers, but to let the sailors on a ship that was in distress know
that help was coming to them, although they wouldn't see the star
in the fog.

And a ship must be in distress. It couldn't be a practice on a
Sunday. Mother was frightened, but I wasn't. I was just excited
and I thought how lucky that it had happened in daylight and not
in school-time. I only hoped that she was not going to stop
me going out. But she didn't. I wasn't in my Sunday clothes

yet, and although she made me put my overcoat on, and a scarf round my neck, she let me go, saying that I mustn't go farther than the dock, and that she would come down herself in a minute or two.

As I opened the street door I saw two fishermen who always went to chapel, and were in their Sunday clothes, running down towards the dock. Old Mrs. Anderson, who kept the King's Head Temperance Hotel just opposite our house, shouted to them from her doorstep :

" Is it a ship ashore ? "

" Aye. It sounds like it ! "

I ran too. Before I got to the dock I felt a strong cold wind, and I heard the sea roaring. The fog was starting to clear too as it usually did when a wind got up.

Already there were quite a lot of people in the dock, most of them in their Sunday clothes. The doors of the lifeboat house were open. The fishermen were moving their cobles up the road out of the way. Every minute more people were coming to join the others and help. The coastguards were helping too although their job was to man the rocket apparatus, which was kept in a place next to the watch-house.

The lifeboat was to be launched first.

There was a lot of shouting and everyone seemed to be talking at the same time but I found out that one of the coastguards who had been on patrol along the Low Batts cliff had heard a signal rocket go off not far from the shore and that he had run back to the village to give the alarm. The fog had been too thick for him to see anything.

Some of the lifeboat crew, including the coxswain, had already got their cork lifebelts on. I saw a funny thing happen. One of the two men who had run down our street from the chapel was just fastening his belt when his wife came up to him with an old jersey, and told him to change his best one for it. They started an argument and got quite angry, but the woman won.

The boat was on a big heavy four-wheeled carriage. It had to be hauled first to the top of the slipway by long thick ropes. When it got to the top the launchers had to leave these ropes and

hold at the stern end of the carriage, to steady it as it moved
with its own weight down the steep slope, and there was a man
at each of the four wheels with a wooden chock to hold it if it
went too fast.

It had just got to the top and the launchers were changing
ends when Mr. Beecham who was carrying a telescope ran out of
the watch-house and shouted :

" Quick as you can everybody. I've just seen her. It's a ketch,
close in to Low Batts scar, and dragging her anchors. It's going
to be touch and go. We'll want the rocket cart out as soon as you're
clear of the slipway."

There were so many launchers that there wasn't room for anyone else on the ropes. Most of the watchers moved towards the
slipway and I went too. The wind was blowing straight up it
between the coastguard's wall and the breakwater. It was so
strong I could hardly move against it but there was a sheltered
place near the breakwater from which I could see what was
happening.

The fog hadn't quite gone yet. It was swirling, one moment
everything would be almost clear, and the next moment hidden
again as though the wind was playing a game of hide-and-seek.
Yet it was getting thinner away from the shore. Now and again the
whole bay except for Low Batts point would be in sight.

The tide was half-way down and still ebbing. The wind was
blowing from the sea, and even far out beyond the scar ends the
sea was almost white with spray. On the scar ends the waves
didn't look so big as I had sometimes seen them but that was
because the wind was whipping them into spray before they broke,
and the spume from them was actually driving up the bare
scars, rolling into thick drifts, then scattering again. The wind
was icy cold. It was a real storm.

At first the only ship I could see was a steamer very far out.
It was rolling and pitching so that its propeller raced out of the
water. It wasn't blowing its horn and everyone was looking
towards Low Batts, waiting to see what Mr. Beecham had seen
through his telescope when the fog had cleared there before
getting thick again.

And suddenly it did clear. It was a terrible sight. There was a two-masted sailing-ship so near to the point that it seemed to be actually on the scar which reached out from the cliff. One of its masts was broken, with a torn sail flapping from it, and the waves were dashing right over it.

Someone near me said :

" She's as good as finished. And so is everyone aboard her unless t'lifeboat looks sharp."

The fog swirled down again, hiding the ship. The lifeboat was now slowly coming down the slipway, and some of the launchers were running ahead with the hauling ropes, ready to pull when she reached the slipway bottom. When she did, there was a great shout of " heave-o, heave-o " and with the launchers actually running, the carriage rumbled quickly over the smooth shale between the two landing scars towards the water's edge.

I ran down one of the landing scars. There were plenty of people and lads there, and I stood among them, in case Mother should see me, for although I couldn't see her I guessed she would have come down to the dock and be looking for me. I didn't want to miss seeing the lifeboat launched.

Although the water in the landing close in was smooth compared with the sea outside, the big waves after they had broken were coming into it in what the fishermen called " runs," so that it would be deep when one of them came in, and shallow when it went back before the next one came.

The carriage had to be dragged in until its front wheels were nearly covered. That meant that the launchers had to wade in almost to their waists. Every regular launcher was paid five shillings for a practice launch, but of course they always wore their oldest clothes for this. They got ten shillings for a real rescue launch which wasn't much if their clothes were spoilt.

Yet some of them who must have been in chapel, or church, were in their Sunday best, and among them was Neddy Peacock who even had his collar and tie on. He was wading as deep as any of the other launchers and when a " run " came in it was higher than his waist. But by then the carriage was far enough.

The crew started to climb into the boat, and get out their oars. And it was just then that I saw Doctor Whittle running down the scar, holding a rum bottle in his hand, and behind him, but only walking, the vicar.

Doctor Whittle gave a shout, holding up the bottle as he did so, and he walked straight into the water until he had reached the back wheels of the carriage, and to my surprise he climbed up into the boat itself, and some of the crew actually laughed, but no one tried to stop him. He had been a ship's doctor. He must have thought that the men in the ship might be injured and would need his help. As he got in the coxswain shouted " Let go ! " One of the launchers knocked out the bolt that held the keel of the boat on to the carriage. She began to move, her bow touched the water, and away she went, the crew starting to pull the moment she was afloat, the coxswain steering straight for the landing mouth and the rough sea.

In summer, when there were plenty of visitors about, there was always one special practice launch on what was called Lifeboat Day. The crew would wear red tam o' shanters on their heads and the coxswain his peaked cap with badge. Before the actual launch the vicar, because he was secretary, would make a speech specially for the visitors, telling them how brave the lifeboat men were and what a noble thing they did in risking their lives to save the lives of others, and he would ask them to give what money they could to support the Royal National Lifeboat Institution. Collection boxes would be taken round among the people watching, and there would always be a loud cheer when at last the boat was launched.

There wasn't any cheering now. Although not one of the lifeboat crew had looked frightened, their wives and mothers and other relations must have known how dangerous it was for the boat to be going out in such a storm, and they must have been thinking about the poor sailors on the ship too.

The vicar stood with them, looking at the boat. He must have stopped the service as soon as he heard the gun, and hurried down from the church as fast as he could. He was wearing his fur-collared coat, and a muffler, but a soft hat instead of his tall top one, and he had a black respirator tied over his mouth because he suffered from bronchitis.

He looked very solemn, and I thought he must have been praying for the safety of the men in the lifeboat and the ship. Every minute the storm was getting worse. The fog had gone, yet the sky was covered with dark clouds like thunder clouds, and the ship was hidden again by a squall of rain or snow which was driving over the cliffs of Low Batts and spreading across the bay too.

The launchers started to haul the carriage out of the water, and the vicar actually seized one of the ropes and helped to pull. But everyone was really watching the lifeboat as she got near to the landing mouth and the big breaking waves.

You could see how big the waves were then for at the first one her bow rose so high that you could see into her, and then the next moment see nothing at all but her stern and rudder and part of her keel.

A coble could not have pulled out of the landing against waves like that, and against the wind too, and I wondered that the lifeboat could do it in spite of there being ten oars and such strong men pulling at them with all their might. Yet she was soon past the two posts that marked the end of the landing scars, almost hidden one moment by a wave, the next moment leaping over another, the crew still pulling in time like on a practice trip. And then she was completely out of sight. The squall which had been driving from the sea reached her, and it reached the landing and the shore too.

It was rain, with flakes of wet snow in it. I was glad that Mother had made me put my coat on. The people on the scars were moving. They weren't going home though. I knew from what they were saying that they were going along the shore to Low Batts, and I was going too unless Mother or Dad stopped me. The rocket apparatus must already be on its way there.

I ran. To get to Low Batts meant going nearly back to the village first because of the water between the other scars. The rain made it almost like fog again, which was lucky for it would be hard for Mother to see me, but, as I reached the place where it was all right to turn, I ran faster, not daring to look towards the slipway.

Mother never liked me to go along this part of the shore. It was supposed to be more dangerous even than Cowling Scar. Just beyond the village the cliffs became higher and steeper and at a place called the Gunny Hole they bulged out seawards, and anyone who was beyond that place when the tide came in would be trapped. If they waited near the foot of Low Batts cliff there was another danger, for pieces of rock often fell down from above.

Yet there were too many people moving along for me to feel frightened, and just as we got to the Gunny Hole, the squall stopped and everything became clear again. Beyond the Gunny Hole was the rocket apparatus wagon being hauled along the beach by another crowd of men including the coastguards, and among the haulers was Dad.

I could see the ship too, clearer than before although I couldn't see any men on her. She wasn't on the rocks. Her anchors were holding. But the waves were breaking over her bow and sweeping along her deck. The lifeboat, tossing up and down, was moving very slowly, and was only about half-way between the landing and the ship. I wondered which would be the first to reach her, the lifeboat or the rocket company. It was like a race. It didn't matter which won though so long as the sailors were saved.

The beach was rough, covered with big pieces of rock that had fallen from the cliff at one time or another, and it got rougher still near the point, so that the wagon could not go farther. It stopped and the men started to off-load the apparatus. There were several lads with them, including Ikey of course, and he was actually helping another boy to carry a stretcher. I would have liked to have helped too, but I was afraid of Dad seeing me and telling me to go home, and I kept behind.

I had seen plenty of rocket practices, with Mr. Tims pretending to be a half-drowned sailor. I had never seen a real rescue. I thought that if Dad did see me and tell me to go back I'd pretend to go, and then just hide behind a rock. Another squall came on and this time it was real snow. I could hardly see the men of the rocket company. Yet it only lasted a few minutes, and when it cleared I saw that everyone had stopped, and that they were starting to rig up the rocket machine.

And there was the ship! The cables holding her anchors had broken at last. She was still afloat, but her stern was only a few yards away from where the waves were smashing on to the outer scars, although she was a long way from the shore. Some men were huddled in her stern. Even above the sound of the waves and the wind I could hear the barking of a dog. I couldn't see the lifeboat. The squall was still moving over the sea.

I moved a little nearer, keeping my eyes on Dad, ready to dodge behind one of the rocks if he looked my way. But he was watching the ship and the rocket machine and he couldn't have guessed how near I was.

Mr. Beecham was in charge of the rocket company. As well as the coastguards, there were several men in the company who attended practices and had special jobs to do. Henry Newton was one of them. It was his job to light the rocket fuse when Mr. Beecham gave the order to fire.

The rocket was an iron tube about a yard long and painted red and filled with gunpowder. It was fixed to a long wooden stick, to which was tied one end of the rocket line. The machine was an open iron tube which had legs to support it in such a way that the head of the rocket (which lay in the tube) pointed upwards at an angle. The rocket line was coiled in a special box which let it go smoothly when the rocket was fired.

They were fixing the machine just clear of the " run " of the biggest breaking waves. Although it was heavy, they were piling big stones round its legs. Mr. Beecham looked very anxious. I heard him say :

" I don't think it's going to be much use until the ship drives closer in. There's too much wind for the rocket to shoot against it. We'll have a try though. And here's another squall. We'll have to wait till it's over."

It began to snow again, and the wind got even stronger. It was fine, hard snow, stinging like hailstones. Instead of falling straight down it was driving sideways, swirling among the rocks, mixing with the spume of the waves. I crouched down behind a rock. I could still hear the dog barking. I wondered whether, if the men were rescued, as I hoped they would be, the dog would be rescued too. How would they get it in the breeches buoy ?

It was a long time before that squall was over. Just as it started to clear, there was an awful bumping sound from the sea that couldn't be just waves.

" She's aground ! " someone shouted.

I stood up, and saw the ship again. She wasn't much nearer in but you could tell she was aground for she didn't pitch and toss when the waves struck her. She just shook, and there was that awful bumping sound. The dog was barking. The men were still huddled in the stern which was the part of the ship nearest to the shore. Every now and then a wave would break over the bow and sweep along the deck. The men must have been hanging on to something or they would have been washed over. One of them must have been holding the dog.

The men were looking towards the shore, watching what was happening, waiting for the rocket which they hoped was to save them. The distance between them and the shore was not much more than that between the beach and the rocket post during a practice, yet it was deep water, with the waves breaking all the way in. Perhaps they didn't see the lifeboat. We saw her now. She was to seawards of the ship, and not so very far away, with the wind now helping her.

I wondered if Mr. Beecham was hoping that the rocket was going to beat the lifeboat. He shouted :

" Stand by now, Henry. I don't think it's going to be much use, but we'll have a try. Light your port fire."

Henry had a thing that looked like a squib in his hand. He held the fuse of it to his pipe. In a moment it started to smoke and splutter, and he went up to the rocket and touched its fuse with the burning end.

Everyone stood back. I put my fingers into my ears while I watched the fuse burning. There was a flash, a terrible hissing, clouds of smoke as the rocket went off, the line moving like a thin snake behind it up and out towards the ship. The smoke was too thick for me to see more. The next thing I heard was a shout from Mr. Beecham : and it was the first time I had heard him swear :

" Fifty yards short. Too much bloody wind. Get another rocket loaded."

The lifeboat was drawing nearer. They must have seen the rocket go off. They wouldn't yet know that it had missed. For a minute or two the sky above was quite clear and blue, but another snow squall was coming and soon the lifeboat was blotted out again, and then the ship.

Another rocket was loaded into the machine, and another line tied to it. Then everyone turned or crouched down as the snow came again.

It seemed longer than ever before the snow stopped and it began to get clear and we saw the ship and the lifeboat. The ship wasn't any nearer in. The lifeboat was almost as near to her as we were on the shore. The lifeboat's bow was pointing out to sea though. The crew were not pulling. They were resting on their oars, letting the wind and the waves move her shorewards on the side of the ship where the waves weren't breaking so fiercely.

One of the coastguards said :

" They're trying to get alongside. They'll never do it, in a sea like this. They'll be on the rocks themselves if they're not careful."

But an old man who had been a fisherman himself and was a relation of the coxswain said :

" Our lifeboat's done worse jobs than this. They know what they're at. They'll get a line on board in a minute. You'll see. The rocket's no use anyway, unless the wind drops, and that's not likely."

The rocket machine and the rocket itself were caked with snow. Mr. Beecham scraped it clear with his hand. Henry was standing ready to light another port fire. Mr. Beecham didn't give the order. He was looking at the lifeboat.

The crew were still resting on their oars. The wind and waves were bringing her nearer and nearer to the ship, and the shore itself. A man in the lifeboat's bow was standing up, with a short stick and a coil of thin line in his hand. I knew from watching a lifeboat practice that the stick was weighted with lead and was called the lead line.

The coxswain was shouting to those on the ship with a speaking trumpet. Two of the sailors ran from the stern almost to the bow of the ship. The man with the stick threw it. It fell on the ship's deck. The sailors seized the line, and hauled it in until they came to a thicker rope that was tied to its end. They hauled this in, and tied it so that the lifeboat was really anchored to the ship.

Everyone ashore seemed to have forgotten about the rocket apparatus. The coxswain was shouting although we couldn't hear what he was saying. The lifeboat was pitching and rolling with the waves. Suddenly one huge wave smashed against the other side of the ship. It broke over the deck, and over the two sailors, and covered the lifeboat with spray. I thought it must have washed the sailors overboard. They were still there, and before the next wave came the lifeboat, with the crew on one side backing their oars had moved so that it was almost touching the ship's side, near to her stern. Two of the sailors jumped and got safely into the boat before another wave swung it away again. The coxswain shouted. The crew backed their oars, the boat got near again and this time three men jumped, and I saw a big black dog jump too, but as it jumped the boat swung out with another wave. It must have missed and fallen into the sea. I couldn't hear it barking any more.

Then everything was hidden in another snow squall. We couldn't tell what was happening, except that now and then we heard the coxswain shouting orders through his trumpet to those who were left on the ship, and there was that terrible thumping and crunching sound of the ship's bottom on the scar.

I huddled behind the rock, shaking with cold, feeling very glad that at least some of the men had got safely into the boat yet also thinking about the dog and wishing I could hear it barking.

And then, as the squall began to clear again we heard a shout from the coxswain :

" Ahoy there ashore ! All hands on board. Rocket not wanted. We're casting off and making for home. Watch out for a dog that fell overboard. We couldn't get hold of it. It may wash ashore."

Again we saw the ship and the boat. The boat was clear of the ship, the crew pulling out against the waves, the men who had been saved lying on the deck between the crew's legs, and Doctor Whittle bending over one of them, who must have been injured.

Mr. Beecham and Henry had already started to move the rocket machine. It was Mr. Tims who gave an excited shout :

" Eh ! There's something washing ashore there. It looks like a dog ! "

The run of a big wave had come up the scar not far from the rocket machine. As it went back leaving the scar bare but for the scum, we saw the dog. It was on its side. But it was alive. It was trying to stand up, but it couldn't and another wave was coming in.

Mr. Tims who was the nearest to it rushed in through the spume. He picked it up into his arms, and started shorewards with it as a run came in, washing high above his knees. Some of the other men went into help him but he wouldn't let go of the dog. He got to the shore. Everyone crowded round him now. He was holding the dog just as though it had been a baby, and he was petting it.

It looked very weak. Its tongue was hanging out. Its mouth was full of spume.

" Let's have the rum ! " Mr. Tims shouted. " And a blanket from the stretcher."

Someone brought a small keg, a tin cup and a blanket. Mr. Tims put the dog down on its side on the blanket, wiped the spume from its mouth and tongue and poured some of the rum down its throat, and closed its mouth so that it had to swallow. Then he wrapped the blanket round the dog and tried to pick it up again into his arms. But as he did so it gave a sudden kick, broke loose, stood up, and shook itself, and then actually barked.

It was wonderful ! I would have liked to have hugged it, I was so glad it was alive and safe. But Mr. Beecham shouted :

"Come on, now. Let's be taking everything back to the wagon. The tide's flowing. We don't want to be trapped at the Gunny Hole, and we may have to help the lifeboat get ashore. Get a move on."

I saw Dad quite close to me. He hadn't seen me and I started to run, back to the village. The other lads were running too. I wanted to see the lifeboat come in. Although I was cold and wet, and hungry too, for it was long past dinner-time, the only thing that bothered me was that Mother might be on the beach, see me and make me go home, change my clothes, eat my dinner, and stay in the rest of the day while so many exciting things were happening.

*   *   *   *

I needn't have worried about Mother. She'd thought that I was with Dad, and Dad had thought that I must be with her, and when she had got down to the dock she had met some other woman who belonged to the Red Cross who told her the vicar had given orders for fires to be lighted in the Victoria Hall, and food and blankets and dry clothes to be got ready for the ship-wrecked sailors if they were saved, and Mother had gone to help.

With most of the other lads I had run all the way back from Low Batts, and we got to the landing, and to the people who were waiting there before the lifeboat was half-way home. They knew that the sailors had been rescued because one of the coastguards had stayed on watch, and in between the squalls he had seen the lifeboat near the ship and some of the men jumping, and the lifeboat pulling out with the men on board. They didn't know that the dog was safe.

The vicar was still on the landing scar, waiting. The snow squalls were coming and going as they had done before, some of them lasting quite a long time, some over in less than a minute and leaving everything clear. The vicar's black coat, and his hat and muffler were caked with snow. He looked very cold. His cheeks were purple, and he kept on dabbing his nose with his handkerchief as though it wouldn't stop running. His eyes were running too, like they had done when I had seen him through

the window, but only with the cold. He wasn't crying. He looked
brave, and I thought that if he hadn't been so old he would have
liked to have been in the lifeboat pulling an oar.

Everyone knew that the danger wasn't over yet. The worst
thing was going to be getting into the landing, where many
fishermen had been drowned in the past. The sea had got much
rougher since the lifeboat had been launched, and the tide had
started to flow. When the squalls cleared, you could see that the
waves were breaking all the way between the posts, which were
bending as the waves struck them, although they were thick oak
trees, cemented into the hard scar.

The lifeboat with the wind and the waves behind was it moving
much quicker than it had done on the way to the wreck. It
wouldn't be long before it reached the place just outside the
posts, where the fishermen when they were coming in with a
rough sea, usually pulled about until their best chance came.
No matter how rough the sea was there was usually a wave that
was smaller than the others, and less dangerous. It would have
to wait too for it to stop snowing, or the coxswain would not be
able to see the posts.

Another squall came, and again it was a fierce one and lasted
a long time. It was thicker than any fog. When it cleared,
although I could see the posts, I couldn't for a moment see the
lifeboat at all. And then just between the posts, it rose up on a
huge wave, so that you could see the front part of its keel! The
wave was curling over, breaking, and the boat was half hidden in
the spray. Then it sank from sight as the wave rushed in and
passed it. Another wave was coming close behind. It was the
stern of the boat that appeared first as it was lifted by this wave.
You could see into the boat, with the crew not pulling their oars,
but holding them ready, and you could see that from the stern was
a thick rope trailing behind to the sea anchor, a canvas bag which,
I knew from watching lifeboat practices would steady a boat
when a big wave struck it and stop it getting broadside on.

The wave curled up, the boat rose with it, until again you could
see under its keel. But this time as it passed, the crew started
pulling again, with all their might and with the sea anchor loose,

H

through the froth of the wave, and before the next wave broke the boat was moving into the landing, past the second posts into smooth water and the shore.

The scar was crowded with people. I thought that everyone would have started to cheer as the boat came in, louder than they had done on Mafeking Day, but it was only the lads who shouted, and although I shouted " hooray " once or twice, the grown-ups were silent and solemn, like the vicar.

As the boat grounded the coxswain shouted :

" Fetch a stretcher. We've an injured man aboard ! "

The launchers were already wading in, dragging the carriage. The crew started to jump out into the shallow water, and so did some of the rescued sailors, but instead of letting them get right down, the crew got them on to their backs and waded with them on to the bare scar. They looked terribly cold and miserable. They must have been wet to the skin. Some of them were carrying little bundles tied up in handkerchiefs. One had a little suitcase, and a small wooden box. Someone said that this must be the captain, and that the box would be his sextant.

The vicar went up to this man, and shook his hand, and then moving the respirator from his mouth said :

" Hurry up to the village. There's food and drink and dry clothes waiting for you."

The man said :

" Thank you, sir. Look after my men, but I'll stand by until my mate's ashore. He's got a broken leg."

Doctor Whittle and the injured man were still on the boat. A man came running down with a stretcher, and he waded in alongside. Soon the injured man was lifted over the side, with Doctor Whittle stepping straight into the water. The launchers started to haul the boat up on to its carriage as the men carrying the stretcher waded ashore. I noticed that Doctor Whittle wasn't wearing his overcoat. It was wrapped round the injured man and that the Doctor himself was just shaking with cold, although he was smiling.

The stretcher men didn't stop. They went on up the scar, with the doctor and the vicar walking alongside. Most of the other people and the other rescued sailors were going too, for there were plenty of men to help with the lifeboat. I followed.

It had started to snow again. The ship was out of sight. As we got to the bottom of the slipway I saw the rocket wagon and company coming along, and the dog with Mr. Tims. It must have been the captain's dog. It must have scented him. It bounded forward, barking excitedly, and leapt at him, trying to lick his face. I had never seen anyone look so happy as the captain did as he patted its head, for he must have thought that he would never see it again, and the dog must have thought the same thing about its master. It was wonderful to think that they were both alive and safe.

12

THE STORM grew worse during the afternoon and evening. The wind got stronger, and although it blew in squalls, it never stopped snowing. We didn't get dinner until nearly four o'clock for Mother had been at the hall, helping to look after the sailors. They had been given dry clothes. Their wet ones had been taken to the gas-works to dry. They had been given hot food and drink, nothing alcoholic of course, and they were all very grateful to the crew of the lifeboat for having rescued them, and to those who were looking after them now. The injured man had been carried to Doctor Whittle's own house, for the doctor to set the broken leg properly.

Mother said that although they were sailors they seemed to be very respectable, not using any coarse language. She was glad though that it was Sunday and that all the public-houses were closed so that they wouldn't be tempted to go there. One sailor had actually asked her where the chapel was, as he was a Wesleyan, and would like to go to evening service.

As I had already changed my clothes and got warm by the fire when she got in, she didn't bother to ask me where I had been. She kept on talking about what she had seen and heard, Dad was also trying to tell her and me about going along to Low Batts with the rocket company, and how he had actually seen the lifeboat rescue some of the sailors from the ship, and how the dog had swum ashore. I didn't tell him that I had seen this myself.

He said that the lifeboat and the ship was a wonderful subject for a picture. If it wasn't Sunday, and daylight gone he would have started to draw it now, while everything was fresh in his mind. It should be an oil painting, on a big canvas. It might easily be accepted by the Royal Academy.

When it was time to get ready for chapel, Mother decided that it was too stormy for me to go. Dad had been downstairs and looked out. Although the tide was now ebbing again he said that the waves were breaking over the coastguard's wall and rushing up the dock and that the snow was at least six inches deep in the street and was still falling.

Mother didn't want him to go to church, and I don't think he wanted to very much, but he said he would have to or the vicar would think he was a coward, particularly when the lifeboat had been out in the storm.

Mother helped to wrap him up with a thick scarf over his head, and he went, and as soon as he had gone, she got very solemn and made me sit down by the fire while she read aloud from the Bible about Jesus curing the leper, and the centurion's servant of palsy, and the woman who was sick of fever, and the men who were possessed of devils : and then of how Jesus had sailed in a ship and the storm had come on, and he had rebuked it and the sea had become calm.

While she was reading this I could hear the wind howling in the chimney, and the waves thumping on the cliff, and I thought it was wonderful that Jesus had been able to stop the storm on the sea of Galilee by just telling it to stop.

She went on to read about the two men possessed of devils who lived among the tombs, and how the devils had asked Jesus to let them out of the men, and let them possess the herd of swine instead, and how when this had happened, the swine ran down the cliff into the sea and were drowned.

I would rather have been reading one of my adventure books, yet I did like it when Mother read the Bible, for she always chose bits that were easy to understand, and were interesting, and although she was solemn, she never read in a gloomy way like the vicar, and some of the chapel preachers did. When she stopped she started to sing hymns, including one with words that were made up from the miracle of Jesus calming the storm which began :

" Master the tempest is raging," and had quite a nice tune and was often sung at chapel on a stormy night. And she sang my favourite of all hymns, " Eternal Father Strong to Save," and I sang too.

It really was nice to be sitting by the fire while the storm was raging outside, and to know that all the men from the ship and the dog too had been rescued, but as it got to the time when Dad should have been home from church, and there was no sound of him opening the street door I knew that Mother was feeling anxious about him. She had got the kettle on, and had laid the table for supper.

If it had been an ordinary night we would have heard his footsteps on the cobbles when he got near to the door. The snow was too thick for that.

She kept on looking at the clock, and humming " Eternal Father Strong to Save," although I thought that " Lead Kindly Light " would have been better as " Eternal Father " was specially for sailors : and at last she said that if he didn't come in another five minutes she would go and knock on Mr. Newton's door and ask Mr. Newton if he would walk up towards the church, and see if Dad had slipped and hurt himself, or got buried in a snow drift. She was afraid though that Henry Newton who only went to church or chapel when there was a funeral or a wedding would be in one of the pubs, which would now be open in spite of it being Sunday night.

I was getting frightened too, for although Dad was strong he wasn't a big man like Mr. Beecham or Mr. Birch, or any of the fishermen. It would be terrible if he was caught in a snow drift and couldn't get out. He would freeze to death.

But suddenly we did hear the street door being opened, and quickly shut again. We ran to the top of the stairs. It was Dad all right, although when he got upstairs into the light he looked just like a snow man, for even his beard was caked with snow. Mother helped him to get his coat off, and gave him a warm towel to wipe the snow from his face, and she wouldn't let him talk until he had been up to the bedroom and changed all his wet clothes for dry ones when she made him sit down by the fire and drink some hot broth we were having for supper. And then he told us what had happened.

He said he had never known such a terrible storm. When he had got to the top of the bank on his way to church, a gust of wind had actually spun him round and knocked him down, and in Church Lane there had been one snow drift as high as the hedges. He wouldn't have been surprised to have found the church empty. Actually it was the smallest congregation he had ever known. Mr. Conyers, the organist wasn't there, nor Captain Redman, and none of the choir boys. Yet the vicar was there all right, and the service had been held without music. The vicar had given quite a long sermon and had spoken about the shipwreck and the lifeboat going off and had said a special prayer about the men who had been rescued.

"Were any of the shipwrecked sailors there?" Mother asked. "One of them was going to chapel!"

"No," Dad said. "I'm coming to that."

After the service, the vicar had asked Dad to go with him to the vicarage. Outside the church, Dad had offered to hold the vicar's arm, but the vicar, who couldn't speak because he was wearing his respirator, had quite angrily pushed Dad away as though it had been an insult. When they'd got to the vicarage, Dad had waited in the kitchen, while the vicar went to his study, and Mrs. Binns the housekeeper nearly filled a big basket with food from the larder.

The vicar returned with a little bag containing five sovereigns, which Dad was to give to the ship's captain to buy things for his crew when the shops opened in the morning, and the basket was for them too.

The basket had been very heavy and there was no one to help Dad to carry it. All the other men who had been at church had gone home. Luckily at the bank top he had been overtaken by one of the coastguards returning from Low Batts from patrol duty, and he had given him a help down to the hall. And when they had got there, there was only one of the shipwrecked sailors left, sitting by the fire. The others, including the Captain, were in the pubs.

" How terrible ! " Mother said. " I suppose that was the nice one who wanted to go to chapel ? "

" Was the dog there ? " I asked.

" Yes, it was. It was curled up by the fire fast asleep."

" I hope you didn't try and find the captain and give him the money from the vicar," Mother said.

" Of course not. That would have meant going into the pubs myself. I left the basket of course, and went with the coastguard to the station and gave the money to Mr. Beecham to give to the captain in the morning. I thought that would be the best thing to do."

And then he said : " Well, it's an ill wind that blows no one good. According to Mr. Beecham and the coastguards who have been on patrol along the cliff, the ship started to break up when the tide came in. She'll be dashed to pieces by the morning, even if the storm is over. There'll be plenty of firewood to pick up. And not only that. She was laden with coal, and that would wash up along the shore."

" Mr. Beecham said that Neddy Peacock had spoken to the captain and offered to buy all the coal for a shilling a ton. That would have given him the right to stop anyone else taking it, and it would have been the duty of the coastguards to see that they didn't. But the captain had said he couldn't sell it. It belonged to the owners of the ship or the insurance company who would have to pay for the loss of the ship and its cargo. But the captain told Mr. Beecham that he was so grateful for what the people of the village had done for him and his crew, that any coal that was washed up on the shore should be free for anyone who picked it up. Mr. Beecham agreed about this, but it would still be the coastguards' duty to write down the name of any-one who took it, and how much they got, so that they might have to pay for it if the insurance company made a claim. Mr. Beecham winked when he said that. It wasn't likely that the insurance company would bother to make a claim against anyone for just a sack or two of coal. I'll have to be on the beach to-morrow as soon as the tide goes down. But I'll have to get on with that picture too. What a subject ! "

13

MOTHER WAS surprised the way I hurried downstairs next morning without being called for breakfast. She knew how I hated Monday mornings and having to go to school. The wind was still blowing and the sea roaring, but it wasn't snowing any more, and looking out of the window I could tell that the sun was actually shining, although I couldn't see the sky because of the houses on the other side of the street. Their roofs were covered with snow, icicles were hanging from their eaves, and these were glittering.

Dad was out. Mother said he had gone over to the studio to see if the storm had done any damage to the roof, and also to light his fire, as he was going to start work on his picture of the wreck as soon as possible. But he was also going on the beach when the tide went down to see what he could get.

Mother gave me some warm water and I washed my hands and face at the sink, and put the rest of my clothes on, quicker than I had ever done on a school day, and as breakfast wasn't quite ready I asked her if I could go out and try and get some coal. She said no, I must wait till I'd had breakfast, and then go straight to school. I would be able to go on the shore at dinner-time for a short while all being well and perhaps later on at tea-time.

I felt vexed with her. It seemed silly when we were so poor, and coal was so dear, to miss a chance of getting some for nothing, but I knew it was no use arguing. I just stood looking out of the window. Old Mrs. Anderson, wearing a shawl over her head, was clearing the snow from her doorstep. The snow was very deep. Henry Newton, although I could not see him, must have been doing the same from the front of his shop, I could hear the sound of his shovel. Some lads were in the street, throwing snowballs at each other, and now two more ran down the street, and one of them shouted very excitedly :

" Eh ! School gaffer has fallen and twisted his bloody ankle. School's shut to-day ! "

I could hardly believe it, it was such good news. Mother hadn't heard it though. The frying pan was making too much noise. I thought I had better not tell her.

In a few minutes Dad came in, looking very cold and hungry.

" Everything's all right," he said. " But *my*—what a job I had to get at the studio door. There was a drift nearly half-way up it, and I had to dig it with my bare hands. It's freezing hard too. I'd left some of my brushes in a jar of water, and they were frozen solid. I've left them by the fire to melt. And what a lot of excitement down in the dock. Everyone's going to be on the shore as soon as the tide leaves the slipway. The ship has smashed to bits, and one of her spars has actually washed up the slipway during the night, and the coastguards have got it, and hauled it up the dock."

We started breakfast, and Dad went on to tell us more news. He had met Mr. Beecham. The shipwrecked sailors were all going off to their homes on the twelve o'clock train. A single engine with a snow plough had been through to clear the line of drifts. The mate, whose home was in Hull, would be carried up on a stretcher. The vicar was going to pay all their railway fares, on top of the money he had sent to them by Dad. The insurance man was expected to arrive by the same train. He would be the one to say whether people would have to pay for any coal or wreckage that washed ashore. But on top of this, Mr. Beecham had said, there were hundreds of pit props floating in the sea, and coming ashore. They must have come from another ship, carrying a deck cargo that had broken loose.

" The tide must be nearly leaving the slipway now. I'll go down as soon as I've had another cup of tea, but I must get on with that picture this morning." And then he said to me. " What a pity it's not a Saturday. You could have come with me."

I didn't say anything to that. I could tell that he hadn't heard about the school-master. The school was only about three minutes' walk away, and it always opened at five minutes to nine. Although it was only ten minutes to nine, I started putting on my outdoor clothes as soon as Dad had gone. Mother hugged and kissed me when I was ready and said I was very good to go off so early.

She didn't come downstairs to see me off, and before I opened the street door, I popped into the coal-house, which was actually under the staircase, for a sack I always used when I went along the beach for firewood. I opened the door then and shut it with a bang, to let her know I had gone. I was tempted to rush straight down to the dock, but thought I had better make certain that school wasn't going to open and I turned up the street, which was thick with snow.

There wasn't a single lad waiting at the school door for the master to come. I ran along Chapel Street for the bridge, and then down the road, past Neddy's coal warehouse, which was shut, and came to the dock.

There was no one in the dock, although two coastguards were standing at the slipway top, and as I got there I saw Neddy Peacock, with a big sack on his back and a bundle of driftwood under one arm, actually running up the slipway, which had no snow on it because it had been washed by the waves at high tide.

The coastguards made him stop and put his sack down. They made him open the sack, which was chock full of wet coal, and made him take some of it out, as though there might be something else inside. I could tell though by the way they were smiling at each other, that they were just doing this to vex him, and waste as much of his time as possible, when he wanted to rush back and get another load. They let him put the coal back and then they lifted the sack, as though to guess how much it weighed. Then they wrote something down in a book, and said he could go.

I hadn't forgotten how Neddy had saved my life on Cowling Scar, but I couldn't help feeling pleased that the coastguards were punishing him for his greediness in rushing to get coal

from the ship when he had so much in his own warehouse,
and there were so many poor people who needed it. He only
wanted it to sell again. He was frightened that if everyone else
was getting it he wouldn't have any customers.

He looked terribly angry as he swung the sack on to his back
again, and rushed on up to his warehouse. But the coastguards
just looked the other way when an old fisherman, carrying a smaller
sack, came up the slipway as I ran down. And they didn't turn
again until he had passed them, and they didn't write anything
in their book.

The wind was still blowing, yet not so strongly as it had done
yesterday when the lifeboat had been launched. The sea was
even rougher. The whole bay was white with roaring breakers.
The tide had ebbed to the bottom of the slipway and from the
coastguard's wall, so that anyone could get along it to the south
cliff without getting wet if they watched the " runs " of the big
waves.

No one could get on towards Low Batts though. The waves
were still dashing along the North Cliff and at the Gunny Hole.
There were lots of people and lads on the shore, some of them
already coming back with sacks or buckets of coal, or backloads
of wood, some still picking things up. Some of the men were
standing near the tide's edge, snatching more pieces of wood from
the water as the run of the waves washed them in. These were pit
props. But the whole beach as far as I could see was strewn with
wreckage, planks and beams and spars, with pieces of sail and
rope still fastened to them, tangled up with seaweed.

I couldn't see Dad. He must have gone straight back to the
studio, thinking that it was more important for him to start his
picture than bother about the coal. I rushed on along the shore,
and I soon found some bits. They hadn't floated from the ship
of course for coal can't float. Yet it was much lighter than stone
and even stones are washed about with a rough sea and a strong
tide. The bits were actually mixed with stones, but it was easy
enough to see them because they were black.

I picked up quite a lot, and then as there were so many more
things to look at and to look for, I decided to leave the coal for

the present and walk along the shore. I had never seen anything so exciting as the wreckage at the cliff foot. As well as pieces
of wood from the deck and sides of the ship and the rigging,
there were barrels and boxes, and ship's furniture, and doors
with lovely brass hinges and handles on them. There were
flags and charts, and clothing. Some of the barrels had contained
salt beef or pork and had broken, and the meat was mixed up
with the other things and the seaweed.

It was just like what happened in *The Swiss Family Robinson*!

But two coastguards, and the police sergeant too were on the
beach watching, and I soon found out that while anyone could
take anything they found, it would have to be shown to the coastguards at the slipway top who would write it down in their book
with the name of the person who had taken it. They might have
to give it up later, but if they did they would also be able to claim
a reward for having saved it from the sea.

Some fishermen were trying to clear a big sail and a spar from
a tangle of ropes. Others were carrying pieces of wreckage up the
cliff beyond high water mark. This was called " laying up."
If you chalked or scratched your name on it, no one else would
be allowed to take it, although even in ordinary times the coastguards could put it down in their wreckage book if it was valuable.

There were plenty of boys rummaging among the weed for
treasures and I joined them. I found a square signal flag, a
leather deck boot, a piece of a chart, and a big lump of salt meat.
The meat was very fat, and it was stuck with sand, and little
bits of seaweed. It didn't look very nice, but it didn't smell bad,
and I thought that as sailors usually fed on salt meat and were
strong and healthy, it would be all right when the sand was
scraped off it, and cooked and that Mother would be pleased
to have it.

I saw one of the coastguards looking at me however, and I
asked him if I could take it home. He laughed and said yes, and
that I should tell my mother to soak it in fresh water for a day to
get the salt out of it, and then boil it with suet dumplings. I put
it in my sack with the coal.

With so many other lads and men looking for things, there

wasn't much chance of finding anything else, and I went farther
along the shore and down to the edge of the tide where the pit
props and still more wreckage was washing by. The pit props
were thick fir-tree poles about seven feet long with the bark still
on them. The men who were here were carrying them one at a
time to the cliff to lay up, and it wasn't long before Neddy Peacock
came running along the shore, from the slipway, keeping to the
water's edge. He must have thought it was no good bothering
about the coal because of the coastguards interfering with him, and
that it would pay him better to get pit props, and he soon got one,
wading into the water almost up to his knees. He didn't take it
to the cliff though.

A horse and cart had come down the slipway and was moving
along the shore towards him. It belonged to Mr. Knaggs, the
milkman and farmer, who was employed by Neddy to bring his
coal down from the railway station every week. Now it was going
to be used to get the pit props, much easier and quicker than the
way the other men were getting them. Neddy threw his first one
into it, and then waded in for another and the carter, who was
Mr. Knagg's son, also got one.

It was a mean greedy thing to do. The other men looked very
angry and I wasn't surprised when Ikey, who of course had been
with the other lads rummaging among the wreckage, started to
shout " Awd Neddy ! Awd Neddy ! " I would have shouted
myself if I hadn't thought of him saving my life, and I hadn't
been so near to him. The coastguards were keeping their eyes
on him though.

I went on along the shore, keeping ahead of Neddy. The tide
was ebbing of course, and some of the scars were baring, yet
things were still washing ashore. There were hundreds and hundreds of pit props. As the big waves broke on the scars, you could
see them being thrown up into the air with the spray and then
falling and spinning round as they washed into shallow water.

I got hold of one myself. I found it was too heavy to lift, and
I wasn't really sorry when one of the fishermen got hold of it to
carry to the cliff. It would be one less for greedy Neddy. And a
minute or two later I saw something in the run of a wave that

wasn't a pit prop. I thought at first that it was a wooden box. I was wearing my best school boots, but I had already got them wet, and I waded in as the run went down and got hold of it and rushed back as the run from the next wave came in.

It was a book-case, made of lovely mahogany, with three shelves, and brass plates to screw it on to a wall. On one of these plates was a bit of broken plank which showed that it had been torn off by the sea. It must have come from the ship, perhaps from the captain's cabin. I was specially pleased because we had no proper book-case at home—only a box that Dad had fixed on the wall by the fireplace. It wasn't heavy, but I knew that I had got as much as I could carry with what I had in the sack, and I started back for the village, steering up for the cliff to avoid Neddy. This meant passing close to the coastguards and the sergeant, but I couldn't have hidden it anyway. I just hoped they wouldn't take it from me.

They saw it, but they didn't say anything at all, perhaps because they knew that the other coastguards were waiting at the slipway top. People were still picking up coal, for as the tide went down more of it was coming within reach. I couldn't carry any more though. Then as I got nearly to the slipway foot, I saw Dad hurrying down.

He was surprised to see me, but he wasn't cross. Someone must have told him about school being shut.

" My ! " he said. " You have got a treasure. But you'll have to show it to the coastguards. I hope they'll let us keep it. What a treasure ! What have you got in the sack ? "

I told him about the coal and the piece of meat, and again he was very pleased, and then he said that he wished he had come down to the beach straight away instead of going to the studio, for when he had started on the picture his hands were so cold he hadn't been able to hold the charcoal, and his brushes anyway were still frozen. He had brought a sack, and so I had better help him fill it with coal, as it looked as though there was still plenty left.

I was very cold myself and would really have liked to have gone home, yet I didn't mind helping him, although I wasn't going to leave my book-case, and I was worried that the coast-guards might want to take it from me. It took us nearly half an hour to fill the sack. I had to help Dad to get it on to his back, for it was very heavy. Just as we started back for the slipway, we saw Neddy coming along with his cart, piled up with pit props. It got ahead of us before we reached the slipway bottom, and we followed close behind, which turned out to be a lucky thing.

The coastguards were waiting, and with them now was Mr. Beecham, and the ship's captain, and a man I had never seen before. I guessed it was the man from the insurance company. The captain had his dog with him, looking very happy.

Mr. Beecham held up his hand as the cart got to the slipway top. Some more men and lads were coming up behind us, all carrying bags of coal or bundles of wood or single pit-props. The cart had stopped.

" What have you got there, Mr. Peacock ? " Mr. Beecham said.

" Nowt but pit props," Neddy answered.

" We'll have to have a look at them. Will you off-load them ? " Neddy scowled.

" I'm in a hurry. I've got to pay for the hire of this cart. You can see them and count 'em without my off-loading them. They're not from the wreck. She was loaded with coal."

" We know that. But they're from another ship and they're wreckage and you know what the law about wreckage is. Get 'em off so as we can count them proper and put them down in the book. I see you've got a lump of meat there. If you're going to take that home it will have to be weighed and put in the book."

" I've only got that for my hens. Gulls and crabs would have had it else. Why don't you stop other chaps taking things ? "

Mr. Beecham didn't answer that.

He said sternly :

" Get your cart unloaded or we'll do it for you and claim the lot."

Neddy began to do as he was told, the carter helping him. While this was happening several men and lads had walked past the cart and the coastguards with their loads and the coastguards took no notice, but Dad had put his sack down which I thought was rather silly, for we could have easily slipped past. I had put my sack and the book-case down too. It looked as though Dad was going to wait until the coastguards had finished with Neddy, and then show them what we had got.

But to my great surprise one of the coastguards came up to us, and said with just a glance at our sacks and the book-case :

" Come on now. You're in the way. Move on. I'll put your name down for two sacks of coal and a bit of firewood."

14

SCHOOL WAS closed all that week, for Doctor Whittle said that the master must on no account try to walk until the swelling on his ankle had gone down and there was no one in the village who could take his place.

It was a lucky week for everyone except Neddy Peacock. The insurance man said that no one who just carried the washed-up coal on their backs, a sack at a time, need bother about paying for it, and although Neddy was down every tide getting as much as he could he lost a lot of trade, as almost everyone was getting their coal for nothing.

Yet when the tide was up he went on delivering coal to those of his customers who were too old or not strong enough to get it from the beach, carrying the sacks on his back up the alleys which could not be reached with his handcart, and several times the lads, with Ikey to lead them, set an ambush for him, and pelted him with snowballs. He couldn't defend himself or chase them with the coal on his back. I didn't go with them though, for I would never forget how he had saved my life.

The gale died away. But the sea was still too rough for the fishermen to launch their cobles, and it never stopped freezing. Except on the beach the snow lay thick everywhere, and it was a wonderful sight when the sun came out, to look across the bay to High Batts and the moors, all gleaming white like the " Greenland's icy mountains " mentioned in the hymn.

Nearly all the lads had home-made sledges. Although he was so busy Dad made one for me, and it was one he had invented himself with two pairs of runners, the first pair bolted to the part you sat on so that they would move from side to side and you could steer it like a boat. It was very kind of Dad to have left his painting to do this for me, and while he was working at it I brought him two half-sacks of coal for his studio fire, from the beach. Even with the grate full of blazing coal it was cold in the studio because of the ceiling being made of glass and his fingers were so numb he could hardly hold his brushes.

He was not very pleased with the way his picture of the wreck was going. He wanted to get everything into it, the rocket apparatus on the shore, with Henry Newton just about to light the fuse, the ship with its broken mast and the waves dashing over it, the sailors waiting on the deck, with the dog too, and of course the lifeboat. But to do this he would need a canvas almost as big as the studio itself and even then if he got the rocket apparatus in he would have to make the lifeboat very small, and the men in her, and on the ship, would have to be just " suggested."

His canvas, which was one he had made himself by stretching a piece of old sailcloth Mr. Beecham had given him over a wood frame and painting it white, was only about a yard square. After several starts he had decided to leave out the rocket apparatus, and just show the ship and the lifeboat, and one of the sailors jumping, and two of the lifeboat men reaching out their arms to catch him.

He wouldn't have to paint the faces of any of the men so that they could be recognised. He couldn't do that unless they sat for him in the studio, with their oilskins and lifebelts on. And there had been fourteen men in the lifeboat alone, including Doctor Whittle. He would have to show them half hidden by the spray, and paint smudges for their faces, although it would be most effective if he could just suggest how calm and brave the lifeboatmen were when they were in such danger, and how joyful the sailors must have felt at being saved.

He had only painted bits of it. The rest was still only charcoal. I thought that he had done the ship wonderfully. He had shown a big wave just breaking over her bow. But the lifeboat looked queer, and he said himself that he hadn't got the " perspective " right. Its stern part looked twice as big as its bow part, and the whole boat looked twisted and bent sideways. And besides he had made it look almost as big as the ship itself instead of being less than quarter its size.

Dad said that it might take him a long time to finish it, and what vexed him was that by working on it now he was missing the chance to do some snow scenes of the village. He couldn't sit outside and do them. But he could make sketches, and notes of the colour. And also he *should* be getting some more coal and not leaving it to me to do this, although actually his time was more valuable making pictures.

There was still plenty of coal and firewood washing up, and hundreds of pit props, although most of these were on the shore towards High Batts. There was quite a lot of meat too, but Mother said she didn't want any more. She had scraped the sand off the piece I had found, and soaked it for a long time in fresh water, and cooked it with dumplings and vegetables. When we had come to eat it she had said she was not feeling very hungry and only took a small piece of the meat. Dad had a thick slice and said it was quite nice, almost as good as fresh pork only a bit salty. It wasn't nice really, I felt a bit sick after I had eaten my slice and I thought that sailors would have to be very hungry to enjoy eating it day after day, and that they must long for something else. I wondered if Neddy Peacock had eaten all the piece that he had found. It would save him buying any fresh meat from Henry Newton for a long time.

We didn't have the salt beef cold, or made into shepherd's pie as we usually did with an ordinary piece of meat. Mother always put breadcrumbs out on the window sill in cold weather for the birds. Usually they were only sparrows that came to eat them. But now there were robins and starlings and jackdaws.

They were so hungry that the crumbs would be cleared almost as quickly as Mother put them out, so she chopped up some of the salt meat for them. They seemed to like this even better than the crumbs, and I did bring some more bits home and Mother cooked them, but only for the birds, and we must have saved quite a lot of them from dying of starvation.

Before the end of the week all the meat had gone from the beach. It had been eaten up by the gulls. And then a very sad thing happened. Thousands and thousands of other birds arrived, flying from over the sea with the strong cold wind. They alighted on the roof tops and in the streets and on the shore when the tide was down. Some of them seemed to fall out of the air, and when they alighted they couldn't move, and you could pick them up. They were almost dead.

Someone told us that they were redwings, and that they came from Russia or Norway. They looked a bit like robins, with red under their wings instead of on their breasts, although they were almost as big as thrushes. Some of them came to our window sill, and Mother put out a bowl of warm water, which they seemed to like as much 'as the crumbs and the bits of meat that were left.

On the beach as soon as the tide left the cliff there were just swarms of them, many of them already dead, some which had got back enough strength to pick for food among the washed-up seaweed. Yet these were not safe. Because of the thick snow covering the fields and woods and moors, the birds that lived there were coming to the shore, and with them came carrion crows and hawks and even owls. It was easy for them to catch the poor redwings and tear them to pieces and eat them.

I felt so sorry for them that one afternoon I got a basket, and lined it with a bit of old blanket and picked up about a dozen redwings that were too weak to fly and hurried home with them. Mother wasn't cooking, but the oven was warm, and she put the basket in it, leaving the door open. The birds were all huddled together, and for a long time it seemed as though they were all dead. Then some of them began to move, and actually flutter their wings.

Mother put a saucer of warm milk on the hearth with some little bits of bread. We helped one of them out of the basket and set it down near the milk. At first it just looked at it, with one eye and then the other, and then it took a sip, cocked its head, and had another look and sipped again, and then snapped hungrily at a piece of bread. Two of those in the basket didn't move at all.

When we picked them out they were still cold, and although we held them close to the fire they still didn't move and we knew they were dead.

Yet the others were all right, and as Mother was afraid that they might fly into the fire when they got all their strength back or into the lamp when it was lit, we took them into the attic, and put out more milk and crumbs for them on the table near my bed.

Dad was in a very good mood when he got back from the studio at tea-time. He hadn't been able to get on with his big picture of the wreck, as he had to wait for the paint to dry, but he had done a water-colour snow-scene, which he said he thought wasn't at all bad. He usually said that when he really thought that what he had done was very good.

Mother had already lit the lamp. As soon as he had taken off his overcoat and warmed his hands at the fire, Dad took out the picture from his canvas satchel, and propped it up on the table for us to see. It was still pinned on to his sketching block. It was a view from the beach, looking towards Low Batts, with the tide half down. It showed the slipway and the coastguard station and some of the cottages perched on the north cliff, including our own and beyond these the Gunny Hole and Low Batt's point. There weren't any boats or figures in it, for he had shown the sea rough, but he had put the ship at Low Batts point, very very small.

I thought it was lovely. Although it was so small, I thought it was much better than the big one, although I didn't say that. He had made it look exactly as it was the morning after the storm, with a beam of sunshine shining between the clouds on to the sea and the cliffs and the cottage roofs, covered with snow, although of course by then the ship had broken up. On the scar where the waves were breaking he had put in a broken mast with some frayed ropes dangling from it.

I kept on saying, " It's lovely, it's lovely ! " Mother praised it too. She said it was one of the prettiest pictures he had ever painted, and Dad said again that he thought it wasn't too bad, and that of course we were seeing it in lamplight, which wasn't fair to the colours. Besides it wasn't quite finished. It needed some figures in the foreground, say an old fisherman looking at the mast. He had been tempted to put in the lifeboat too, and he might do the whole thing again in oils, perhaps as a companion picture to the big one he was doing, showing the return of the lifeboat, but as it stood it wasn't too bad. It was a selling subject too.

Mother hadn't told Dad yet about the redwings. She said that tea was ready, and Dad said he must first go upstairs for a dry pair of socks, and he opened the door to the bedroom staircase. He got a fright. There was no door to the attic. One of the birds had found its way downstairs, and as he opened the door it flew straight into his face. Then it flew round the room and almost hit the lamp.

We managed to catch it all right. Dad wasn't cross, and when Mother told him what we had done he seemed really pleased, and said that in the morning we must try and rescue some more of the poor little birds. There were tears in Mother's eyes when she showed him the two that were dead and I thought that Dad sniffed a bit when he looked at them. As we began tea he looked at them again and he said :

"We mustn't throw them away yet. I think they'd make a rather nice little picture, sad of course, but that might make them appeal to some sort of customers. I'd paint them lying in the snow, huddled close together. The red feathers would make a nice contrast with the snow. I'll do it on a small panel."

We didn't get any more redwings. Those which hadn't died of cold or starvation, or been killed and eaten by bigger birds, must have gone on flying to a warmer part of England. Even those we had saved tried to get out of the windows, although they became quite tame and they perched on the ends of my bed, and one actually fed out of my hand. They made an awful mess of course.

Dad did a lovely painting of the two dead ones. He had them snuggling up to each other in the snow, but lying in such a way that you could see some of the red feathers under their wings. Their eyes were closed and they were on their backs with their little feet sticking up. He said that he might sell it to some firm who published Christmas cards. It would be a change from the usual picture of a robin redbreast. But Mother, although she praised it, said it was too sad for a Christmas card. It went in the shop window, together with the snow scene, and a lot of people admired it, but no one seemed to want to buy it, and in the end Dad hung it up in the studio with other pictures which he said were among his best works although he could never find customers for them.

I hoped that the cold weather would go on, perhaps even to Christmas, particularly if school went on being closed. But on Saturday afternoon the north wind which had been blowing all week changed to south, and the snow and ice began to thaw and change to slush. It started to rain, and it rained all night.

I was awakened just at daybreak on Sunday morning by the redwings fluttering about my bed and the skylight window. Although it was still rather cold, I jumped out of bed and opened the window, and one of the birds flew out straight away. It was still raining. All the snow had gone from roofs of the opposite houses, and I could see the red tiles again. I shut the window so that the other birds would have a chance to eat some food before they set off. Although there were crumbs and bacon rind on their plates, they just fluttered at the window so I opened it again. I felt rather sad and a bit vexed to see them go so eagerly, without as much as a chirp to say " thank you," even the one which I had fed out of my hand and I had really got quite fond of. But I knew it was silly to expect anything like that from dumb animals. I went back to bed.

Dad always had to get up at seven o'clock, and go off to early communion on Sunday morning, no matter what the weather was like. Breakfast was ready, and I had just got downstairs when I heard him opening the street door, then coming up the stairs. I knew there was something wrong as soon as he opened the living-room door for he just stood there, without starting to take off his overcoat. Mother looked at him.

" Is anything the matter ? " she asked. " Why are you looking so bothered. Have you got bad news ? "

"Yes," Dad said. "I'm afraid it's very bad news indeed. The vicar has had a telegram from the War Office. It was sent to the coastguard station, as the post office was shut, and Mr. Beecham sent one of the coastguards up to the vicarage with it. The vicar's son is in hospital at Pretoria. Enteric fever. His condition is very grave."

Mother looked terribly sad.

"Oh the poor boy," she said. "And his poor poor father. What a mercy, in a way that his mother has been taken to be spared such terrible news. But the poor vicar. His only son!"

Dad had started to take off his coat, which was dripping wet.

"He's a very brave man," he said. "It must have come as a terrible shock, for he has been hoping since Mafeking Day for a telegram to say that his son was on his way home, and perhaps he thought this was it. Yet his voice never shook when he told us the news before the service, and he carried out the service just as though nothing unusual had happened. A special prayer was of course said for the major's recovery. Perhaps the worst won't happen after all. Many soldiers *have* recovered from enteric fever. Well, we must just hope for the best."

"And pray too," said Mother. "We must pray now, instead of just saying grace, before breakfast, and pray for the vicar himself as well as his poor sick son and for the horrible war to be over."

We did pray, and yet although I repeated every word that Mother said, and meant it too, I couldn't help thinking what a disappointment it would be for everyone if the major did die, and there was no big "do" for his homecoming, which might have been even more exciting than Mafeking Day. And if he died too, Dad would never get the chance to do a picture of him in uniform.

God must have heard our prayers, and the vicar's, for the major didn't die. The next news that came was that he was out of danger, and being moved to a convalescent camp at Durban. And before Christmas came the news that he was on active service again, fighting the Boers. There was nothing about him coming home. But to show how pleased he was, the vicar gave special parcels of Christmas food to everyone who went to church and to all the poor people in the village whether they went to church or not, and he gave Dad a special present of a big goose, which was very lucky, for he hadn't sold any pictures for a long time, or made any money out of his inventions and we couldn't have afforded a real Christmas dinner.

15

ONE OF the exciting things to look forward to in Bramblewick during the winter was the Shepherds' Walk. It was to be held on a Wednesday late in January.

The Ancient Order of Shepherds was a friendly society. Those who belonged to it paid so much money every week and if ever they were ill, so that they couldn't work, they were given enough money to buy food and perhaps pay the rent of their homes. If a Shepherd died, money was also given towards the cost of his coffin and funeral.

They hadn't to be real shepherds to belong to the society. Although some of them were farmers (including Gow Pickering) most of them were fishermen or sailors.

The Walk always began and ended at the King's Head Temperance Hotel, just opposite our shop and house. There was one big room in the hotel, which was called the Shepherds' Lodge, and when the walk was over the Shepherds had a great feast in the Lodge. Mrs. Anderson had to have at least six women to get the feast ready, and for two days before it happened she would be preparing for it.

It would have made anyone's mouth water to see the things that were being taken into the hotel the day before the feast : geese and hare and rabbits, ducks and chickens and cheese, great lumps of beef and pork, sacks of vegetables ; pies and cakes already cooked, and to be warmed up, as Mrs. Anderson's ovens weren't big enough to cook everything. There was a barrel of beer and bottles too, in spite of it being a temperance hotel, and Mrs. Anderson herself being against strong drink.

The men wore their Sunday clothes for the Walk, and a broad silk sash over one shoulder and across their chests. They had white gloves on their hands. Each man carried a long wooden stick with a crook at the end. But the crook of the chief Shepherd was thicker than the others and the crook was made to look as though it was made of gold. Only one of the Shepherds had no crook. He had to carry the banner, which was made of silk and shaped like a shield something like the Royal Coat of Arms, only with different things on it, and a different motto.

Dad had been paid to paint this banner from a design that had been lent to him. But he wasn't a Shepherd himself. It was only for those who had been born and brought up in the parish.

First of all the men gathered in front of the hotel. The band would be getting ready higher up the street. Then the Shepherds would form up into two lines, reaching almost down to the dock, each Shepherd facing another one. They would raise their crooks and hook these together to make an arch wide enough for the band to pass through.

At a signal from the chief Shepherd, the band would strike up and come marching down the street. The banner bearer would get in front of it, then the chief Shepherd, and they would march through the arch, and as they went through each pair of crooks, the men holding them would lower their crooks and rest them like guns on their shoulders and join the procession which would go on through the dock and up the road for the bank.

It wasn't like the Mafeking Day procession of course. Although the pubs were open, no one was ever drunk at first, and there was no singing or shouting, except from the lads who always joined in at the end of the procession, some of them wearing sashes on their chests in imitation of their father's, and home-made crooks. The Shepherds always looked solemn and a bit shy.

School was closed of course and so were all the shops, even Neddy Peacock's coal warehouse, for he was a Shepherd and wore a sash and white gloves and carried a crook like the others.

The band played all the way up the road. When it got to the

bottom of the bank though it had to stop for those who played the wind instruments couldn't have got their breath, and the procession just walked slowly until they got to the top, and usually had a rest then before it went on, with the band playing another tune.

It went along Church Lane past the vicarage and the church, under the railway bridge and then on to Thorpe, with the Thorpe cloggers gaping at it, but not showing any signs of quarrelling if there were plenty of bay bumper lads behind the procession. Then the procession would turn round, and march back to the church for the special service.

The band would leave their instruments in the porch, and the Shepherds would leave their crooks there too. Even the Wesleyan Shepherds would go in to the service, but I never did, and I never saw or heard what happened, although Dad, who had to go, said that the vicar always preached a short sermon, and brought in something about Jesus being a Good Shepherd and that the Order of Shepherds had a religious meaning, particularly as it helped the sick and the dying and the dead.

Of course all the Shepherds must have been thinking about the feast that waited for them at the Temperance Hotel. When the procession formed up again after the service, everyone seemed to look more cheerful. It marched down to the village much quicker than it had come up and at last stopped in our street, and the Shepherds after handing their crooks to their wives or other relations, hurried inside to get their seats at the table. The bandsmen went in too, after they had played one more tune.

Although we could not see through the windows of the lodge from our living-room in daylight we could hear most of the things that went on.

They didn't start eating straight away. They had to wait for the vicar. He usually came down on his horse which he would leave at the blacksmith's stable, and walk the rest of the way. He was the chairman like he had been at the concert.

You could tell when he had entered the room, for there was a dead silence. Then he would say grace. All the Shepherds would say " Amen " and the feast would begin, and I could imagine the plates, piled up with food being set down in front of the hungry men, and them stuffing themselves. I could see the thick slices of roast goose, the legs and wings of duck and chicken, the slices of beef and pork, the rich gravy, and then the puddings and pies and thick cream waiting for them when they had eaten all the helpings they could manage of meat.

It was said that the Shepherds never had any breakfast on the morning of the Walk so that there would be nothing to spoil their appetites. You couldn't hear much talking or laughing at first. They were all too busy. But the beer was being handed round too, and gradually the noise did begin, just like a wind getting up, and the waves starting to break on the scars. The men would start joking and laughing and even shouting and singing bits of songs. But you would never hear any bad language while the vicar was there.

The feast would go on for nearly an hour. Then the vicar would rap on the table, and there would be shouts of " Order, Order," and then complete silence. The vicar would call for the first toast, Her Gracious Majesty Queen Victoria, and you would hear the Shepherds saying in their rough voices, " The Queen, the Queen—God bless her "—as they drank, then one of the bandsmen would start " God Save the Queen " on the piano, and they would all sing the first verse.

Mother said that she was sure that the Queen herself in her heart would not have approved of her health being drunk in strong drink. She was such a good good woman. And she could never really understand how the vicar could do it, for he must have known what an evil thing strong drink was. She was very glad when Mrs. Anderson told her that not all of the Shepherds did drink the toast in beer or spirits. Some, and Neddy Peacock was one of them, just drank water.

When the Anthem had been sung, the vicar called on the secretary to read the report, and of course we could not hear this. Then there were other speeches, including one from Doctor Whittle who was always there. When these were finished, the man would go to the piano again, and there would be a sort of concert with solos and choruses. But very soon after this started we would see the vicar coming out, to go home, and things would get noisier and noisier, and we would hear plenty of bad language and sometimes the sound of quarrelling, although usually everyone was in a good humour. Neddy would have left to open his warehouse again as soon as the eating was over, in case he missed any trade.

But the best thing about the Shepherd's Walk and Feast was what happened when it was all over. In spite of the men having such appetites, there was usually plenty of food left, and Mrs. Anderson would fill a basket with things like goose or chicken carcasses with lots of meat on them, pieces of sweet pies and portions of trifle and give them to Mother. This year I was looking forward more than ever to the Walk for although we had done well at Christmas with the vicar's goose we were still very poor and although I always had enough to eat I was sure that Mother and Dad hadn't.

In spite of it being winter, the weather wasn't cold. There hadn't been any more snow or frost since the storm. It was raining on the Saturday before the week of the Walk, and Mother had made me stay in. Dad was still working on his picture of the wreck and he didn't want me in the studio because of my disturbing him. It was the lifeboat that was bothering him. He had scraped it off at least four times and he hadn't got it right yet.

It was nearly dark and we had started tea when he came home. When he opened the living-room door, he stood and he looked exactly as he had done when he had told us about the news of the major's illness.

" Have you heard ? " he said, in a very low solemn voice.

Mother looked frightened.

" Heard *what* ? " she asked.

" About the Queen."

" *What* about her ? " Mother said quickly. " She's not—she hasn't passed away ? "

I think that Dad was really a bit pleased, that Mother hadn't heard anything. He liked being the first with news, even if it was bad news.

" She's very very poorly. A bulletin was issued by her

doctors at twelve o'clock to-day. It was Mr. Beecham who told me. He said that the very fact that a bulletin had been issued, pointed to it being serious."

" Did it say what was the matter with her. Is she in pain ? "

" The doctors haven't said what her complaint is. Just that she is exhausted and that her symptoms cause anxiety. Mr. Beecham had heard that the Prince of Wales has been summoned to Osborne and that the German Kaiser, who is the Queen's nephew by marriage, has left for England on his yacht. She's very old of course, eighty last birthday, a day older than George the Third was when he died. Mr. Beecham had been looking that up in a history book. It looks as though the worst is going to happen."

Dad sat down to his tea.

Mother didn't seem quite as upset as she had been about the major, and as she'd already said grace she didn't pray again. Yet she seemed very sad, and she kept on saying what a good woman the Queen was, and what an example she had set to all her subjects.

Although she had only been a girl when she had ascended the throne, she had shown from the start that she was going to rule wisely and in a true Christian way. Apart from being a good queen and always doing her duty, she had been a good wife, and a good mother. Of course she had never known what it was to have money troubles, but she had been full of compassion towards the poor, and she had always sent large sums of money when there were disasters in the land, and relief funds opened. She had sent money to hospitals and orphan homes and other charities, and to foreign missionary societies who spread the Gospel among heathen people.

She'd had her own troubles. She had lost one of her married sons and one of her married daughters. She had lost her beloved husband, Prince Albert the Good, and that perhaps must have been the greatest sorrow of her life, yet she had taken that blow bravely, believing that it was the will of God.

" Well let us hope and pray that in spite of her great age, she will be spared to reign many more years."

" Yes," Dad said. " We must all hope for the best. The

vicar is going to be very upset. I thought of going up and telling
him but Mr. Beecham said that everyone in the place must know
about it by now. It's going to upset the Marquis too, with him
knowing Her Majesty so well. It looks as though it's good-bye
to my hopes of the Queen seeing one of my pictures. It would
have been a wonderful thing if I'd been able to do a good portrait
of the Marquis, and I am certain the vicar could have persuaded
him to sit for me once I had done a good one of the vicar himself."

Mother looked vexed. "We shouldn't be thinking of that.
We must think only of the dear Queen herself, and her anxious
family. How good of the German Kaiser to be hurrying to her
side. No one in the world has ever been loved as she has been.
If she does pass away the whole country, and the Empire too will
be in mourning. I shouldn't be surprised if all places of entertainment are closed, and all festivities put off for the time being at least
as a sign of mourning and respect. It would be a good thing if
all public houses were closed too."

"I don't suppose that will happen, unless a special law was
passed," Dad said. "But we're talking as though she had already
passed away. She may get well again. I'm sure there will be
special prayers at all places of religious worship to-morrow, for
her recovery. And by the way. It's the Shepherds' Walk next
Wednesday. I suppose that would be put off if the worst happened."

I couldn't feel sad about the Queen being ill. I wouldn't feel
sad if she *did* die. You could only do that if it was someone
you really knew and liked who was ill or dead. I'd never seen her.
Neither had anyone else in Bramblewick, except the vicar, who had
been to the jubilee service in London, but hadn't seen her close
up. I'd seen plenty of pictures of her of course. Her head was
shown on all coins and postage stamps, some coins as she was
when she was young, some when she was old. She looked pretty
on the very old coins but not on the new ones. She was nothing
like as good looking as Mother was, and she didn't look very kind
either, in spite of what Mother said.

I'd felt really sad about the major being ill, because of having seen the vicar crying that time, and because I thought that he would never see him again. I did feel sorry for Dad though and his disappointment, for it would have been a wonderful thing if a picture of his had been seen by the Queen and she had liked it. And it was going to be another disappointment if the Shepherds' Walk was put off. I hoped that if she was going to die, it wouldn't happen until after the Walk.

We didn't get any more news about the Queen until Sunday afternoon, and it was brought by Mr. Beecham. It was good news too. Her health was slightly improved, and she was keeping up her strength. Dad told us that the vicar had said a special prayer for her at morning service, and that there had been an unusually large attendance at the church. The vicar had seemed very grave, and everyone had seemed gloomy. He had seen two old women actually crying as they left the church.

When I got home from school at Monday dinner-time there had been another message. It just said that there wasn't much change, but by tea-time news had come to say that she was becoming weaker and that she couldn't take any food. And then came another message. She was a bit better. She had taken some food. She'd been to sleep and she wasn't any weaker.

On Tuesday morning when I went off to school I saw Henry Newton carrying a big basket of meat into the Temperance Hotel. He looked quite happy and I felt it was going to be all right about the Walk and the Feast. When lessons were finished that afternoon the master told us that there would be no school next day because of the Walk, and when I got home there was even better news. The Queen had gone on improving. She had taken more food and had actually spoken to some of her family who were at her bedside.

" It looks as though our prayers are going to be answered," Mother said. " It looks as though she is going to be spared."

All that evening things were being carried into the hotel for the feast and there was a delicious smell of cooking coming out of the kitchen door. There were lights in the Lodge room. Peering between our own curtains I could see the women getting the tables ready.

Dad hadn't been to see Mr. Beecham since the afternoon as Mr. Beecham had promised he would let us know if there was any important news. It was just about seven o'clock, when Dad, who had been sitting by the fire, got up and said he would take a stroll down to the dock and ask the coastguard on watch if anything had come through. And just then we heard a single church bell starting to toll, not quickly as it had done on Mafeking Day morning when the vicar had rung it himself, but slowly as it did for a funeral.

The women in the Lodge room must have heard it too. One of them was peering through the window, and Mrs. Anderson herself appeared at the hotel door, looking up and down the street.

Dad rushed downstairs and he crossed the street to speak to Mrs. Anderson, and Henry Newton without his hat on, joined them. They all stood listening to the bell which kept on tolling. Then a coastguard came quickly down the street. He didn't stop but he said something to them, in a low voice as he passed.

Mrs. Anderson put her hands to her face and went indoors again. Dad and Henry said something to each other in low voices, and then Dad came slowly up the stairs, and opened the living-room door, and stood like he had done before, only sadder, and actually with tears in his eyes.

" Well, it's all over," he said. " The Queen passed away at half past six this evening. It's all over."

16

I DIDN'T feel sad about the death of Queen Victoria. The Shepherds' Walk and Feast were put off. But there was no school, and instead of us just getting "leavings" from the feast Mrs. Anderson gave us a whole hare pie that had already been cooked and was to have been warmed up, and a big bowl of delicious trifle.

Besides, the death of the Queen meant that her eldest son, the Prince of Wales, had already become the King of England and that before very long he would be crowned in Westminster Abbey at the Coronation ceremony, like the Queen herself had been crowned many years ago. By that time, although many people including the King himself would still be feeling sorry that Victoria's reign was over, there would be great rejoicing everywhere, and it was almost certain that there would be a holiday, and a procession through the village, and decorations, and a special tea in the vicar's field, and perhaps another bonfire.

When Dad said anything about the Coronation, Mother got vexed. It wasn't decent she said, even to think about rejoicings at a time of sorrow like this, nor indeed until long after the funeral.

She didn't know much about the new King. She had heard however, that he was far from being a total abstainer. In fact she had heard that in his younger days, although he had been brought up very strictly by his parents, he had caused them much anxiety by the company he had kept. Among other things he was very fond of horse racing, and all that meant. She had heard that he had often travelled on the Continent, using an assumed name, and that he had been seen even at Monte Carlo, which was supposed to be one of the wickedest places in the world. It was only to be hoped that, now that he had become King, he would follow the examples set by his parents, that he too would one day be known as King Edward the Good.

We didn't get a newspaper every day like some people did, but Dad got one the day after the Queen's death. It was a picture paper too, called *The Graphic*. On the front page, surrounded by a thick black border was a big picture of the Queen herself, taken from a photograph and showing her wearing ribbons and stars and more medals than any famous general or admiral. She wasn't wearing a crown though, or sitting on her throne.

Inside the paper were pictures made from drawings which showed all the important things that had happened to her during her reign, starting with her being told about the death of her uncle, William IV, and that she had become Queen, and her being crowned in Westminster Abbey. It showed her being married to Prince Albert and then with her first baby, a girl, who, when she grew up, became the mother of the Kaiser of Germany. It showed her sitting on horse-back, and dressed in uniform, reviewing her troops, and visiting sick and wounded soldiers from the Crimean War, and then from the Indian Mutiny, and the wars in Egypt and other countries.

There was a picture showing the funeral procession of her husband, Prince Albert, with her dressed in mourning and looking very sad, but there were also pictures of her at the Diamond Jubilee Thanksgiving Service, with a group where she was surrounded by all her sons and daughters, and their children who were alive, in which, although she looked very old, she didn't look so sad although she wasn't smiling.

Another picture showed her on the royal yacht, *Victoria and Albert*, steaming between the ships of the Royal Navy anchored at Spithead for the Jubilee Naval Review, with the ships decked with flags and guns firing a salute. All the pages of the paper had thick black borders round them, and there were some pictures quite up to date, showing a crowd of people standing outside the gateway of Osborne House, waiting the latest news of the Queen's health. Another of a messenger on horse-back, riding out through the gate, with men in the crowd standing with their hats in their hands, as though they knew the bad news had come.

The paper wasn't all pictures of course. There was lots of reading matter, chiefly about the Queen and the royal family. There wasn't any news about the South African War but on a back page was a big list of soldiers and officers who had been killed or had died. Most of them had died of fever.

There were advertisements too, including those of London theatres and one of the things that Mother noticed was a theatre where a Gilbert and Sullivan opera was running, only it said, as it did with the other theatres, that it was being closed on account of the Queen's death. There were also advertisements of London shops which sold mourning dresses for ladies, and firms who could dye coloured dresses black in a very short time.

As Mother always wore a black dress for chapel, because she thought it was more respectful to God, there was no need for her to get anything dyed, but Mr. Beecham said that he and all the other coastguards would have to wear a sign of mourning, and that would be a piece of wide black crêpe stitched on one arm of their uniforms, and Mother did the same for Dad's best jacket and overcoat. She didn't think it was important for me to have this done, but she told me that until after the funeral I mustn't play at any noisy games, or behave in any way that showed disrespect for the royal family and the memory of the Queen.

Mrs. Anderson had lowered the blinds of all but her living-room windows. Mother did the same with our bedroom window, and she kept even the living-room window half-way down, which made it very gloomy inside. She thought that the shop blind ought to be down too, as it was on Sundays, but Dad said it should be all right if it was only half-way down, for it wasn't as though the shop was a place of entertainment.

" I think though," he said, " it would be rather nice if I cut out that picture of the Queen on the front page of the paper, and mounted it on a card, keeping the black border of course, and put it in the middle of the window among the other pictures. I could put a wreath of evergreen leaves, ivy or laurel round it."

" That would be nice," Mother said. " Only it would be more

respectful if you took all the other pictures out, then passers-by wouldn't think you were using the Queen's picture as an advertisement."

" Couldn't you show just the picture of the two dead redwings lying in the snow ? " I asked.

" That's an idea," Dad said. " I wish I'd finished the picture of the wreck, that I started at the same time as I did that nice little one of the birds. I wonder if the Marquis is as friendly with King Edward as he was with the Queen. He would know him of course because of all the royal family going to Divine Service at Windsor Chapel."

" That is where the dear Queen will be laid to rest, I suppose," said Mother. " In the family vault, next to her dear husband. I think, after all, we should just keep the shop blind down until after the funeral. I am certain that would be best."

All the other shops in the village had their blinds down, so we kept ours down too. The flag at the coastguard station was at half-mast, and people who had flag-poles in their gardens did the same as the coastguards, and quite a lot of men in the village, including the sergeant, had black crêpe sewn on their sleeves. The schoolgirls had black ribbons in their hair. But Miss Lawson of course didn't look any different from what she always did.

The fishermen didn't wear any signs of mourning of course on their rough clothes. They went on fishing just as though nothing sad had happened. The pubs were still open. There wasn't quite so much singing and laughing inside them as usual, but one night just after closing-time there were the sounds of quarrelling and then of a fight.

We heard next day that the fight had been between Ikey's Uncle Jake, the sailor who we'd thought was going to fight Gow Pickering on Mafeking Night, and a farm labourer who was tramping round looking for a job. He was an Irishman. He had boasted that he was a home ruler, and that the English were no good and that the Boers were going to drive them out of South Africa, and that one day the Irish would drive them out of Ireland too. And then he had said a terrible thing about the Queen. He said he couldn't understand why everyone was making such a palaver about the old woman having kicked the bucket. She was only a German anyway on one side of her family, and had no more right to be Queen of England and Scotland and Ireland than the Shah of Persia.

I wish I had seen that fight. The Irishman was very big and strong, but Jake had knocked him down several times before giving him the final blow. It had ended with him being carried to the police station and locked up in the cell. He was summoned later and sent to prison for being drunk and disorderly and using insulting language. Jake wasn't summoned of course.

Apart from this, and having to go to school every day it was just like having one Sunday after another for the rest of the week, and the next week too, for the funeral wasn't going to begin until Friday. We read in the newspapers what was going to happen. On Friday afternoon the Queen inside her coffin was going to be taken on a gun carriage from Osborne House to Cowes and put on a paddle steamer. The warships of the Royal Navy, and ships from foreign countries too including Germany, France, Russia, Italy, America, Spain and Japan would be anchored in two lines between the Isle of Wight and Portsmouth, like the ships of the Royal Navy had been for the Jubilee Review, and the paddle steamer would go very slowly between them, with the guns of the warships firing a salute every minute.

The paddle steamer would stay at Portsmouth all night, with sailor sentries mounting guard over the coffin. Next morning it would be put on the royal train at the station, and the train, with the King and his family, and all the other famous mourners on it would travel to Victoria Station, London. And then another procession would begin, with the coffin on another gun carriage, through the streets of London past Buckingham Palace to Paddington Railway Station, where the funeral train would be waiting to travel to Windsor.

All sorts of famous people would be in the procession, including Lord Roberts who had got back from South Africa just in time. As well as the Kaiser, and his son the Crown Prince of Germany, there would be the Kings of Greece and Portugal and Belgium, the Crown Princes of Denmark and Norway and

Sweden and Siam, and the Archduke Ferdinand of Austria, and of course the Prime Minister and all the members of the Cabinet.

The King would be mounted on his charger, but Queen Alexandra and the other ladies would be in carriages. There would be four military bands to play music.

The streets would be decorated with wreaths and cloth trappings but Mother was very surprised to read that instead of the trappings being black they were to be purple, by special orders of the King. She said that she was sure that Queen Victoria could not have approved of that. She had worn nothing but black since Prince Albert had died.

It was going to be a wonderful sight. Although I didn't like funerals, I would have loved to have had a good view of this one, and seen all the warships firing their guns, and then the procession through the streets of London. I had never been to London of course and neither had Dad or Mother.

On top of the coffin would be the Crown of England, and the Orb and the Royal Sceptre, which were always used for the Coronation of British Kings or Queens, and would be used next for the Coronation of King Edward. As well as the four military bands, there would be Highland pipers from Balmoral.

It would be wonderful. But there wasn't going to be any procession or anything like that at Bramblewick. We were not even going to get a holiday on Friday afternoon, or leave school early. On Saturday morning while the grand funeral procession was passing through London, with the bands playing, there was to be just a memorial service at the church, to which, as it was the Parish Church, all loyal people, whatever their religion, were asked to go and show their respect and sorrow.

Mother didn't like going to church any more than I did, and she often argued against Dad about it. She said it was wrong to bow down to a Cross, as though it was a graven image and that in many ways the church service was near to being Roman Catholic. But, because it was for the Queen, she would go, for this once, and let me go too. She wasn't going to let anyone in the village think she was not loyal.

Even at breakfast-time on Saturday morning Mother was in

one of her most religious moods, and talked in a low solemn voice, and now and again started humming a gloomy Moody and Sankey hymn.

I didn't want to go to church a bit. It was a nice day, just right for going along the shore treasure-hunting, even if the sea hadn't been rough. But Mother wouldn't let me go out, in case I was late for getting ready, and because she had to get ready herself I had to help her in the house. I felt awful having to put on my Sunday clothes on a Saturday morning.

The church was packed of course. There were plenty of Wesleyans there, but I didn't see Neddy Peacock. Dad told us later the attendance had beaten all records. He and Captain Redman had had an awful job finding seats for everyone, and there hadn't been enough hymn books and prayer books to go round. It was lucky that they hadn't to take a collection, in spite of all the money that would have made for the church.

Actually it was just like an ordinary Sunday morning service, except for the sermon which the vicar preached, and that was nearly all about the Queen and what a good Christian woman she had been. Mother had read all this aloud to us from the newspapers, not exactly the same words of course, but really the same thing, and it wasn't easy for me to keep listening, for I was thinking of the procession in London, and other things like how nice it would be to be going along the shore in my old clothes, and wishing for something really exciting to happen like another big storm and a wreck.

I had never known such a long sermon either. The vicar always spoke slowly when he was preaching, but this time he was slower than usual. Perhaps he thought that by doing that he was being more respectful to the Queen.

I was glad when it was all over, and we started going out, with the organ playing. I would have liked to have run home, but I couldn't do that because of Mother and Dad, who like everyone else who had been to the service, went on looking solemn.

But she had to change her clothes before she could get dinner ready, and she made me change mine, and she didn't say anything when I got my oldest boots on. When we'd finished dinner I told her that I was going to have a walk along the beach to see if I could get some wood for the fire. All the coal from the wreck had either been picked up or washed out to sea long ago, and I knew there wasn't much chance of finding any wood, but it was a good excuse.

" I'd much rather that you went for a nice walk than played any noisy games with the village boys," she said. " The funeral of our dear Queen isn't over yet. It won't be until she is laid to rest in the Royal Chapel beside her dear husband, and I don't think that will be until to-morrow or perhaps even Monday. It is still a time of mourning. I hope you will find something nice on the shore, a real treasure."

I wonder what she would have said if she had known what I was going to find on the beach that afternoon. Perhaps if she had, she wouldn't have let me go at all, for it was going to be a lot of bother to her, although everything was going to come right in the end. In one way it was more exciting that the wreck.

17

THE TIDE was ebbing, but it wasn't far enough down for the lads to be playing football yet, and although there were a few old men sitting on the slipway seat, smoking their pipes, there was no one on the shore.

It was a neap tide too. The sea wasn't calm. There were little breakers on the scars, but the wind had been blowing from the land and I was more certain than ever that I wasn't going to find anything washed up. There were only a few bits of dead seaweed to show where high-water mark had been, and the tide hadn't even reached the foot of the clay cliff.

Yet there was always a chance of finding something interesting if you looked closely. Although there were patches of sand, the beach between the cliff foot and the scars was nearly all gravel that had washed out of the clay when the sea was rough.

One day when I had been on the beach I had seen an old gentleman with a long white beard, and wearing a knicker-bocker suit. He had a haversack on his back and a hammer in his hand. He was looking closely at the cliff, where the sea had washed the soft clay away, and now and again he would pick one of the stones out of it with the pointed end of his hammer.

He saw me staring at him, and he smiled, and spoke to me in a very kind way and offered me a piece of chocolate. Mother had told me that I must never accept sweets or money from strange people, for the sweets might be poisoned, but as this man ate a bit of the chocolate himself I thought it would be all right, and I took a piece.

He went on talking to me. He told me that he was a Professor

of Geology at a university and that he was making a special study
of clay cliffs like the one here, and the stones that were in the
clay. He showed me one big round stone just at the foot of the
cliff which I had seen dozens of times before without thinking
there was anything special about it. He said that it was a piece
of granite, quite unlike the shale that made up the scars. He
pointed to some long scratches on it, and then he told me that
the stone had come all the way from Shap Fell in Westmorland
and was called Shap granite. The scratches on it were made *by
ice*.

He told me that hundreds of thousands of years ago, during
what was called the Ice Age, all this part of England and the
North Sea too had been covered with frozen snow and ice just like
Greenland and the Arctic Sea were to-day, and as more and more
snow fell and was frozen it made glaciers, which moved slowly
south over the land, grinding it away, but bringing the pieces of
hard rock with them.

When the climate got warmer the glaciers melted, and the
hard rocks and the softer rocks that had been ground up fine were
left behind, and this was what the clay was, and it was called
boulder clay because of the hard boulders found in it. Some
of these boulders came from as far as Norway, and it was by
studying them that the geologist could make a map showing
just where the glaciers had moved.

He showed me some red stones which he said were jasper,
and some which because of their greenish colour he knew had
copper in them, but when I asked him if there was a chance of
finding any that had gold or silver, or if there were any diamonds
he said he didn't think so, but there just was a chance. I had
already found agates and cornelians, and he said they came from
rocks that sometimes had gold and silver in them, only these rocks
were in Wales and Cornwall, not where the glaciers had moved.

He was only staying one day in Bramblewick, and I never saw
him again, but when there wasn't any wood or floating treasures
to look for, I always kept a sharp look-out for gold and silver
nuggets, and many times I found what I thought might be a
diamond only it turned out to be just a bit of broken glass.

It was very nice to be on the beach. Although I would have liked to have seen the funeral procession in London, I was really sick of hearing about Queen Victoria, and the Coronation was too far ahead for me to feel excited about that. To-morrow was Sunday too. I wouldn't have to go to church again, but I would have to go to Sunday School and chapel in the evening. Except that when I looked back at the village I could see the flag at the coastguard station flying at half-mast, there was nothing else to show that everyone was in mourning. And I was glad too that there was no one else on the beach.

I wandered on and on, searching every patch of gravel, and looking at the cliff itself too, and I was quite a long way from the village, when I saw, running along the beach from the opposite direction, a small dog. It stopped just a few yards away from me.

I didn't know much about dogs. I didn't know what breed it was. It was just the size of a terrier, but it had a thick coat, black, with brown patches on it, and a foxy-looking face, with a pointed nose. It was panting a bit, with its tongue hanging out, and it just stood looking at me, as though trying to make up its mind whether I was a friend or an enemy.

I was a friend of course. I loved all animals. I remembered that Mother had given me a little bag of broken biscuits in case I got hungry on my walk. I held some out in my hand, and said coaxingly:

" Come on, come on."

The dog seemed almost to smile at me. It came up to me, wagging its tail, took the biscuits, and then barked quite softly, and stood up on its hind legs with its front paws on mine pressing on my thighs, and it tried to lick my hands as though to say thank you. I gave it the rest of the biscuits. Then as it looked as though it wanted to play I got a bit of tangle, and threw it along the beach. It scampered after it, picked it up in its mouth, brought it back and put it down at my feet for me to throw it again.

I noticed that it hadn't got a collar on like most dogs. I wondered whose it could be. I was certain that it didn't belong to anyone in the village. I knew every dog there, and I had never seen this one before. There still wasn't anyone on the beach as far as I could see, but there were plenty of footprints on the sand patches and I thought that perhaps it belonged to someone who lived on a farm, who had been to the church service, and had walked back along the beach just as the tide had got low enough. Yet they wouldn't have taken a dog to church.

I was excited but also a bit worried. I'd always wanted a dog. It would be wonderful if no one claimed it, and I could keep it. I went on playing with it. Then I thought I would try and find out if it really wanted to come with me, and I pointed towards High Batts and said to it, as sternly as I could :

" Go home. Go home ! "

It didn't take any notice, so I ran along the beach in that direction. It just scampered after me, thinking this was a new game and when I turned and ran in the direction of the village it just followed until it came to the piece of tangle. It picked it up and showed that it wanted to play with that again.

I had forgotten all about treasure-hunting. The tide was getting lower, and there was a pool between the scars. I threw the tangle in, and it went after it picking it up from the shallow bottom. There was no doubt that it liked me, and had completely forgotten about its real master whoever that was. I was certain that it would follow me home.

I wondered whether I should start for home now, and that was when I began to feel bothered. What would Dad and Mother think about it ? Mother was very fond of animals of course. So was Dad in a way but not so much as we were. One day I had found a stray cat and taken it home. It wasn't a very pretty one and I think it was rather old too, for it never wanted to play like some cats do. It was black with patches of white on it.

One evening it was lying on the hearth rug fast asleep when it suddenly got up and made a queer howling sound. And then it started to scamper round and round the room. It had gone mad.

Mother was really frightened. Dad tried to get hold of it, but it was too quick for him, and all he got was a scratch. It leapt on to the table, sending the crockery flying, but going round and round all the time, just as though it was chasing something, although there was nothing to chase. It wasn't howling, but its eyes were flashing in a most terrible way. It leapt on to the mantle-shelf, knocking a vase off but not stopping there, then it rushed half-way up the window curtains and leapt from there over Dad's head on to the table again, and then luckily through the door, which Dad had opened, and downstairs to the shop, where we heard it scampering round and round, knocking things over for quite a long time before everything was quiet.

When Dad went down at last we found that it had smashed the glass of two of his pictures, and that it was lying in the shop window dead.

Dad had gone to Doctor Whittle, to get something for his scratch for he was afraid that it might have given him hydro-phobia, but the doctor had said that you only got that from mad dogs. But Dad had said that we must never keep a cat again, and I was very much afraid he wouldn't want a dog. He mightn't think so when he saw this one though.

I thought of a name for it. Aunt Annie had once sent me a book as a Christmas present. I hadn't read it all for it was very sad and religious. It was called *Lost Gyp*, and I thought Gyp sounded just right for my little dog, and I tried calling it several times, and it seemed to understand.

I started for home. Gyp picked up the tangle. I told it that we couldn't go on playing that game, and I took the tangle from it but just carried it. It tried to persuade me to throw it but in the end it understood, and it just walked alongside me, wagging its tail, and now and again looking up at me in a very happy way.

Although it wasn't raining, the sky was cloudy and it was beginning to get dark. As we got nearer to the village I saw that some of the lads had come down and were playing football or shinny ower, and while I was very proud of having Gyp with me I thought it would be best not to let them see him, or they might try to entice him away from me. So instead of going along towards the slipway I climbed up the clay cliff. There was a path half-way up to where the fishermen kept their small boats which they only used in summer-time. This path led to an alley and some steps down to the dock.

Gyp kept close to me all the time, although by the way he kept looking at me, I think he was wondering where we were going. Luckily there was no one in the dock when I came in sight of it and I ran down the last flight of steps, Gyp running too.

We crossed over to the beginning of Chapel Street, and I saw the sergeant walking down it. There wasn't time to turn and go back to the dock. I wished that Gyp then wasn't walking so close to me, but I didn't look at him, pretending that it was just by accident that he was so close, and I didn't look at the sergeant as we passed, but I felt he was staring both at me and Gyp although he didn't say a word.

Instead of going straight into our house I went on up the street, looking slyly round to see if the sergeant had gone. He had gone, so I turned round quickly, ran back opened the street door, and Gyp followed me inside. I shut the door at once. Mother had opened the door at the top of the stairs. She must have thought it was a customer. I shouted to her that it was only me, and I bent down and patted Gyp's head, hoping that he wasn't feeling frightened.

I didn't know whether it would be best to tell Mother first before I went upstairs about him, or just walk up and let her see for herself, but Gyp gave himself away by suddenly barking, not very loud but enough for Mother to know it was a dog. I heard Dad's voice then, and I thought I'd better get it over, I went up the stairs and Gyp followed me. Mother stood looking at me in great surprise.

I didn't give her time to ask me questions. I told her straight away when I got to the landing, that the little dog had run up to me on the beach, and tried to make friends with me. There had been no one else on the beach, so it must have lost its master, and didn't know where to go. It was lost. And it was hungry too. It had eaten all my biscuits. Although I had tried to shoo it away, it wouldn't go, and it had followed me home. If it hadn't come with me it would have had to wander about the beach all night with nowhere comfortable to sleep, and it might even have been drowned when the tide came in. I didn't believe this,

L

for it hadn't been a bit frightened of going into the pool for the tangle and I was sure that Gyp was a good swimmer, but I wanted to give every excuse I could for keeping him.

Gyp seemed to understand that too, for he nudged Mother gently with his head and wagged his tail and whimpered, and then he went over to Dad, who was sitting by the fire and put his paws on his knees and looked up into his face, like he had done with me at first. Then he sat down on the hearth rug, where the cat used to sleep before he had his fit, and Dad actually bent down and patted him.

" It's a nice little doggie," he said. " I should say that who-ever owns it was having a walk along the beach or the cliff top and it ran away after a rabbit, and got lost. I've heard of that happening. It doesn't look as though it's been ill-treated. It's owner is probably very worried about it."

Mother had shut the door, and was looking at Gyp, and I could tell that she liked him, and wasn't upset by what I had done.

" Poor little thing," she said, " I expect he's hungry too. I'll find him a bit of bread or something. We must look after him until we find out whose it is. I suppose we ought to tell the policeman."

" The policeman saw him with me as I came up through the dock," I said quickly. " So there's no need to tell him again ! "

" It would be the policeman's duty to find out who the owner is," said Dad. " We've got to remember too that no one is allowed to keep a dog unless they pay a licence. I believe that costs five shillings. A lot of money. I hope he's well behaved, and hasn't dirty habits, like that cat had."

" I'm sure he's well behaved," I said. " He's very obedient too. I've called him Gyp, and look if you say Gyp, he'll come to you."

Gyp did cock his ears and came to me, as I said that word, and wagged his tail, and when I pointed to the mat, and said " Down Gyp " he did sit down, and then he turned round two or three times and curled up in the way dogs do when they want to go to sleep.

Dad picked up the newspaper again, and started to read, and Mother although she looked a bit bothered didn't say anything else about Gyp just then, and I felt it was going to be all right with them anyway. Mother told me to take off my boots, and change into my slippers for she was sure that my feet must be cold, and I asked her if she would like me to run any errands for her before I did so because of it being Sunday to-morrow with the shops closed. But she didn't. I didn't want to go out again really. It was just wonderful to see Gyp going to sleep so happily, to feel that if nobody claimed him, he would be mine for keeps.

18

GYP WAS well behaved. Although he liked to play, he never scampered about the house or barked. He wanted to sleep on my bed, but Mother said he mustn't do that in case he had fleas, so I made him a bed of his own close to mine with a box and an old blanket. There was a little yard at the back of our house, with a wall protecting it from the cliff, and I took him out there before his bedtime, and first thing in the morning.

Mother didn't mind him being in the living-room when I went off to Sunday school next day, although he did want to come with me. He certainly barked when we came back from chapel, and made a great fuss but that was only because he was so pleased to see us.

The Queen's funeral wasn't quite over yet. The coffin was still in the Royal Chapel, but there wasn't going to be another real procession, when it was taken to its last resting place on Monday, and on Tuesday the flag at the coastguard station was at full mast again and most people in the village had their blinds up. Everybody seemed more cheerful especially mother. She was even humming " Dear Little Buttercup " at breakfast-time.

I could tell that she was getting very fond of Gyp, and that Dad liked him too, but I was certain that Gyp liked me best. They hadn't said anything more about telling the sergeant, or about the dog licence. It was no good trying to pretend though that Gyp wasn't living with us. He couldn't help barking when I got back from school at dinner-time and tea-time, so that anyone who was in the street could have heard him. Besides, although I had to leave him behind when I went to school, he went with me everywhere at other times, even when I was just running errands for Mother.

Henry Newton of course saw us together, and I had to tell him how I had first met Gyp on the beach, and he gave me some nice bones for him. He frightened me a bit because he said that although he hadn't any idea whose it was, I mustn't be surprised if someone did claim him one day, for it was a very nice little dog. But he also said that it might have belonged to some stranger who had been just visiting the district, or even someone who had stolen it from its real master and it had run away from him, and I hoped and prayed too that this was what had really happened. Perhaps it had been with the Irish tramp who had been locked up.

It was just before supper-time only two or three days later, when there was a loud rap on the street door. I was sitting with Gyp on the mat before the fire. He jumped up at once and barked but not loudly. Dad went downstairs, leaving the living-room door open, and I went to the landing and looked down. Dad opened the door, and although I couldn't at first see who it was, I knew by his voice that it was the sergeant.

He said, quite politely, " Good evening," to Dad, and then he said :

" I understand that your son has found a stray dog, a small black and tan mongrel, and that you have it in your keeping. This gentleman here, Colonel Watson, D.S.O., who lives on the other side of High Batts, has lost such a dog. Have you any objection to his having a look at the one you've got ? "

I looked at Gyp, who was cocking his ears as though he was actually listening to the sergeant and understood what he was saying. I wondered if I could rush upstairs with him, and hide him, or let him out at the yard door. But it was too late. Dad said he had no objection of course, and then he said " good evening " to the man, and asked him to come upstairs. The policeman said he would wait.

Dad came first. He waited by the door for the gentleman to come in. He was a gentleman. You could tell that by his clothes, and the polite way he took off his hat, and said " good evening " to Mother. And he actually smiled at me. He was tall and straight and had a moustache. He was dressed like the professor had been, except that on one shoulder of his jacket there was a patch of leather which I knew would be for resting a gun on when he was out shooting rabbits or pheasants. He hadn't a gun of course, but he was carrying a basket, with a lid and a handle. It was just big enough for Gyp.

Mother asked him to sit down. He said he mustn't do that as he wanted to catch the last train for High Batts station, and he hadn't much time. Could he just look at the dog ?

Gyp had been on the mat when Dad and the gentleman had started coming up the stairs. I looked under the table. He wasn't there. And then I saw him, hiding under the sofa. I called him. He wouldn't move. And then although I didn't want to, I reached under the sofa and pulled him out by the scruff of his neck.

I was still hoping that Gyp wasn't the gentleman's dog. I thought that if he had been he wouldn't have tried to hide from him. He would have run to him, like he had done to me. He didn't want to go to him now. He tried to get back under the sofa, and the gentleman looked puzzled. But he said :

" That's Brownie all right," and he held out his hand to him, and said coaxingly, " Brownie, Brownie."

Gyp didn't go to him. The gentleman made a grab and then picked him up in his arms. Gyp actually growled, and looked at me as though he was asking me to save him, but it was no good.

" Would you mind opening the basket ? " the gentleman said to Dad. " I'm very sorry that I've got to take him away like this, for it looks as though he's got very fond of the boy. You must have looked after him very well. I wouldn't bother about him if it wasn't that he belongs to my little daughter, Penelope. She's got two other dogs but Brownie is her favourite and she's been very upset about losing him. I'm very grateful to you all for looking after him so well, and I'd like your boy to have a reward."

He put Gyp in the basket, closed the lid, and fastened it with a bit of string. Then he took a little gold case from his waistcoat pocket, and took from it a small coin, and put it in my hand, but I was nearly crying and I didn't see that the coin was

actually a sovereign. Mother was nearly crying too. Dad said :
    " You shouldn't give the boy money for what he's done. He's
been very happy looking after the little dog."
    " That's all right. He well deserves it, and I'll get Penelope
to write him a letter of thanks. Well, I must hurry or I'll miss
my train. Don't bother coming downstairs with me. I can
find my own way. I wish you all good night ! "
    He picked up the basket. As he walked passed me he patted me
on the shoulder, and said something, but all I heard was Gyp
whimpering, and then barking loudly as they went downstairs,
where the sergeant was waiting. Mother put her arms round me
then, and I really did cry, for I had never felt so sad in my life.

19

DAD SAID that the colonel must have been a very rich man to have given me a whole sovereign as a reward for finding Gyp, but I felt that if he had given me a hundred sovereigns it wouldn't have made up for my losing him. It was just awful to look at the bed I had made for him in the attic alongside my own, and to wake up in the morning and not to see him curled up in it, to look at the bones he had gnawed at, and remember the games we'd had together on the beach.

I was certain that the colonel's little girl could not have loved him as much as I did, and that he couldn't have been very fond of her, or why had he run away? I hated her. I was certain that she was horrible, more horrible and silly than any of the girls who went to Miss Lawson's school, or any of the summer visitors' girls with their penny shrimping nets.

If her father was so rich she'd have hundreds of toys. She had two dogs anyway. Why should she have Gyp too? I hoped that he wouldn't be pleased when he saw her again, that he wouldn't play with her, that he wouldn't answer to the silly name of Brownie. I even hoped that he would bite her, not really hard, but just to show that he didn't like her.

I did get a letter from her two days after Gyp had gone. The envelope had a crest, coloured red, on the flap, and Dad said that it showed that the colonel came of a very good family. He had already found out that he lived in a big house about three miles on the other side of High Batts, and although he hadn't been there long he was a squire and owned a large estate including part of the moor for shooting grouse.

There was the same crest on the writing-paper, and a telephone number, but someone must have drawn pencil lines on it for the writing to keep it straight. It was very poor writing, with a lot of spelling mistakes. I would have been ashamed of it. And all it said was thank you for looking after Brownie, who was very pleased to be home again and that she had two other dogs and a cat and some pet rabbits. She spelt rabbit with only one b.

That letter made me madder than ever against the girl. I couldn't believe that Gyp was pleased to see her again.

I couldn't bear to walk along the beach at dinner-time or after school for the rest of the week, for I knew it would remind me of the first day I had seen Gyp. But I didn't want to play games with the other lads, either on the beach or in the dock or the gas-works. I'd been very proud of Gyp. None of the other lads, not even Ikey had a dog of their own. All of them knew now the sergeant had brought the colonel to our house for him, and how he had been taken away, although none of them knew about the sovereign (which Mother was keeping for me, although she gave me an extra penny on Saturday for pocket money). I didn't want to have them laughing at me or sneering.

It wasn't until Saturday afternoon just a week from the day I had found Gyp that I did set off along the beach, and I wasn't a bit excited about it. The sea hadn't been rough. The cobles had been out fishing in the morning. Now they were all hauled up into the dock, and there was no one on the beach, for the craze among the lads was hoops and whip-tops, which could only be played in the dock or the road where the ground was hard.

The tide was flowing but only half-way up, and as it was still a neap tide, it would be a long time before it was up to the cliff bottom. I went down the scars first, looking in the pools where sometimes even in winter there was a chance of finding a fish or even a crab that had been trapped when the tide had ebbed. I had once found quite a big cod like this. It had a hook and a bit of snood in its mouth and must have broken away from one of the fishermen's lines.

I didn't find anything this time, and I soon gave it up and

went back to the beach near the cliff and started to search the patches of gravel for precious stones. I didn't have a bit of luck, and I felt more and more miserable when I came to the very place I had been searching when I had first seen Gyp. I remembered how he had stood looking at me, making up his mind whether I was a friend or not.

I looked along the beach to the cliff of High Batts. Three miles beyond that and of course out of sight was the house where the colonel lived. At this very moment, Gyp would be there with that horrible little girl. But I was sure that he wasn't playing with her as he had done with me. Perhaps she was even beating him with a stick because he would not play or answer to the name of Brownie. I imagined seeing her do this, and imagined myself going up to her and taking the stick from her and perhaps giving her a whack with it, and then Gyp bounding up to me, barking with pleasure.

I wondered whether I dare walk as far as High Batts, and then to the colonel's house. If it was a very big house I would be sure to see it from the top of High Batts. But I had never been even half as far as that. I would have to start very early in the morning, and even then it would be no good, for although I might see Gyp he wouldn't be allowed to come home with me. If I tried to steal him I would only get into trouble, and Gyp would be taken away from me again.

I walked on to the next patch of gravel. Again I found nothing worth putting in my pocket, but I did find an old rusty tin can at high water mark, and I put this up on a boulder and started to throw stones at it, like an Aunt Sally, only instead of it being an Aunt Sally I pretended that it was the colonel and I was having my revenge.

I soon got sick of this game. I went on walking towards High Batts, thinking about Gyp, and feeling more and more miserable. I came to a place called Mill Beck Nab, where the clay cliff ended and the shale began. The Nab jutted out like the Gunny Hole and just beyond it there was a sort of cove, called Boggle Hole with the beck running through it down to the sea. You couldn't get round the Nab when the tide was up, even at neap tides.

But it wasn't dangerous like the Gunny Hole for if you were trapped you could go up the cove and along the cliff tops.

Yet I wasn't supposed ever to venture round it by myself, although I often did, and I didn't turn back now. The Nab actually hid the rest of the beach just beyond it, and it wasn't until I had got round it that I saw it reaching away towards High Batts, still a good two miles away.

There was no one on the beach. It wasn't a good place for finding things, for there were no gravel patches, and as it would be too late, with the tide flowing, to try to get to High Batts, I thought I might as well turn back after all.

And it was just then that I thought I saw something moving, far along the beach. It was only a dot. Yet it *was* moving, and moving my way quickly, getting bigger. It looked like a dog. It *was* a dog. *It was Gyp!* Running as fast as he could go.

I ran towards him, shouting, " Gyp, Gyp," at the top of my voice. I saw that he had a collar on, with a leather lead trailing from it.

He was already barking. He had seen me of course, and he knew me. He ran right up to me, stood on his hind legs, actually jumped up and licked my face, and I didn't mind his tongue being wet, and I hugged him before setting him down, and then he started dancing round me, barking excitedly, wanting me to play. But there were no tangles to throw for him. I didn't want to play that game anyway. I wanted to get him home, and I started to run, shouting " Come on, Gyp, let's have a race," and I don't think that I had ever run so fast or ever felt so happy, for I hadn't begun to think yet about what would happen when I did get home.

*　*　*　*

I thought that I was being extra lucky. It was tea-time, and there were no lads playing in the dock. There was no sign of the sergeant either. The only person who could have seen me with Gyp was the coastguard on duty, and as I wasn't carrying anything that looked like wreckage he didn't seem to take much notice of us. Henry Newton was chopping some meat when I passed his shop and had his back towards me, but I was very glad when I got to our door, opened it and closed it again. Gyp must have heard Mother and Dad in the living-room for he scampered upstairs ahead of me, and barked and tried to open the door himself, and when I did open it for him he ran to Mother and tried to lick her, and then did the same thing to Dad and then ran back to me before I had time to say anything, and I was certain that at first they were as glad to see him as I had been.

It was only when I started to tell them what had happened that I saw that they were both worried. Although they had *looked* pleased they didn't say so. I told them that I was certain he had run away because he wasn't happy. That it was quite likely the little girl had been cruel to him, and that he preferred living with us. It was very likely that he had been trying to get back ever since the colonel had taken him home. That's why there was a lead on his collar. He must have dragged it out of her hand when she was taking him for a walk.

" Oh, I'm sure that no little girl would be cruel to a small dog like Gyp," Mother said. " You mustn't say things like that. The colonel said how very very fond she was of him. She may be just as sad now as you were when he had to go back."

" It's her dog of course," Dad said. " Both she and her father will be worried that he's run away again."

Gyp had stayed with me, and he was looking at Dad and Mother as though he just knew what they were saying. I was sure that if he had been able to talk he would have told them how glad he was to be back.

" I bet he's hungry," I said. " Can I go and get him a bone from Mr. Newton ? "

Mother had some bones she had bought to make broth, and she gave one to Gyp. He only licked it, so I got him a basin of water which I put near the fire. He just took a few licks at that then looked up at me in a very funny way. I was sure that he was worried. The next thing Dad said was :

" This has put us in a very awkward fix. Now we know whose the dog is we can't pretend he's just a stray, without an owner. The colonel was very generous. And it was very good of his little girl to write such a nice letter. He's a wealthy man. We mustn't offend him. He might even prove to be a customer," and Dad said to me, " Did the sergeant see you with Gyp this time ? "

" No. I don't think anyone did, except one of the coast-guards."

" But he'll soon find out. I think the best thing would be to make a clean breast of it at once. We'll have to tell the sergeant so that he can telephone to the colonel and set his mind at rest. He wouldn't be able to come for him to-night, or to-morrow with there being no trains on Sunday, so you'll have Gyp to play with until Monday at least."

Mother was looking sad, and even Dad was a bit, but neither of them could have felt as sad as I did.

Mother put her arms round me, and said in her religious voice :

" Dad's quite right, you know. We mustn't keep anything that isn't ours. I am sure that the little girl would be kind to Gyp. I think that Dad should go round to the sergeant at once and let him know. That would be much better than letting him find out from someone else. Come on now and change into your slip-pers and then get your tea. You'll have the whole of to-morrow to play with Gyp."

Dad put on his coat and hat and went out. I was hungry, but I just couldn't eat any tea. I kept on looking at Gyp, who was now sitting down on the mat, but not trying to sleep, and he actually barked when he heard Dad coming back up the stairs. Dad came in and said :

" It was a lucky thing. I actually found the sergeant talking to the coastguard on watch. Whether the coastguard had said anything to him about the dog I don't know. Anyway he said he would call up the colonel on the telephone, and let us know what the colonel said about coming for him again."

It was about an hour later, when there was a loud knock on the street door. Gyp not only barked, his mane bristled, and I think he would have rushed downstairs if I hadn't held him tight and petted him. I was sure that he was remembering the last time the sergeant had called. Dad went down. It was the sergeant of course.

He didn't say " Good evening " to Dad. His voice was very gruff and bossy and loud and I heard every word he said.

" I've come about that dog. I've been on the telephone to Colonel Watson. He wasn't in first go, so I had to call him again. He's says he's had enough bother with it one way or another, and that if your lad wants to keep him he's welcome, and that his little lass whose dog it is agrees. But I'd best remind you you'll have to get a dog licence for it, or there'll be the police court and a fine for you. That's all."

I took Gyp in my arms and hugged him and hugged him and actually kissed the back of his head, and then I put him down, and held his forepaws and danced with him. He was barking with excitement and pleasure and I was certain that he knew what had happened. That he was mine for keeps.

20

It was spring. The war in South Africa wasn't over yet. Mother had kept on making things for the Red Cross, but none of the lads had worn buttons of generals on their jackets since Mafeking Day. They had swapped them for marbles or tops with anyone who would take them, and the grocers had stopped selling new ones. There was still a bit of a craze for cigarette cards of generals and other war pictures of course, and I had quite a good collection.

These cards were very small, just the size of a cigarette packet. Yet Dad had copied one of General Baden-Powell full size, head and shoulders, and it was so good that it looked almost alive. It showed the general with a felt hat and khaki tunic with medal ribbons on his breast. Everyone in the village came to look at it when it was framed, and put in the middle of the shop window, and everyone praised it, even the vicar, who actually said that Dad ought to send it to the Royal Academy. Dad said he couldn't do that because it was only a copy and that would have been against the rules of the Royal Academy, although the colouring was all his own work. He couldn't do an original portrait, unless the general actually sat for him and there wasn't much chance of that.

Dad told us that it had been on the tip of his tongue then to ask the vicar if he would sit for him, but he had still been too frightened to do so.

He had given up the picture of the wreck and the lifeboat as a bad job. He just couldn't get the composition right. He had sold a few pictures to local people who wanted them to give away for wedding presents, but we were still very poor, and would be until the first visitors came at Easter. After she had paid for Gyp's licence, Mother had been forced to use the rest of the money the colonel had given me for food and other things. She did say though that she had only borrowed this from me and that one day she would pay it back. I didn't mind, so long as I had Gyp.

Dad hadn't finished his washing machine either, or the tricycle. I was hoping that he would give up the tricycle altogether and let me have the wheels to make a little cart, which I could use for getting firewood, but he hadn't lost hope of getting another wheel for it. Now, when he wasn't painting he was trying to make a patent folding easel out of an old deck-chair, for using when he painted country subjects.

One evening Dad came home with some very exciting news. He had been to see the vicar on some business about the church, and the vicar had told him that he had received a message to say that his son, the major, had been given sick leave and was now on his way home from Cape Town. His ship was expected to arrive at Southampton in three weeks' time.

Dad said that he had never known the vicar in such a good mood. He had taken him into his library and actually offered him some port wine, and when he had refused this because he was a total abstainer, the vicar had actually laughed, and got his house-keeper to make Dad a cup of cocoa, and bring him a slice of cake.

It was the first time that Dad had been in the vicar's library. I felt myself blushing when he started to describe it, for it made me think of the night I had gone to play pin-and-button and had seen it through the chink in the curtains. It was worse still when he went on to say that the vicar had shown him two photographs that were on his writing-table, one of his son who had been lost in Australia and the other of the major.

It was the photograph of the major that had interested Dad most. It was only head and shoulders, like the cigarette card photo of Baden-Powell, but it showed him in the full dress tunic of the Huzzars, and that would be either blue or red, a splendid subject for a real painting.

Although the vicar had been in such a good mood, Dad still hadn't enough courage to ask him straight out if *he* would sit for his picture, but he had said that he would like very much to do one of the major, using the photograph first, and then perhaps having a real sitting when he got home, if the major himself would agree.

The vicar hadn't even stopped to think about it. He had said straight away that it would please him very much to have the portrait painted, that the major would be pleased too, if it turned out as well as the portrait of General Baden-Powell, and he was sure he would give him a sitting. Not only that. He said he would buy the picture and pay ten pounds for it, without a frame. And he would pay Dad five pounds on account, the rest when it was finished.

He had lent Dad another copy of the photograph, which he showed us. The vicar had told him that it had been taken when he was only a lieutenant, two or three years before he had gone to South Africa. We had never seen the major himself. In the photograph he was staring straight at you. I thought he looked very stern, just like the vicar did, in spite of his being so much younger. But Mother said he was very very handsome, and that it was no wonder the vicar was so proud of him. She was very pleased about the money.

I was more excited about what was going to happen on the day that the major arrived. I thought that it was bound to be nearly as exciting as Mafeking Day. I was glad that I had kept some of my " general " buttons to wear. If only there had been one of the major himself. What a pity that he hadn't become a general, and won the Victoria Cross, or at least the Distinguished Service Order, like the colonel.

A meeting was held to decide what should be done to show how glad everyone was that the Major was coming home, and show their admiration for him. The vicar wasn't there, of course. The chairman was Captain Redman, and I was a bit disappointed when Dad told us what happened. Because it was Lent, and because everyone was still supposed to be in mourning for the Queen, there wouldn't be a tea party, or sports, or a real pro-

M

cession through the village, although everyone would be asked
to put out flags if they had them. Nothing was said about having
a bonfire.

But there would be a procession from the station to the
vicarage. The station would be decorated, and so would the road
to the vicarage. There would be an open carriage for the major
and the vicar to sit in when they got out of the station. Instead
of being drawn by horses, it would be dragged by the lifeboat
crew with ropes. The band would lead the procession. The
coastguards should be in it, so should the Shepherds with their
banner and sashes and crooks, and the girls of Miss Lawson's
school, dressed like they were for May Day if the weather was
fine, and anyone else who liked to join in, only they must be
respectful, and not noisy. I expected that this meant we wouldn't
be allowed to have drums or rattles or bells, like the one Ikey
had on Mafeking Day.

It was also decided at the meeting to make a money collection
in the village and district to buy the major a present which would
be given to him when the procession reached the vicarage, and
Captain Redman (who was quite a rich man) had said he would
open the fund with a gift of five shillings.

Henry Newton was to arrange the procession. Dad was asked
to paint a special banner to be hung across the road. Mr. Beecham
hadn't been at the meeting however. Dad said he was still
feeling huffed about the concert. When Henry Newton had asked
him next day if the coastguards would take part in the procession
and form a guard of honour he had at first said no, and had been
quite rude. He had told Henry that he couldn't see why there
was to be such a big welcome for someone who hadn't done anything special. He wasn't the only one who had been in the war.
There were plenty of soldiers who would never come back at all.

As for giving him a present and asking everyone to give money
to buy it, wasn't the major the son of the richest man in the spot?
He was paid by the Government for being a soldier and was
getting at least ten times as much as a common soldier or a naval
rating would get.

Henry had repeated all this to Dad, and Dad had told us

what Mr. Beecham had said. Mother was upset. She said that
although she would never believe that the Church of England
was the true religion there was no doubt that the vicar was a good
man. Although it was true that he was rich, he wasn't mean.
The rejoicing would be for a son returning safely to his father.
We must certainly give at least something towards buying
that present. It wasn't the present so much as the thought
behind it.

I was glad when Dad told us a few days later that Mr. Beecham
had changed his mind. He would let the coastguards take part,
if only to show how smart they could look, but he still wouldn't
give any money, and there were lots of folk in the village, he said,
especially the Wesleyans, who wouldn't either. Were any of the
collectors going to ask Neddy Peacock ?

Dad had bought a new canvas out of the five pounds the vicar
had paid him, and he had started on the picture straight away.
He wouldn't let me see him working on it in the studio, but he
told us every day when he came home, how it was getting on.
He was sure the vicar was going to be pleased with it, and that
quite apart from the money it was going to be a splendid advertisement for him. It was the thin end of the wedge. It was almost
certain to lead to him doing one of the vicar himself and very
likely the Marquis.

He was also working on the banner to go across the road.
He wished in many ways that he hadn't been given this particular
job, for it had to be done on a long strip of calico, which was
very difficult to paint on. He had to paint on it the words
WELCOME HOME, as big as possible. He would have liked
to have painted Union Jacks on each side of the words, but
that would have taken too much of his time from the portrait,
and anyway real flags could be pinned on to the calico, before it
was hung up.

It was about a week before the major was expected that he
brought the picture home to show to us, and as he often did when
he thought he had done something very good, he pretended at
first that he was not really pleased with it himself. He said he
wasn't at all sure now that the vicar was going to like it. He had

waited until after dark to carry it across from the studio, and had wrapped it up carefully, so that no one could see it.

He told us before he took the wrappings off that he wouldn't be surprised if we didn't think that it was one of his best portraits but we must remember that we were judging it by artificial light.

It was wonderful. It was much better than the one of Baden-Powell. Although the face and the uniform, and the way he was looking were all exactly like the photograph except in size, the way the face was painted make it look alive, with real flesh. It looked as though any moment the major would move and open his mouth and speak. And it was better than the photograph in another way, for Dad had given it a background, with hills and some palm trees, and a blue sky with little white clouds to make anyone think it was South Africa.

Mother was so pleased that she hugged Dad and gave him a kiss, and Gyp who had been sitting on the mat barked, because he saw that we were all excited. I had never seen Dad so pleased with himself. He said that he would take it up to the vicar at once, and if he liked it, he would ask his permission to put it in the window as soon as it was framed, and keep it there until after the major returned.

He was even more pleased when he came back.

The vicar, he said, had seemed delighted with it. He'd said that he could hardly believe that Dad had been able to do such a fine painting with only a photograph to copy from. It was a wonderful likeness too. He was sure that his son would think the same. Dad must order an English gold frame for it at once, and it was quite all right for him to put it in the shop window.

The vicar had been having the whole of the vicarage re-decorated. He had taken Dad upstairs and showed him the major's room, all ready for him, with new carpets on the floor, and new curtains. He had said that although he was only coming home on sick leave, it wasn't likely that he would be going back to South Africa for many months and it was almost sure that the war would be over by then, especially as Lord Kitchener was now commander-in-chief. The vicar was hoping that really his son was coming home for good.

Again Dad had been tempted to ask the vicar if he would sit for his portrait, but he had decided that the time wasn't quite ripe for that. It was the thin end of the wedge. The next thing would be to do another one of the major, full length and from *life*. The vicar hadn't paid him the other five pounds yet, but seeing that we had got the first five pounds, we ought to give at least five shillings towards buying the major's present.

2 1

I was afraid that the day of the major's arrival would be a Saturday, so that like it had been for the Queen's funeral service we
wouldn't get an extra holiday.

Luckily it was a Thursday, and the weather was fine, with the
sun shining. We were to have a holiday of course, in spite of
ours being a Wesleyan school.

The major's ship had arrived at Southampton. The vicar had
gone to Southampton two days before to meet him. They were
going to travel all night, and their train would arrive at Bramblewick at one o'clock so that everyone would have time to get
dinner.

We were all in our Sunday clothes. I was sorry I couldn't
have my tin-can drum, but I had my wooden sword, and all my
" generals " pinned on to my jacket. I tied a piece of red white
and blue ribbon round Gyp's neck. He didn't like being on a lead,
but I was afraid of him getting run over by the train, so he had
to have it.

I had never seen so many people as there was at the station.
Most of them were in the road outside the station entrance,
where the open carriage, decorated with garlands of flowers were
waiting. The lifeboat coxswain and crew were wearing lifebelts,
over their best Sunday clothes. The men of the crew had red tam
o' shanters on their heads, and they had ordinary boots instead
of sea boots which made them look a bit funny.

The coastguards were in their best uniforms too, and wearing
their medals which they had earned when they had been in the
Royal Navy. They carried cutlasses at their waists, but Mr.

Beecham had a real sword in a scabbard, with golden tassels. I thought that he was looking a bit vexed, as though he still couldn't see why there should be such a " do " to welcome the major. Most of the shepherds wearing their sashes and white gloves and carrying their crooks were there, although I didn't see Neddy Peacock, and of course Miss Lawson was there, in a black dress, with all her girls in white and wearing garlands of flowers. And the band was ready with all the bandsmen quite sober.

Scaffold poles had been fixed on each side of the station road with flags and bunting draped between them. Just outside the station, stretched across the road, was the banner Dad had painted with the words WELCOME HOME. But the procession hadn't formed up yet. Everyone was just standing about waiting.

Dad had told us that unless we wanted to be in the actual procession, we had better go into the station, so that we should actually see the major getting out of the train. Only those who were to shake hands with him would be on the platform, close to, but it would be all right if we stood well back. Doctor Whittle would be the first to speak to him and shake hands, then would come Captain Redman and Mr. Conyers the organist and choir master, and one or two others including Dad.

It was only a single railway line. There were two platforms, and we had to cross the line to reach the one where the train was to arrive. I held Gyp very tightly when we did this although there was no sign of any train yet. I had heard of dogs being run over.

We found a good place to stand near the waiting-room. It wasn't long before we saw the train itself coming out of the tunnel at High Batts, three miles away. The line curved inland from there along the slope of Stoupe Brow, and there was another little station where the train had to stop, which was hidden in a wood, although you could see the steam and smoke from the engine rising above the trees, and hear its whistle as it started again.

I was very excited. Dad had taken his picture to the vicar before he had left for Southampton and had got the rest of the money for it, but it had been in the window for several days. Everyone who had seen it had admired it. I was certain that as soon as the train stopped, I would recognise the major just from his face in the picture, quite apart from his officer's uniform. I wondered though whether he would be wearing his sword, and have a revolver in his belt.

Everyone was looking along the line. We could hear the engine puffing, but there was a deep cutting about half a mile from the station, and it wasn't until it had passed it that the train came in sight again. I thought I had better hold Gyp in my arms. Before the train got to the first signal post there was a loud bang, and then another and another, that made me and Mother jump and made Gyp bark. They were fog signals, and the station master had put them on the line as a first welcome to the major.

And then the train drew into the station, and came to a stop. Almost straight opposite to us was a first class compartment, and looking out of the open window was the vicar, his head bare, and of course without his respirator, and smiling happily. The station master himself touched his hat respectfully and turned the handle of the door. Those who were to welcome the major gathered round while the vicar got out, and all touched their hats to him, and the vicar smiled at them.

Then he looked into the compartment, and made a sign with his hand and out stepped a man, not in uniform, but wearing an ordinary suit of clothes and a bowler hat, and I could hardly believe that it really was the major. He didn't look one little bit like Dad's picture. He didn't look like a soldier at all.

He wasn't tall like the vicar. He was very broad though. He wasn't young. His hair was grey. He didn't look kind either as even the vicar did sometimes when he was in a good humour and smiled. He didn't look happy or a bit pleased to see anyone. There was something funny about his eyes. He kept on blinking them, as though he was dazzled, and it wasn't until Doctor Whittle reached out his hand to him, that he reached out his own hand.

I couldn't hear what Doctor Whittle said to him because of the engine panting, or what he said to Doctor Whittle, but when he had shaken hands with Mr. Conyers, he turned away as though he didn't want to shake hands with anyone else, and I thought that Dad looked a bit surprised and vexed.

A porter had stepped into the compartment for the luggage, and another porter was getting things out of the van. The doors were all shut again. The guard blew his whistle and waved his flag and the train moved away so that we could see the crowd on the other platform and on the road outside the station, and they could see us, and of course the major.

Henry Newton who was standing there, gave a shout.

" Three cheers for the major and the vicar ! " and everyone shouted " Hip—hip—hooray ! " three times. The vicar waved his hat and smiled, but it seemed to me that the major himself still wasn't feeling pleased. He didn't smile anyway, and kept on blinking his eyes, and when the last cheer was given they all began to move along the platform to the crossing, and it was then I noticed that the major, who had a walking stick, was limping.

" The poor man," Mother said. " He looks quite ill. He *must* have been wounded."

We followed. Again I was glad when we got safely across the line, and I could put Gyp down. We got out of the station through the luggage entrance, and were just in time to see the vicar and the major move out of the ordinary door, to where the carriage was waiting. On each side of it were three coastguards standing to attention and Mr. Beecham, with his sword drawn, giving a salute.

The vicar smiled at Mr. Beecham, but the major didn't take any notice of him. He didn't seem to look at the banner with Welcome Home on it. He just got into the carriage, and the vicar followed him and they both sat down.

Then Henry Newton gave another shout. The band started to play and march off. The lifeboatmen pulled at the ropes fastened to the carriage, and it moved under the banner and along the road, with the coastguards on each side and the Shepherds following behind, and then the schoolgirls and the lads, all waving flags and shouting and cheering, but not playing any drums, or ringing bells or blowing horns or making as much noise as we had all done on Mafeking Day.

Doctor Whittle and those who had been on the platform, including Dad, didn't join in the procession. There were two ways from the station to the church and the vicarage, one to the left which led to Bramblewick, and then branched into Church Lane, and one to the right which led to Thorpe, but also branched into Church Lane. The procession was going to the left, and Dad told us that if we were to get a good view of the presentation, which was to be on the lawn of the vicarage, we should go with him and the platform party, the other way, which was a bit shorter, only we must hurry, so as to get there before the procession arrived.

I wasn't feeling so excited now. As we hurried along with Dad, Mother said :

" The poor man. I'm sure that he is ill. I'm sure that all this excitement can't be good for him. He needs rest and good nursing. He looks unhappy, and yet he must be glad to be home after all he has gone through in the war, and how glad and proud his father looks."

" I think that he's just shy," Dad said. " Soldiers are like that often. I don't suppose he expected a welcome like this. He certainly looks very different from the photograph and the portrait. I wonder what he will think of his portrait when he sees it ? I expect the vicar has put it in the library."

We got to the vicarage just as the band was turning into Church Lane. There were people on each side of the lane. They were cheering and waving their hands to the vicar and the major as the carriage passed, and the vicar was raising and lowering his hat to them, but the major didn't seem to be taking any notice at all. He was just sitting still, and staring straight ahead but with his eyes blinking.

Dad made us hurry to the lawn. Some people were already there, including Mrs. Binns, the housekeeper, and her husband Tom, who was the gardener and groom. They were waiting at the front door which was open.

I felt myself blushing when I looked at the very window that

I had peeped through and seen the vicar crying. I wondered what Mother would have said if she had known what I was thinking about. But the band was getting near, turning into the carriage drive. It came round the corner of the house, followed by the lifeboatmen and the carriage and the rest of the procession. The band stopped playing. The carriage stopped just opposite the front door, and everyone crowded round, cheering again, for the major at last was home.

The vicar was smiling. The major wasn't though. He seemed to be in a daze. Neither of them got out. The vicar must have been told what was to happen next. Dr. Whittle was standing on the steps of the house. Tom Binns opened the carriage door, and the Doctor got in, standing between the vicar and the major. He had a little box in his hand.

I wondered if he was going to tell us about the bombardment of Alexandria again, and Lord Charles Beresford and the *Condor*. But he had been drunk that night at the bonfire, and now he was quite sober, and he made just a short speech, that was interrupted by cheers, whenever he mentioned the major's or the vicar's name.

He said how pleased everyone was to welcome the gallant major home again from the war. The war wasn't over yet, but thanks to the courage and skill of men like him, under generals like Lord Roberts, and Buller and Baden-Powell, and now Lord Kitchener, Kruger had been beaten, and the rest of them would soon be wiped out and the Union Jack flying again over the whole of South Africa, which belonged and always would belong to the glorious British Empire.

It was sad that our late Queen had not lived to see the day of victory that was coming soon. But in her son, King Edward, we had a man in every way worthy to succeed her. The major had been lucky to escape being wounded in the war, but he had suffered from fever, and hadn't yet quite got back his health. Everyone who was listening to him now would join with him in wishing him a complete recovery. It was now his pleasant duty to present to him a small gift which had been bought for him by his many friends in the district, as a mark of their respect.

While the doctor had been speaking the major had kept on blinking his eyes, and biting his lips. I noticed too that he was clenching the handle of his stick very tightly, as though he would like to hit somebody with it. Yet he wasn't really looking at anyone.

When the doctor stopped, the vicar gave him a nudge, and whispered something to him. He stood up. I saw that he was actually *trembling*. Doctor Whittle opened the little box, and took from it a gold watch and chain. He held it up for everyone to see, and then he offered it to the major.

Everyone cheered and clapped their hands again. The vicar was smiling, but the major stood looking more dazed than ever. He took the watch though, and he looked at it, and I think he said " Thank you very much," but that was all. He sat down again, and everyone went on clapping and cheering until the vicar stood up, and raised his hand for silence.

He put his hand lovingly on the major's shoulder. Then he said that this was one of the happiest days of his life. He was very pleased with the great welcome that had been given to his son, and by what Doctor Whittle had said, and by the handsome present that had been given to his son, which he knew he would treasure more because of the kindly thoughts behind it. But his son was more accustomed to the battlefield than ceremonies like this. The time had now come for him to go indoors to his own home. The most fitting way to bring everything to a close would be for us all to join in the singing of the National Anthem.

The band started to play. The major stood up to attention, and so did all the other men in the crowd. But I noticed that several people who were near us sang the words " God save the *Queen* " instead of " God save the *King*," as it ought to have been.

When it was finished Doctor Whittle got out of the carriage, and then came the vicar, who stood to help the major out. There was more cheering. The major, leaning on his stick walked through the door without even glancing at Tom or Mrs. Binns who were standing there. The vicar followed, turned at the threshold and smiled again. Then he went in, followed by Mrs. Binns. The door was shut, and we all started to go home.

22

I WAS very disappointed about the major's homecoming. It hadn't been in any way like Mafeking Day. I felt that I didn't like the major himself a bit. I began to think that Mr. Beecham had been quite right about him. He wasn't a hero. Why should he have had such a welcome home and been given a gold watch which he hadn't seemed pleased to get anyway.

Dad was disappointed too. For although he had seen the vicar next day, he hadn't as much as mentioned the portrait. Mother said it was hardly surprising. Probably the poor man had gone straight to bed after he'd had dinner with his father, for there could be no doubt that he was poorly. She hoped that Mrs. Binns would be looking after him properly, giving him the right sort of food. What a pity his own mother wasn't alive. She would have been the one to nurse him although there was no doubt that the vicar loved him very very much. What was the matter with him, she wondered ? Apart from his lameness, he seemed to be quite strong in his body. Yet he'd seemed so nervous, as though his mind was affected in some way, as though he couldn't collect his thoughts. He wouldn't have stood up to take the watch from Doctor Whittle, unless the vicar had nudged him.

Dad hadn't seen the major himself next day. He wasn't at church next Sunday either at any of the services. Dad hadn't dared to ask the vicar if the major *was* ill in bed, but he'd had a word with Tom Binns, who'd said that as far as he knew the major was all right, only he'd been keeping to himself since he'd got home. His charger, which had come with him on the ship from South Africa, had arrived and was now in the vicarage stable. The major had given orders for it to be corned up, so that

it looked as though he would be out riding soon. Dad said though
that he had the feeling that Tom was keeping something back.

It was Ikey who brought the next news about the major, and
he told us lads about it at school play-time. He was boasting as
usual, but I didn't think he was telling lies. Because he was such
a good runner, and because he was going to the shop as apprentice
as soon as he was fourteen and left school, Ikey was often given
a job to deliver the telegrams from the post office. He'd get a
ha'penny for doing this if it was to anyone in the village, a penny
if it was Up-bank, and tuppence if it was Thorpe. He was the
only lad who would go to Thorpe by himself, because of the
cloggers.

He'd had to take a telegram to the vicar. Of course he didn't
know what was in the telegram. He'd gone to the back door,
which was the one nearest the lane. He couldn't make anyone
hear, so he had gone round to the front door. And then he had
heard shouting inside the house, in the front room. It was the
major shouting at the top of his voice, and swearing at his own
father, the vicar, calling him all sorts of names. He'd actually
called him a bloody bastard !

Ikey had heard the vicar too, only talking softly, as though he
was trying to calm the major down, and then he had heard a
crash like glass being smashed up, and just then Tom Binns had
come out of the stables and seen Ikey and taken the telegram from
him, and told him to run off.

I didn't tell Dad or Mother what Ikey had told us, for I
knew it would upset them, yet I think they must have heard
something, for Mother told me that I must on no account go
near the vicarage at present, and that if I saw the major out, I
must avoid him, although she didn't say why.

I was having a walk with Gyp along the beach after school a
few days later when I saw a man on horseback come down the
slip way. Usually when the farmers from the moors or High
Batts, who had been to the village on horseback to do their
marketing, rode back along the beach they came very slowly down
the slipway, because it was so steep. But this one galloped down,
then came tearing along the shore in my direction.

Gyp wasn't on his lead. I ran up towards the cliff out of the way, shouting at him to follow, for I was terrified the horse would run over him. Before we reached the cliff it galloped past, only a few yards away. The man on the horse was the major. He was whacking it with a hunting crop, shouting at it in a fierce voice just as I used to imagine him charging into battle against the Boers slashing with his sword, shouting to his men to follow him to victory.

I *was* frightened, especially as Mother had said I must avoid the major if I saw him outside. I watched him galloping along the beach, past Mill Beck Nab and along the hard beach beyond. There was another cove and stream before High Batts cliff began with a lane that led up to the moors and he turned up the lane and was then out of sight.

I thought I had better go home, in case he came galloping back and I put Gyp on his lead.

There were some men and lads standing on the slipway, with Mr. Beecham among them. They must have been watching the major. I stopped among them and listened to them talking. I found out that the major had actually galloped down the road and through the dock where some little boys had been playing hop-scotch, and had nearly knocked some of them down, and had so terrified an old woman she had screamed.

Everyone seemed angry. I heard one of the fishermen say :

" He's either tight, or he's taken leave of his senses. It's lucky he didn't kill one of them bairns, riding full go like that. He'll likely break his own neck anyway."

" And what about his brand new gold watch, eh ? " Mr. Beecham said sarcastically. " If it was anyone else but the vicar's son he'd have been summoned for riding like that. But it's my opinion he's off his chump. I thought so when I first saw him. He's off his chump."

It was just then we heard the sound of another horse, coming through the dock, only trotting. It was the vicar himself. In spite of what he had been saying, Mr. Beecham saluted him respectfully and everyone stood back. The vicar had pulled up.

" Have you seen my son on horseback ? " he said. His face

was very pale, and he looked anxious, yet bossy too, as though he
expected everyone to be humble, and no one said anything about
the way the major had galloped through the dock.

"He went riding along the beach a few minutes since, sir,"
someone said. "I reckon he's turned up Stoupe Beck Lane."

The vicar didn't look at the man who had spoken, or say
thank you. He made a clucking sound to his horse, which started
off again, walking down the slipway, then, on the level beach,
breaking into a gallop, although not such a fast one as the major's
charger, and away they went until they too were out of sight
where the lane went up towards the moors.

I thought I'd better go home, for although I didn't really like
either the major or the vicar, I didn't like to hear even Mr.
Beecham talking against them, for the vicar had been kind to us,
and in many ways he had been Dad's best friend, and Mother's
too. I thought that if they hadn't heard what had happened, I
wouldn't tell them. I would keep it to myself.

*   *   *   *

But whether they'd heard anything or not Dad and Mother
stopped talking about the major or the vicar in front of me. I
couldn't help listening to what the lads were saying though, or
overhearing scraps of news from grown-ups. All sorts of tales
were going about. I'd heard that the vicar had got back to the
vicarage just before dark that night by himself, but that it was
nearly midnight when the major returned, with his charger
covered with froth and mud, and almost winded, as though it had
never stopped galloping.

Everyone knew that there was something the matter with him.
Although telegrams were supposed to be secret, it was known
that the one that Ikey had taken to the vicar was from someone
in London, and that it said he could be expected at Bramblewick
the next day. Doctor Whittle wasn't one to talk about other
people's business, at least when he was sober, but he'd let somebody know that the man was a very clever doctor and specialist
and that it must have cost the vicar a big sum to have him come
from London.

It couldn't have been just because of the major's lameness the other doctor had come. That was only rheumatics, which he'd got by sleeping without a tent in the war, and getting wet and cold. It must be something to do with his nerves, the way he had seemed dazed by the procession, and the people cheering, and trembled when he had stood up to take the watch, and hadn't been able to make a proper speech. And then the quarrelling with his father that Ikey had heard, and his galloping through the village.

In spite of Ikey being so brave, when another telegram had come for the vicar a few days later, he wouldn't take it, because he was afraid he might meet the major himself.

The next news we heard was that both Mrs. Binns and Tom had given up their jobs at the vicarage, and gone to live in a cottage in Thorpe, and that two strange men had arrived. They were both very tall and strong. They had both come to live at the vicarage, and one of them had been seen out riding with the major on the vicar's horse. The major's charger was a bit lame, and they hadn't been galloping.

I could tell by the very way that Dad and Mother never mentioned what was happening in front of me they did know quite a lot and were very worried. Whenever Mother mentioned the vicar's or the major's names, she always said, the " poor " vicar, or the " poor " major, and when the news came that the vicar himself was actually leaving the vicarage, and going to live in a small house just on the Thorpe side of the railway station Mother did tell me in a very sad voice, that this was because the major's mind was affected owing to what he had gone through in the war. The vicar was moving so that his son could be looked after better by the two men who had come to stay there.

She said that it was a very sad thing indeed that this had happened, seeing how deeply the vicar loved his son, and how eagerly he had looked forward to him coming back from the war. It showed what a really kind and loving man he was, giving up his nice comfortable home with its beautiful garden for his son's sake. It would have been so much easier to have let him go to a hospital, or some place where he could have got treatment for his

N

nerves. She was glad the vicar hadn't done that. We must pray that in time the major would get completely well again, but that when he did he wouldn't have to go back to the war. What a terrible thing it was that the fighting was still going on, men trying to kill or wound each other, instead of making things up and being friends.

And then she said that when men's minds were affected they sometimes became violent and even dangerous, and that although there were two men to look after the major, I must never go near the vicarage at present. Even Dad, when he went to church, went to it round by the station, instead of along Church Lane.

I had never told mother what a fright I'd had when the major had galloped past me on the beach that day. I didn't need either to be told never to go near the vicarage, for I had heard lots of other frightening things from the lads that she didn't seem to know about.

Ikey didn't say just that the major's mind was affected. He said he was *mad*. He'd heard that from someone talking in the post office shop. And it had come from one of the men who was looking after the major, who had been in a pub drinking. The man's name was Macdougal, and he'd told everyone in the pub that although he'd once been a policeman, he was a private lunatic asylum attendant, and so was the other man, Mr. Perkins. They'd often had to take on jobs like this, where the parents or relations of the person who was mad didn't want to put them in an asylum.

The major wasn't as mad as some they'd had to look after. In some cases the only thing was the asylum, where they had padded cells to stop the man from injuring someone or himself, during what was called a brain storm. The major hadn't got to that stage yet, but it seemed that he'd taken against his own father, which was a thing that often happened when a man was out of his senses. He imagined that those who were his friends were his enemies, perhaps trying to murder him, so that he might try to murder them.

The man had said that the vicar hadn't been afraid of this happening. He'd wanted to stay and help to look after his son. It was the specialist from London who had said it was best for him either to keep away, or allow the major to go to an asylum until he got well again, as he might do in time if he was looked after the proper way and given certain things in his food to keep him calm. He wouldn't know that these things were really medicines the specialist had ordered.

There were no weapons left in the vicarage, that the major could get at. His sword and revolver, which had come in his luggage from South Africa, had been taken away without his knowing it. Things like sharp knives or axes, or even pokers weren't left lying about. The best rooms in the vicarage were locked up, for the major had done a bit of damage in the library.

Yet no one need feel frightened about him. He was being looked after properly. If he went out riding one of his keepers would always be with him, and now that his horse was lamed there was no fear of him galloping off. He was a strong man, but he wasn't really dangerous. And if the worst came to the worst, they had got a straight jacket, which of course the major didn't know about.

I didn't tell Dad or Mother what I had heard. I thought it would have made Mother sadder than ever if she had known that the real reason why the vicar had moved was that the major might kill him, his own father. I think that she was more sorry for the vicar than for the major himself, and she actually cried when Dad told her how brave he was being, and not showing anyone how unhappy he must be feeling. He said that although he looked more than usually pale when he was carrying out the church services, his voice never shook either when praying or preaching.

I felt very sorry for the vicar too. I did pray that the major would get well again, and that the vicar would be able to go back to the vicarage, especially as the King's Coronation was going to take place next year and there would be another procession and decorations, and tea for everyone, and sports in the vicar's field and of course a bonfire. This had happened at the Queen's Jubilee, before we had come to Bramblewick, and at the tea party every boy and girl (including Wesleyans) had been given a mug by the vicar with the Queen's picture on it. It was expected he would do the same for the Coronation, only the mugs would have pictures of the King and his wife, Queen Alexandra.

If the major wasn't all right by then it wasn't likely that the vicar would want to give a tea party, and certainly not so close to the vicarage.

I was glad anyway that the two men who were looking after the major were so big and strong, and that one of them had been a policeman. The other one, Mr. Perkins, had been a sergeant-major in the army, and had won a medal for bravery. I was glad too that the major's charger had gone lame, and also that they were keeping all weapons from him. I wondered if they carried weapons themselves just to be ready.

Ikey said that his uncle had told him that a straight jacket was a thing they put on a man when he got really violent, that made him so that he couldn't move at all, and was better really than handcuffs or leg irons, which they used for convicts in the old days. It was made of strong canvas so that it didn't hurt the man himself, no matter how he struggled.

I'd try not to think about the major at night when I was in bed, after I had said my prayers, and Mother had kissed me good night and gone downstairs, leaving me just a night light floating in the wash bowl. I could hear her and Dad talking together, and although I couldn't hear what they said, especially if the tide was high and the waves thumping against the cliff that did help to stop me from feeling frightened.

But the best thing was having Gyp in the room with me, and if I couldn't get to sleep I'd just say very softly, " Gyp, Gyp " and he'd jump on to the bed and snuggle up almost on top of me. As soon as I began to feel really sleepy I would tell him to go back to his own bed.

One night I had a terrible dream. I was in church. The vicar was in the pulpit, preaching. Then walking down the aisle I saw the major, with the two keepers walking one on each side of him, carrying torches in their hands, with the flames from them reaching up to the church ceiling just like the flames coming out of the gas-works retort when Mr. Birch shovelled in the coal.

The major had a black mask on his face, like the vicar's respirator, only it was higher up, and there were two slots for his eyes so that he could see. Over his shoulder he was carrying a huge axe, the one I had seen in a history book, used for the execution of Charles the First.

The three men walked right up to the altar table. Then they stopped and turned round facing the congregation and the keepers set down their torches on each side of the cross. Then leaving the major they went to the pulpit, got hold of the vicar and marched him down to the altar. The vicar didn't struggle. He knelt down before the altar, and put his head on the table. The major lowered his axe, felt the blade with his fingers to make sure that it was sharp and then he raised it and struck and cut the vicar's head off with one blow.

I must have shouted out in my dream and frightened Gyp, for he was on my bed, barking, when I woke up, and the next moment Dad and Mother came upstairs, asking me what was the matter with him. Dad said it sounded as though he was having a fit, and attacking me. Really he should have a kennel out in the yard. I dare not tell them that I had been dreaming that the major had chopped off his father's head. I stuck up for Gyp though and said I'd had a nasty dream and must have shouted and that was why he had barked. He had stopped barking and was back on his own bed.

Mother tucked me in again, and petted me a bit, and they both went downstairs again. But as soon as they'd gone I whispered to Gyp to come back on to my bed, for, although I knew it had been a dream, I was still feeling frightened, and wished that it was daylight.

23

THE EASTER holidays had come. The weather was fine and warm. The tides were spring and the sea was calm. It was too early in the year for crabs and lobsters to be caught down the scars, and the water was still too cold to wade for flatfish, although I had seen Neddy Peacock having a try for crabs, and even wading in his old clothes and boots. He hadn't caught any.

The days were getting longer. It wasn't dark until seven o'clock, and Mother didn't mind my being out till then, only she liked to know where I was, and she still forbade me to go along the beach towards Low Batts farther than the Gunny Hole or beyond Stoupe Beck in the other direction. It was all right if I went into the country, but never as far as the moors by myself. I had been to the edge of the moors with Dad to look for painting subjects and once nearly to the top of High Batts, but it had started to rain and we'd had to turn back. I had never seen what the country was like beyond High Batts and the High Moor.

I had heard that there had once been a Roman fort at High Batts top, and that on the moors there were the burial places of Early Britons, and that you could find flint implements, arrow and spear heads, near these places. There was also a quarry with sandstone cliffs where jackdaws built their nests and a cave where there were bats. Of course Ikey had been there, or boasted that he had, and had climbed the quarry cliff and found a kestrel's nest as well as a jackdaw's, and on the moor he had even found a curlew's nest, only the eggs had been deep-set so that he couldn't blow them.

Ikey couldn't go birds' nesting now. He had left school and

started as apprentice at the post office shop. The shop opened at eight o'clock in the morning and didn't close till eight at night. When he wasn't serving behind the counter he had to carry out groceries, and do this sometimes after closing time. He wore long trousers and a collar and tie, and he never looked happy.

A few visitors had arrived for the holidays. Dad was busy painting subjects in the village, in the hope that some of the visitors might see him and admire what he was doing and want to see more of his work and go to the shop and perhaps buy a picture. Mother had to look after the shop.

One day, I decided I would have a walk to High Batts top and see all the things that Ikey had boasted about. We'd had dinner. I told Mother that I was just going to the woods to look for birds' nests, and also to try and get her some daffodils. She said that she'd certainly like some daffodils, and would have come with me if it hadn't been for the shop, for it was such a lovely day. She gave me an apple and some bread and cheese to take with me, and some crusts for Gyp, and I set off along the beach, for the tide was only half-way up.

She wasn't afraid about the major now, and I wasn't either, in spite of my awful dream. Although I hadn't seen this for myself, I had heard that barbed wire had been fixed all along the top of the garden wall, and iron bars across most of the windows. The big iron gate to the carriage drive was locked. So was the back door. No tradesmen called. Either Mr. Macdougal or Mr. Perkins did the shopping, and even got the milk and their letters.

The only person who did call was Doctor Whittle. Although he was only a small man he didn't seem a bit afraid. According to what Mr. Macdougal had said in the pubs, the major liked him and would talk to him in just an ordinary way. But the doctor had to be careful not to say anything about the vicar. That was like a red rag to a bull.

One of the things the major had done when he'd had one of his brain storms was to start pulling up the rose bushes in the garden, just using his bare hands. That must have been just to spite his father. Another thing he had done, but not in a rage, was digging a hole in the garden. He thought he was in Kimberley, and that he was looking for diamonds. He had found an old spade to do this, and Mr. Macdougal and Mr. Perkins hadn't interfered with him. They'd even pretended to help, so as to keep him in a good mood. They'd hidden the spade later on though, just to be on the safe side and he'd had to go on digging the hole with his hands.

It was a lovely day. There were a few visitors on the beach, and some children were playing by the pools with toy boats and shrimping nets and one little girl was in her bare feet but not actually paddling. Gyp was delighted to be going for a real walk. He kept on running ahead, then stopping, to see if I was following, then running back past me, turning and going on ahead again.

With the sea so calm I didn't bother to look for any treasures on the shore. I walked as fast as I could go without running, for I had a long way to go, and I wanted to have plenty of time when I reached the moors and High Batts top to see things, and find things that I'd never seen or found before. Really I was going exploring.

I got to Stoupe Beck Cove and was tempted to stop there a bit ; for just where the beck got to the beach there was a long pool, in which some little trout were jumping for flies. How I wished that I had brought a hook and line.

But I went on, up the steep lane on the other side of the beck where the major must have gone after he had galloped along the beach. There were level fields and a farmhouse at the top. There were sheep, with lambs, in one of these fields. I put Gyp on his lead in case he was tempted to run after the lambs, and we sat on a wall watching them jumping up in the air, and playing " follow my leader," and then rushing to their mothers to get milk, and I thought what a pity it was that lambs had to grow up into sheep, for the sheep didn't seem in any way happy. They just went on munching at the grass, and looked so stupid.

I went on, past the farm. I was now about a mile away from the nearest edge of the moor. There was heather on the top, but between the heather and the first fields there was rough ground, with bare sandstone rock, and clumps of whins, some of them yellow with blossom. The railway from High Batts ran along this rough part, with cuttings and embankments.

The lane began to climb. The sun was so hot I had to take off my jacket. But I wasn't feeling tired yet, although it did look a long way to the moor and longer still to High Batts top. I got to the whins, and then to the bridge over the railway line. I did have a rest then, and ate my apple and gave Gyp a crust. I had kept him on the lead because of being near the railway line, although there wouldn't be another train until five o'clock.

There was a wonderful view. I could see all the south part of the bay, with the red roofs of the village and the bank and the new houses at the bank top and the church and the vicarage itself, only they were all too far away for me to see people. The tide was now almost up. The sea was smooth, although there was a bit of wind ruffling it, so that it wasn't like it was on a really hot summer's day. There was a coble near Low Batts, and a sailing ship and steamers, far out. I looked at the vicarage and I thought that if I'd had the coastguard's telescope I might have been able to see the garden, and perhaps the major himself digging for diamonds, with one of his keepers watching him.

Suddenly Gyp barked and his mane bristled. I heard the clumping of a horse's hooves, coming down the lane from above the bridge. I ran back, and got over the fence into the whins, Gyp following me, and I crouched down, really frightened, for I thought that it might be the major himself in spite of what I had heard about his horse being kept away from him. But as the sound of hooves drew nearer, I peeped through the whins, and saw it was only a farmer on a cart-horse. When he had passed, I went back to the lane and this time crossed the bridge and went on up the lane.

Very soon it joined another lane which went left towards High Batts, and right along Stoupe Brow, following the railway.

Just opposite to me was a steep rough path which led up to the moor. There were no more whins here, only heather, growing very thick, but without flowers, as it would be in summer. I started up this path.

I took Gyp off his lead as we were now well away from the

railway line. He scampered up the path ahead of me, just like he had done on the beach, but not going very far before he stopped and ran back, and it was just as though he was doing this to make certain there was no danger for me on the way. I was very glad to have him with me, for I had never been so far from home by myself, and I might have felt frightened without him and even turned back.

The path got steeper, yet it was not so steep as a real cliff and at last it became almost level. I had got nearly to the top of the moor. I was disappointed. I'd thought that when I'd got as far as this I would only have to walk a short distance to be able to look on the other side of the moor, and see all the country to the south. Instead of that the moor reached for a very long way in that direction, still rising gently. I wouldn't be able to see beyond until I had reached the highest point, and the path didn't go that way.

Yet I had reached the moor. I had done something I had never done before, even with Dad. There was heather everywhere, and it wasn't so thick that I couldn't walk through it, although Gyp had to jump, just like a kangaroo. I aimed for what I thought was the highest point.

There was plenty to see. I hadn't gone very far before a grouse flew out of the heather just ahead of us. Gyp barked and tried to jump after it. I looked at the place it had flown up from, hoping I might find a nest. All I found were some droppings. A peewit was circling overhead, making its queer call, and I heard a curlew calling far off. A lark was singing too, in the air.

I hadn't gone very far before I came to a bog, with sedges growing round it instead of heather, and between the sedges was moss and a plant with little red leaves covered with hairs which I knew was a fly-catching plant. There was sticky stuff on the leaves which attracted the flies and when one alighted on a leaf it would stick on the hairs and the leaf would curl round it like the tentacles of a sea anemone. The water in the bog was the colour of strong tea. It swarmed with tadpoles. I saw a lovely green dragonfly hovering over its surface.

I found a way round the bog. A little farther on where the

ground was quite dry, were three curious mounds, two close together, one some distance away. They were circular in shape and about six feet high at their middles, and each was about twenty feet across. They were nearly covered with short heather and here and there the sides were bare, showing that they had been built of heaped stones and soil. I was certain that they were the burial places of Early Britons, that inside of each of them would be the bones of a man, and perhaps weapons and jewellery. I wished I had brought a spade with me so that I could dig into one of them.

I hunted the ground round them hoping to find some sort of treasure. I wasn't lucky. I started off again for the highest point. Several more grouse flew up. Gyp got very excited about them. And he got more excited still when a hare jumped up out of the heather just in front of him. He chased it for quite a long way but it ran twice as fast as he did, and he came back when I called him, looking very disappointed.

Before long I got out of the thick heather. It looked as though someone had burnt it, for the ground was black, with newish shoots of heather growing from it, so that it was like walking on a carpet. In patches even this had been taken off, and I saw why when I came to some little stacks of what I knew were turf, used for burning in the fireplaces of the farms near to the moor. The smoke from these had a lovely smell, and I put some pieces of it in my pocket to take home as a present to Mother. She wouldn't know exactly where I had got it from.

I wasn't far off the highest point now. I was out of sight of the bay and the village, even of the sea. To right and left, and behind was nothing but moor, ahead some more stacks of turf, and I guessed that when I reached them I would be able to look down on the other side. I actually ran the last few yards, with Gyp again going ahead, as though he wanted to be the first to get there.

I was right. When I got to the first stack there was a wonderful view before me. I saw the sea again, not Bramblewick Bay, but the sea beyond High Batts, and the coast reaching for miles and miles to the south. Although the moor stretched away as far as I

could see inland, it ended not far ahead in fields and woods like
those at home, and there were farms and cottages, even a village
a long way off.   And about a mile away, there was a big house,
much bigger than the vicarage, with trees and a garden and farm
buildings near it.   I guessed that this was the very house where
Colonel Watson lived, Gyp's old home.

I sat down on a heap of turf that came from a stack that must
have been blown down by the wind. Gyp who was panting with all
the running he had done squatted down beside me. I took out my
sandwiches, and offered him his share, which he seemed very
glad to take. I patted him and while I ate I went on looking at
the view, feeling very pleased and proud that I had done what I had
set out to do. I wondered if Ikey had ever walked as far as this
by himself.

Actually I had come farther than High Batts top. I could
see the railway station there when I looked to the left. You
couldn't see this from Bramblewick. It was at the other end of
the railway tunnel.

I thought that when I'd had a bit of a rest, I'd walk that
way, see if I could find the Roman fort, and then the quarry,
which I believed was between the moor edge and the railway line
on the Bramblewick side, and would be on my way home. I
didn't know what the time was but as the sun was still hot it
couldn't be very late.

I was eating the last of my sandwiches. I broke off a bit for
Gyp. He was standing away from me though, and he was looking
down the moor towards the big house, in a rather funny way.
He was trembling, and jerking his tail from side to side. I called
him. He didn't take the slightest notice. And then suddenly he
bounded off straight down the sloping moor towards the first
field, just as he had done after the hare.

I got up and shouted at him, " Gyp—Gyp " as loud as I
could. He didn't turn round. He just went on running, and I
started after him.

I was terrified. Never once, since I had first found him, had
he disobeyed my order. He had stopped chasing the hare, as
soon as he had heard my voice. Had he known that the house was

his home ? Had he heard the voice, or scented the little girl who had once been his master ? Was he sick of being with me, and wanted to go back to her ?

I went on shouting as I ran although I was soon nearly out of breath. I saw him reach the first field, which had a stone wall. He just jumped the wall, and then tore down the next field where there was a clump of trees. He was out of sight when I got to the wall myself.

I knew it was no use shouting now. He was too far ahead for him to have heard me. I climbed the wall, and went on running until I came to the trees and found a barbed wire fence, which he must have got through easily because he was so small. I just couldn't do it without tearing my clothes, and I had to run along it until I came to a gate.

The next field was almost level. There were some more trees at the far end of it, and still another barbed wire fence. And in the next field were some cows, and what looked like a bull, for it had a ring in its nose. They were running about as though Gyp had frightened them. I was certain that if I had got into that field the bull would have chased me.

I was nearly crying now. I could never catch up to Gyp no matter how fast I ran. I tried shouting again. It was no good. Then I had an idea. One of the trees was an ash, with low branches. It had no real leaves on it. I climbed up it, and before I was half-way up I saw that next to the field I was in, on my right, was a lane, and that not very far away was the big house.

I climbed down, ran along the fence of the lane, looking for a place I could get through. There were thick thorn bushes as well as barbed wire, with young nettles growing between the thorns. I had to go back a long way before I found a small gap. I got through it all right, but my jacket was torn and my hands and knees were scratched and nettled.

I started off down the lane. I heard the bull bellowing as I passed the field it was in. Soon I saw a barn ahead of me, on the right-hand side, and when I got to it, there was the back part of the big house, with more farm buildings and a stack yard with a wall round it, but a big archway into the yard with double doors, one of them wide open. And then I heard from inside a voice speaking very angrily :

" Why didn't you keep her locked up ? You knew she was that way."

" I had her fastened up, sir, I had her in the loose box. The stable lad must have let her out, not knowing she was there. It wasn't my fault, sir."

The second voice was rough, like a farmer's. I was sure that the first voice was Colonel Watson's.

" Whoever's fault it is a damned nuisance. I'd have had her mated to-morrow to a champion, and her pups would have been worth ten pounds a piece. And to think it happened with a mongrel. How did the damn thing get here. I've half a mind to shoot it."

I couldn't make out what had happened, but I knew they must be talking about Gyp, and when I heard the word " shoot " I was just terrified. I went through the archway into the yard, and there was Colonel Watson holding a small dog which I knew was a spaniel, on a lead, and a man in farmer's clothes, holding Gyp, with a piece of string tied to his collar. Gyp was cowering, but as soon as he saw me he barked, and tried to run to me.

The colonel looked at me in surprise, and I thought with anger too.

" Well I'm damned. Aren't you the Bramblewick boy who found my dog when it strayed a few months ago ? "

" Yes, sir," I said. " But please don't shoot him. I'm sure he didn't mean to do any wrong. He's a good dog. He never runs after sheep or hens or anything like that. He never bites anyone. Please don't shoot him."

The colonel didn't look quite so angry, but his voice was very stern :

" How did you get here ? " he said.

" I was having a walk on the moor, and I wanted to see this side of the highest point. I was just sitting having a rest, when Gyp, I mean Brownie, suddenly dashed off, and he wouldn't stop when I called him as he usually does, for he's very obedient. I ran after him as fast as I could, and I thought that this was the place where you lived, and that he wanted to come and see you and your daughter, because this was once his home. I don't know what he's done wrong, but I hope you won't punish him for it. I'm sure he didn't mean to do wrong."

I was nearly crying again, for Gyp was still trying to get to me. But Colonel Watson stopped looking angry. He actually smiled.

" You don't know much about dogs my boy, and you're too young to understand if I told you. I'm not going to harm Brownie. He was only obeying the call of nature. But you keep him on his lead in future, especially this time of the year when there are lambs about." He turned to the man. " Here," he said. " You take the spaniel and lock her up, and let the boy have the mongrel," and to me he said, " Come on now, put him on your lead."

I fixed the lead on Gyp. He licked my hand, and I was certain that he was feeling sorry for disobeying me, and causing such a lot of trouble, although I still didn't know what he had done wrong.

Then the colonel said :

" You're a long way from home. How do you think you're going to get back. You look a bit tired too."

" I'm going to walk back, sir."

The colonel pulled out his watch, and looked at it, and I saw the same little gold case he had taken the sovereign from when he'd come to take Gyp away.

" You're not going to walk all that way back," he said. " Come into the kitchen now, and have a wash, and I'll get the cook to give you something to eat and drink. When you've done that I'll take you to High Batts station and put you on the train. I've got to go there to meet Mrs. Watson and my little girl. But you hold on to that dog. He looks as though he'd like a drink of water and a biscuit to eat. Have you ever been in a motor car ? "

" No, sir," I said. " I've never seen a motor car. I have seen a picture of one though."

He laughed again. I followed him into a big kitchen. There

was a nice, kind looking woman in it. The colonel just told her to let me wash and then to give me some tea as quick as she could, for there was only twenty minutes before he must leave to catch the train. There was a drinking bowl on the floor by the sink, and while I washed, Gyp drank, and the colonel himself gave him a biscuit, and then walked out. The woman gave me tea and a slice of ham, and put some cakes down on the table in front of me. I was very hungry and thirsty, and I had finished the ham and got to the cakes, when the colonel came in again, and told me to put the cakes in my pocket, as he was ready to start.

I followed him round to the front of the house where there was a drive like the one at the vicarage. And there at the front door was a motor car. It was true that I never had seen one before and certainly none of the other lads at Bramblewick had. Its engine was going, and clouds of smoke were coming from a pipe at the back end. It had four seats, two in front and two behind, and it had a canvas top.

The colonel climbed into one of the front seats, where there was the steering wheel, and told me to get into the one next to him. Gyp was very frightened, so I took him in my arms, and the next moment with the engine making an even louder noise we started off down the drive and out into the lane.

I *was* frightened. The lane was very rough, and we kept bouncing from side to side. I had heard too that motor-car engines sometimes exploded. Yet I was excited. We were moving faster than any horse, as fast even as a train. I really had something to boast about now to the other lads, although I supposed that none of them would believe that I had not only seen a motor car, but had a ride in one.

And the colonel didn't seem angry about Gyp any more. He asked me questions, about where I went to school, and what games I liked best, and what I wanted to be when I grew up. He said that he hadn't been in the district long, and he had been too busy with his estate to see much of Bramblewick, and now that he had got this motor car, he would take his wife and little girl there, as it seemed to be a very interesting place. He didn't know the vicar, as he lived in a different parish. He had heard about him and his son, and it was very sad that the son was so ill, and needing keepers to look after him.

It wasn't easy to talk, with the engine making such a noise and the motor car bouncing up and down, but I told the colonel about Dad, and his portrait of Baden-Powell, and the one he had done of the major, for I thought that this might lead to him wanting Dad to paint a portrait of himself, or of his wife and little girl, and be very good for business.

He didn't say anything to that though, for now we were getting near the railway station, which wasn't such a big station as the one at Bramblewick, although it had two platforms. We stopped outside the WAY IN. When he turned off the motor-car engine, I heard the sound of the train puffing up the hill from the south, and I gripped Gyp very tightly.

The colonel went to the ticket window, bought my ticket and gave it to me.

The sound of the train was getting louder, but we couldn't see it yet. It was to come in at the other platform, and I was very glad when we had crossed the line. Then the colonel said :

" You must leave me now. You go to the far end of the platform and mind you get into a third class compartment near the engine. I don't want my little girl to see Brownie, or there may be trouble. Keep him under your jacket when the train comes in. Good-bye. And here's something to buy sweets with."

He took my hand and put a shilling in it, and I did try to tell him I didn't want it, he had been so kind. But he wouldn't take it back, so I just said, " Thank you very much, sir," and I hurried along the platform, just as the train came in.

The station master and a porter were waiting. It was the porter who opened a door for me, and shut it again when I got in, with Gyp hidden under my jacket.

It was not until the train started that I dared to peep out of the open window. I saw the colonel, standing with a lady, in very nice clothes, and a girl who was younger than I was, also in nice clothes, and with long plaited hair. I guessed that like the vicar and the major they had got out of a first class compartment. I couldn't see the little girl's face properly, but I did see that she

o

was wearing spectacles and wasn't pretty, and although I thought that the colonel was just about the nicest and kindest man I had ever met, I thought that she looked very stuck up.

I was more certain than ever that Gyp had run away first because he hadn't liked her. I still couldn't make out what Gyp had done to make the colonel so angry. It must have been something to do with the spaniel. Anyway he hadn't run away from me because he wanted to go back to the girl. If he had been he would have scented her now, and wanted to jump out of the window on to the platform. Instead of that he was trying to lick my face and showing in every way he could that he was happy.

24

I DIDN'T tell Mother and Dad the exact truth when I got home,
that I had actually been on the moor top when Gyp had run away
from me. I made it sound as though I had just been on the beach
when this had happened, and that I had gone up to the moor
because Gyp had run that way, and that I had guessed he'd been
aiming for where the colonel lived.

I told the truth about everything else, although Dad kept
interrupting me, and asking me questions, as though he just
couldn't believe it, especially when I came to the ride in the motor
car. He had never seen a motor car of course, and he made me
describe it, as though he was trying to trip me up and prove I
was inventing it. He didn't ask any questions about the spaniel,
although I told them what I had overheard the colonel saying to
the man, and that the colonel had told me I was too young to
understand what had happened and that Gyp had only been
obeying the call of nature.

I told them how the colonel had asked me questions while we
were riding on the motor car to the station, and that I had told
him about the portraits of Baden-Powell and the major.

" What did he say to that ? " Dad asked.

" He didn't say anything, because we'd nearly got to the
station then, but he did say before that he would be coming to
Bramblewick in his motor car with his wife and little girl one day."

" Did you tell him that the portrait of Baden-Powell was still
in the shop window ? "

" No. I didn't think of that. The motor car was bumping
about, and I was a bit frightened really."

" I'm very glad I didn't see you," Mother said. " You must never *never* go so far from home again, and do anything so dangerous as riding in a motor car. You might easily have been killed."

" I don't suppose there was any real danger of that," Dad said. " But the boy certainly must never go off on his own like this again. Really I should go and thank the colonel for being so kind to him. He must be very wealthy indeed to own a motor car."

For days after this Dad went on asking me questions about the colonel, and his wife and the little girl, and although he didn't say so, I knew that he was hoping that the colonel would prove to be a customer. He didn't go to thank the colonel. But he did set out one day for the high moor on a sketching trip, and I was sure he was hoping that the colonel would see him painting, and perhaps invite him to go to the house and have a ride in the motor car. A thick fog had come on before Dad got as far as the moor edge so he had turned back without making even one sketch.

The Easter holidays were soon over. All the visitors had gone, and Mother hadn't done much business in the shop, and we were still very poor.

There wasn't so much talking about the major now. Everyone seemed to have got used to the idea of his being shut up in the vicarage and the garden with the two keepers to look after him and see that he didn't escape.

Doctor Whittle was still going to see him every day, and the specialist had come again. The vicar never said anything about the major to Dad. But Mr. Conyers told Dad after the specialist had been that unless a miracle happened the major would never recover. He was almost healthy in his body. He had got over the lameness in his leg, and could now walk without a stick. It was his brain that was diseased. He might go on living until he was an old man. But at any time he might have a stroke and drop dead. The only way to prevent him becoming violent was a soothing medicine, and for his keepers to humour him. He must never see his father. The vicar had to pay the specialist fifty guineas every time he came, yet he was going to come in another month.

It made Mother terribly sad to hear all this. If only a miracle could happen she said, like the one in the Bible where Jesus had cast out the evil spirits that possessed the men who were living among the tombs and made them enter the swine. It must be an evil spirit to make a man hate his own father, as the major did the vicar.

Mr. Conyers had said that it was a good thing that the major seemed to get on quite well with the keepers. One of the rooms in the vicarage which hadn't been shut up was the old nursery, where the vicar's two sons had played as children. As it was on the second floor iron bars had been fixed across its window for safety in case they might fall out, and the bars were still there.

The vicar had kept many of their toys. Among them was a big box of lead soldiers, all painted in exact imitation of British regiments, cavalry, and artillery and infantry. There were model forts and cannons. On wet days, the major would play with these toys, with one of the keepers taking part in the game, and they would pretend they were having a battle. What he liked best though was digging in the garden for diamonds, and the keepers had thought it was safe enough to let him have the old spade.

There didn't seem to be any danger now of the major escaping or doing harm to anyone, yet few people would walk along Church Lane unless they had to, especially after dark, and I wouldn't have dreamt of going near the vicarage even in broad daylight. Dad always walked round by the station on his way to the church and back and the vicar himself went the same way, not because he was afraid, but because he didn't want to run any risk of upsetting his son.

There was a garden at the house where he was now living. It wasn't as big as the vicarage garden. As the house had been empty for two or three years, the garden had been overgrown with weeds. Tom Binns had cleared the weeds and dug the soil, and planted it with flowers. The keepers had brought him the prize rose bushes which the major had uprooted, and these had been replanted with the vicar telling him exactly where to put them.

The vicar went out on his horse every day, visiting the sick people in the village or country, and taking presents of food to those who were very poor, or giving them money, and at church he took the services and preached just as he always had done, and although he never seemed to smile, he never said anything to show how worried and sad he must be feeling in his heart. Mother said that she had never heard of anyone being so brave.

*   *   *   *

As the Coronation wasn't to take place for another year, the next thing to look forward to was the Whitsuntide holidays and Bramblewick Fair, which was held in the dock, and on the beach, when the tide was down. There would be swings and a round-about, and coconut shies, and stalls selling sweets and toys, and a gypsy fortune teller. There would be sports for the children, and a greasy pole with a leg of mutton for a prize, and horse racing along the beach, and in the evening a singing com-petition in the dock. The pubs were always very busy at Bramble-wick Fair, and as all the farmers came down for the horse racing, and the clogger boys too, there was usually some quarrelling and fighting.

It was just before Whitsuntide that a very exciting thing happened.

This was the time that the fishermen started getting ready for salmon fishing. They would start cleaning and painting their small cobles which were laid up the cliff all winter.

The boat Neddy Peacock used for salmon fishing wasn't a coble, but a ship's boat he had bought cheaply many years ago. The fishermen used bright colours for their cobles, each plank a different tint, and each coble had a name.

Neddy had no name for his. It just had his salmon licence number and letters painted on it, and it was tarred inside and out as tar was so cheap.

It needed two men for salmon fishing, one to shoot and haul the nets, while the other pulled the oars. Neddy always had a job to find someone to go with him, because he wouldn't pay a fair share of the money he would get for the catch. Usually it would be some sailor who was out of a berth and had spent all he had earned from his last job on drink.

If the weather was fine enough the salmon cobles would be launched down and anchored in the landing before fishing began, to tighten up their planks. The weather was fine. There hadn't been any rough seas for a long time, and all the cobles, and Neddy's old boat were anchored.

As there hadn't been any rough seas no drift wood had been washed up, at least near the village. Neddy knew there was always plenty of this at High Batts point. It was too far for even him to fetch a big load of it on his back. What he did was to walk there whenever the tides were right early in the morning, collect it and lay it up above high-water mark. Then on a really calm day he would go and get it in his boat.

The sea had been calm that morning when I had gone to school. There hadn't been a breath of wind. But just as we got out of school at dinner-time, the lifeboat gun went off. I ran down the street, without stopping at our house, down to the dock. The lifeboat house doors were open. The crew were putting on their life-jackets. Some other fishermen were hauling their boats out of the way. I ran to the slipway top. There was a strong wind blowing from the sea. It wasn't so strong as it had been when the ship had been wrecked and the sea wasn't so very rough, but the waves were breaking on Cowling and the landing scars. All the cobles which had been anchored in the landing had been hauled up again.

I saw nothing else at first. There was no ship on the rocks, or making signals of distress. I wondered if it was just a practice lifeboat launch. And then I did notice, just beyond where the waves were breaking on Cowling Scar, a small black boat, with a man in it pulling at the oars, against the wind and the waves. It was Neddy Peacock. And it was no wonder I hadn't seen it at first for it was loaded with wood, and it was so low in the water that it was only when it was on top of a wave that you could see it at all.

The tide was flowing and nearly up to the bottom of the slipway. When I moved back to the dock, the lifeboat was already out of the house, moving to the slipway top. And holding on to one of the ropes I saw Ikey, wearing his collar and tie and his grocer's white apron, and looking very excited as all the other lads were. I got hold of the rope myself, and all round me I heard people saying things about Neddy, calling him a greedy old b——, and an old fool, and that it would serve him right if he was drowned, and things like that. Everyone seemed angry with him.

I didn't feel angry with him. I was thinking of the time he had saved me from drowning at Cowling scar, and I hoped he wasn't going to be drowned, even if he was the greediest and worst tempered man in Bramblewick. I hoped the lifeboat would save him and I was glad that in spite of what people were saying it was being launched quickly.

Already it had got to the slipway top. The launchers got hold of the ropes that were to steady it down. I got hold too, and so did the other lads too. Ikey was pulling so hard that he didn't notice Mr. Thompson, his new master, hurrying across the dock. He came up to Ikey, and shouted at him angrily :

" Eh—you ! Get back to your job. I don't pay you your wages for playing on like this ! "

Ikey looked angry too, angrier than I had ever seen him look in a fight, and not a bit afraid.

" I'm not playing on," he shouted without leaving go of the rope. " Lifeboat's got to be launched hasn't it ? Mind your own business. I'll do what I bloody well like ! "

I thought this was an awful thing for a boy even of Ikey's age to say to a grown-up, especially his own master, and while some of the men who were pulling at the rope laughed, one of them said :

" Cheeky young beggar. You'll get the sack for that ! "

Ikey just laughed.

" What if 1 do ? " he shouted back. " I don't want to be a grocer. I want to go to sea. Heave away, lads, or poor awd Neddy's going to be drowned."

Mr. Thompson must have heard what Ikey said, but he had

turned away, muttering to himself, and was walking back towards his shop. I was certain that Ikey *would* get the sack.

Soon the lifeboat had reached the slipway bottom. I ran back to the breakwater wall to get a better view. I could see Neddy again. He was still pulling hard, yet he didn't seem to have got any nearer to the landing mouth. It seemed as though it was taking him all his strength to keep the boat away from where the waves were breaking on Cowling Scar. A man who was near me said :

" He'll never make it, loaded as he is. Why doesn't he throw some of his wood overboard and lighten her ? "

Another man said :

" He'd have to leave go of his oars for that, and he'd drift to leeward and the scar ends. Besides Neddy doesn't want to loose his load. He's aiming on t'lifeboat towing him in, load an' all. But if they do, they'll want some brass out of him for salvage."

There was only a short distance between the slipway bottom and the edge of the tide. The carriage was dragged in, with the launchers nearly up to their waists, and again I saw Ikey with them just like a grown-up launcher, wading over the knees of his long trousers.

The crew climbed in. There was no sign of Doctor Whittle or the vicar. The boat was launched, and away she went, the crew pulling with all their might, and I felt that no matter how they hated Neddy it wasn't making any difference to them wanting to save him.

I knew there was not much danger for the crew. It wasn't a storm. The wind was strong and cold, but it wasn't a gale. I had seen the cobles come into the landing with the waves just as big as they were now. But there were always two and often three men in a coble, and they were never loaded as Neddy's boat was.

The water on the landing was almost calm. As the lifeboat got near to the outer marking posts it started to pitch with the waves. They weren't big enough to hide it when it rode over them, but they were hiding Neddy's boat every time it got between two of them, and they had white tops too where he was, although they were not breaking until they reached the end of the Cowling

Scar. He was still pulling, trying to keep head on to the waves, and not getting any nearer the landing mouth.

He must have known that the lifeboat was coming to his rescue. He must have seen it, for it was soon out of the landing mouth, and had turned towards him, moving even faster with the wind and waves. Yet it had still a long way to go.

And then the terrible thing happened. His boat had gone over one wave, which wasn't a very big one. The next was big, with a curving white top. Neddy must have seen it coming, and given an extra spurt with his oars, and that must have done it. One of the oars broke. The boat slewed round so that it was almost broadside on. The wave lifted it up, then rolled the boat right over. When the next wave came it was the right way up, but full of water, with only its gunwales showing and scattered round it were the pieces of driftwood which had been in it, but no sign of Neddy himself.

The crowd was silent. Everyone must have thought that Neddy had been drowned. I felt *awful*. It had happened almost in the very place where I had searched for the captain's money-box when I had been trapped by the flowing tide and Neddy had saved me. I imagined him now sinking down, and the tangles wrapping round him. I was glad when I heard one of the men who was near me say :

" He must have gone down. But a chap usually rises three times before he sinks for good, no matter how heavy he is. There's plenty of wood floating about for him to hang on to. Lifeboat's getting closer."

The lifeboat was getting closer. It was too far away for us to hear but it looked as though the coxswain was shouting at the crew, telling them to pull harder than ever. A man was standing in the bow with a boat hook in his hand. I could tell he was looking for Neddy, and that the lifeboat hadn't given up hope anyway.

I could still see Neddy's boat. It was now actually among the Cowling Scar breakers, every wave washing it nearer in. The lifeboat got up to it. The bowman actually touched it with his boat hook, as the lifeboat passed it, but he didn't hold on. The

next moment he was waving his hand to the coxswain, then pointing shorewards. The lifeboat turned, with the men still pulling,
and then suddenly the coxswain signed to them to stop, to back
their oars. And as the boat slowed, the bowman and two of the
crew, leaned over the side as though trying to lift something
out of the water. And when they stood up I knew that it was
Neddy himself, still hanging to a piece of driftwood.

I shouted "hooray" but no one else did. Everyone in the
crowd was silent again and I thought that quite a lot of people
were feeling a bit disappointed that he hadn't drowned. There
was no doubt that he was alive for as the lifeboat turned and
started pulling for the landing, I saw him standing up, near to the
coxswain coughing and spluttering but pointing to his boat as
though he was trying to persuade the coxswain to save the boat
too, before it washed on to the scars and dashed to pieces.

The lifeboat kept on towards the landing mouth. Everyone
rushed down the slipway to see it land, and I saw the vicar too,
who must have arrived too late to have seen what had happened.
He was talking to one of the old fishermen, asking him questions.
But Doctor Whittle hadn't come. He was probably out on his
rounds in the country.

He wasn't needed anyway. For as soon as the lifeboat grounded
Neddy jumped out. He'd lost both his jacket and his hat. His
face was whiter than I had ever seen it, even on a Sunday when
he was in his best clothes for chapel. He looked very cold too. But
he also looked angry. Perhaps he had thanked the coxswain and
the crew for saving him. He didn't say anything to them as he
started to wade ashore ; or to the launchers and lookers-on who
were waiting. He walked straight past the vicar. And instead
of going up the slipway to go to his home and change his clothes
and get warm, he turned and walked as fast as he could go along
the beach, where some of the driftwood that had been in his
boat was already washing up. He'd soon picked up a piece.

And that wasn't the only wood that was washing towards the
shore, with the wind and the waves and the flowing tide. Half-
way out to Cowling Scar, in the broken water, looking like a
black rock was one side of his boat, no use now for anything but

firewood. Even as firewood Neddy was going to make sure that no one else got it.

I was glad though that he had been rescued, and I felt sorry that the lifeboatmen hadn't saved his boat. I was sure they could have done if they'd wanted to. If there hadn't been so many people about, and most of them sneering and laughing at him, I would have gone and helped him. They would only have sneered at me. Besides it was nearly school-time, and I hadn't had any dinner, or seen Gyp, so I set off for home. There was nothing very interesting in watching the lifeboat being hauled up, only I did notice that Ikey was helping again instead of being at the shop.

25

IKEY GOT the sack of course. We heard that his mother cried and cried about it, and that his Uncle Jake had given him a beating. But they must have seen that it was no good trying to make him into a grocer when all he wanted to do was to go to sea like his father and brothers had done, and before Whitsuntide came he went off to Hull, to join a ship as cabin boy.

I was sorry in a way that Ikey had gone for although he had never been nice to me, and was always swanking, I really liked him, and he was very brave. I hoped he wouldn't be drowned or die of fever in a foreign place as his mother was afraid would happen, and that she would be left with no children at all.

Yet in another way I *was* glad. Last year and the year before Ikey had won the greasy pole prize at Bramblewick Fair. I was a good climber myself. I'd never tried the greasy pole, but this year I would have a go, and with Ikey out of the way I felt that I might win. The prize was always a leg of mutton, given by Henry Newton.

Although the fair didn't begin until Whit Monday the gypsies and other people who owned the swings and merry-go-round and coconut stalls always arrived on the Saturday. The gypsies were allowed to put their caravans on the drying ground behind the gas-works. They had piebald ponies for hauling these caravans and the drays which carried the frames and boats for the swings, and the wooden horses for the merry-go-round. They also had lots of donkeys, for children to ride on, a penny a time, when the fair began.

The gypsies had dark skins and hair and flashing eyes. All

the women had gold rings hanging from their ears, and even some
of the men had ear-rings too. The women wore bright clothes.
But the men looked shabby and dirty and they had bare feet.

I was a bit afraid of them. Gypsies were supposed to be
thieves and even murderers, and to kidnap children. I didn't
think they were as bad as that, but decided to keep Gyp on his lead
whenever I went out with him until the fair was over.

The weather was foggy when Whit Monday came, but the fog
was thick only on the moors. The sea was calm and the tides
were neap, so that even at high water you could walk along under
the coastguard's wall to the beach. I was out early. Already
there were crowds of people in the dock and on the shore. I
had left Gyp at home to be on the safe side. Mother had to look
after the shop, anyway, as there were visitors about. Dad was
painting a subject up the road, where he knew the visitors would
see him as they walked down to the dock and beach.

Mother hadn't been able to let me have any money to spend
on the fair as Dad hadn't made any since Easter. All I had was the
shilling the colonel had given me, which I had kept in my money-
box with some foreign coins I'd found on the beach at one time
or another. She'd had to use what had been left from the colonel's
sovereign after getting Gyp's licence to buy food, but she said
that she would pay this back to me one day, as it was really mine.

I clutched the shilling tightly in one hand and kept that
hand in my trousers pocket, and I thought that I would have a
good look round both the dock and the beach before I spent
anything. There were only stalls in the dock. The cobles had
been launched down again so there was plenty of room for them.
They were just like shops, without windows, and they were full of
exciting things which you'd never see in the Bramblewick shops.

There were all sorts of sweets, not in big bottles like they
were in the shops, but on trays, heaped up. There were big slabs
of toffee, some hard and the colour of treacle, some which were
soft and the colour of butter, and were called clagum by the
lads, because they stuck to your teeth when you chewed them.
There were toys, engines, and boats, tops and marbles, pistols,
swords and guns, and even sets of soldiers' uniforms, that a boy

could wear. There were things for girls too, like dolls and skipping ropes, and bracelets and toy wrist watches, which wouldn't go of course. There were balloons and flags, some with pictures of King Edward and Queen Alexandra on them, ready for Coronation Day, although it was such a long way off.

Some of the stalls had things for grown-ups, like dresses and hats and boots, and things for farmers like harness and leggings and whips. One sold ice cream, ginger beer and lemon pop. The one that excited me most had a big glass tank and small glass bowls with goldfish in them. The bowls were sixpence, with one goldfish, but if you had a jam jar, you could buy a goldfish for just a penny. I decided that whatever else I bought or spent my shilling on I would have one goldfish. Mother would like that too. But I would get it later when I'd been home for a jar.

I would have liked a ha'porth of clagum, and an ice cream cone, and a top, and several other things, but there would only be elevenpence left when I'd got the goldfish, and I went down to the beach with my shilling still in my hand.

The swings and merry-go-round and coconut shies had all been set up near the cliff foot clear of high-tide mark. There was just room for the donkeys to ride.

The gypsy fair men were all shouting or using rattles to attract customers. I noticed several Thorpe cloggers among the lads. I was careful to keep clear of them, for without Ikey to frighten them, they might easily start trouble. There were some visitor children too, boys and girls, and they seemed to have plenty of money to spend, for they were having donkey rides and going on the swings and merry-go-round.

I didn't think much about the merry-go-round. Really it was only for girls and small children. There were twelve hobby horses, painted various colours, and one of them had lost its head, and the reins were nailed to its neck. There was no machinery to make it go. The thick wood post that supported it was fixed to a four wheeled cart. When all the riders had mounted and paid their pennies, two of the gypsy men would start to push with their hands on the back of a " horse," walking at first, and then running, and although some of the little girls screamed and seemed quite frightened and looked as though they might be sick, it wasn't a bit dangerous, and the gypsy men never went round more than twenty times, for that would have been bad for trade.

The swings were more exciting and they *were* a bit dangerous. Each boat held two persons sitting at opposite ends, and each with a rope to pull at. Although they started off with a man giving a few pushes, you could make them go higher and higher by pulling at the ropes in turn. At one Bramblewick Fair a boy had actually fallen out, and had been struck on the head by the boat before he could get out of the way and had been killed. But he couldn't have fallen out if he hadn't left go of the rope. I decided I would have at least one go out of my shilling but not just yet.

I went up to one of the coconut shies. The man in charge of it was shouting :

" Roll up—roll up. Three shots a penny. Lovely coconuts full o' milk. Three shots a penny."

The coconuts were fixed on iron posts stuck into the beach, each with a cup like an egg cup at its end, half filled with sand. They were quite near to where the customers had to stand, and it looked as though it would be quite easy to knock one of them off, and of course every one you knocked off you kept. I watched a farmer boy, too grown-up to be a real clogger having a go. He paid his penny and the man gave him three wooden balls, a bit smaller than cricket balls. The boy took very careful aim, and threw with all his might each time, but he didn't hit one nut, and the man shouted at him :

" Have another go, and your mother won't know. Have another go."

The boy did have another go, and this time with his first shot although he didn't hit a nut he hit one of the iron posts and the nut fell off. I thought that the gypsy would say that this wasn't a fair do and that he wouldn't give the boy the coconut, but when he'd had his other two shots, he went and picked it up and handed it to him. And the next moment, before I had time to think, I was holding out my precious shilling to the man.

" Please I'd like a go ! "

He looked at my shilling, to see if it was a bad one or not, then he gave me my elevenpence change, and the first of my three balls. There was quite a crowd round the shy, and I felt myself blushing as I took aim at the nearest one, for I knew they were all watching me. I was certain that if it had just been a tin can I was throwing a stone at, I could have hit that nut. But I missed, and I heard some of the lads in the crowd (I guessed they were cloggers) laugh. I missed with the second ball too, and I missed with the third and like he had done with the farmer boy the man shouted :

" Have another go and your mother won't know," and he handed me another ball. " Next time lucky. Where's your penny?"

I gave him the penny. I aimed again and I missed. With the second ball I did hit a coconut, but not the one I had aimed at, and although it moved it didn't fall off. I missed with the third ball and I think I'd have cried if there hadn't been so many people watching.

The man offered me another ball, and said what he had said before, but someone else was waiting to have a go, and I moved away feeling that everyone was laughing at me. It would have been so lovely to take a coconut home to mother, for I knew she liked them. I had spent tuppence all for nothing, and now if I bought the goldfish I would have only ninepence left.

I didn't look at the other coconut shies. I walked along the beach, passing the donkeys which were being ridden backwards and forwards along a bit of sand that wasn't much bigger than a cricket pitch. I certainly wasn't going to waste any of my money on a donkey ride. I began to wish that the fair was over, that I was just starting along the beach on a treasure hunt, with no one else on it except Gyp. And then I noticed beyond where the donkeys turned some men digging into the sand and gravel.

I went up to them. They were digging a hole, and already it was quite deep. Close by was a long coble mast, and a tin of soft soap, which looked like thick brown treacle. There was a little flag tied to the thin end of the mast. I knew that it was to be the greasy pole. The men would smear it with the soft soap all the way up to the flag. Then they would fix it upright in the hole, like

P

a flag staff. The first person to climb up and touch the flag would get the leg of mutton.

There were posts on the drying ground that were just as tall as this one. I had swarmed up them dozens of times. I had never dared to do what Ikey had done, just for swank. He would get to the top of one, then turn upside down and come down head first. But next to Ikey I was certain that I was the best climber among the lads.

I began to feel excited and happy again. The sports for children wouldn't start until the afternoon, when the tide was down. The greasy pole came at the end of the sports. There were money prizes for all the children's events, just running, and egg-and-spoon and potato and wheel-barrow, and three-legged and sack races and high and long jump. With Ikey out of the way again I ought to win some money. The first prize for a race was always a shilling, the second sixpence and the third threepence. I had only to win one third prize to more than make up for what I had wasted on the coconut shy.

And if I won the greasy pole, and the leg of mutton, that would be worth more than coming first in every race that I was allowed to enter.

I thought I'd go back now, and have one go at the swings, then go up to the dock, buy just a ha'porth of clagum and a ha'porth of chocolate for Mother, an ice cream, or a bottle of pop, then go home and get a jam jar for the goldfish, and not spend any more of my money until after the sports, when I'd know how much I could afford.

*   *   *   *

I didn't tell Mother about the greasy pole, although it worried me when she made me put on my best breeches and jersey after dinner. She said that all the other children would be in their best clothes for fair day and she didn't want to be ashamed of me, especially as there were visitors about.

I felt sorry in a way that she couldn't come and watch the sports because of having to look after the shop. But I was sure she would have stopped me having a go at the pole, and anyway she was feeling a bit excited for she'd had two visitor ladies in looking at the pictures, and although they hadn't bought anything they had " nibbled " at one half-guinea water colour, and had promised to come back after they'd thought it over.

She'd been very pleased with the chocolates, and the goldfish. She promised to look after it and Gyp, while I was out. I daren't have Gyp with me at the sports, for if he'd seen me running he would have wanted to run too and besides I didn't trust the fair men.

Dad hadn't come in for his dinner. I supposed that he was still hoping to have someone admire what he was painting, so that he could send them on to the shop. I got back to the beach before the sports had started, and there was a bigger crowd than ever about the swings and coconut shies and merry-go-round.

I had told Mother I was going in for the races, and as the weather wasn't cold she had let me wear my summer sandshoes, and no stockings which made it much easier to run in than boots.

It wasn't long before Henry Newton walked along the beach, ringing a bell and shouting to everyone that the children's races were to begin, and most of the crowd began to follow him along to where the greasy pole now stood upright. The tide was nearly half-way down and beyond the pole there was a patch of hard sand where the races were to be held.

Henry was in his best clothes. I could tell by his red face and the way he shouted that he'd been having a few drinks. He had a piece of paper in his hand with the list of events on it, and also a real pistol, which fired blank cartridges.

Sports weren't very interesting, except for the events you took part in yourself. The first races were for girls starting at " under sevens." The mothers of the little girls who entered had a job to make them race at all. Some of them sulked or even screamed, and they were terrified when Henry fired the pistol, although it didn't make a very loud bang. Only two of them ran the whole way to the flag and back to Henry, yet one little girl who started off and then turned and ran to her mother was given a " booby " prize of a ha'penny.

The other girls' races weren't any more interesting. There was only ordinary running and skipping, and egg-and-spoon and sack, and as I didn't like any of the girls who took part I didn't care who won. And it was a long time before the boys' races started.

I'd noticed among the lads who were waiting to take part several Thorpe cloggers. Some about my age. They were wearing their clogs too, and although they looked strong and healthy, I thought I'd have no trouble in beating them at running, with my sandshoes on. Two of them were the young brothers of Joe Pickering, the boy Ikey had fought on Mafeking Day.

Yet when the boys' races began they took off their clogs and stockings and were in their bare feet. I think they must have been practising too. The first running race that I was in was won easily by one of the brothers, and I didn't even come in third, although I ran just as fast as I could. And it was the same with all the other races. The only thing I won was the booby prize in the sack race. The other lads *had* practised of course. I didn't know that in a sack race you had to pull the sack up to your waist, and jump with both feet at once. I tried to run and just fell over, and everyone in the crowd laughed which made me feel very angry.

I didn't do any better in the high jump or long jump either.

But between the races I kept on looking at the greasy pole. No one would laugh or mock at me if I won that. It would make up for everything if I did.

The men's races came next. They were the same as the children's, except that there were no prizes, and they ended with a tug-of-war between Bramblewick and Thorpe, which really meant the farmers.

Big Gow Pickering was in the Thorpe team, and Ikey's Uncle Jake and Mr. Tims were pulling for Bramblewick, and they nearly all seemed a bit drunk although there was no quarrelling, and it was quite funny, for just as both teams were pulling with all their might the rope broke and all of them fell on their backsides in a heap. Bramblewick won in the end.

And at last came the greasy pole.

I had already moved near to it, to make sure that I was going
to have a try. It was open to persons of all ages, but they had
to belong to Bramblewick or district, so that none of the fair-
men or any visitor was allowed to try.

You were allowed to have as many tries as you liked, but you
had to go in turn, and Henry Newton was the one to say in what
order the competitors should go. He wrote the names down on
his piece of paper.

There were never many competitors, in spite of the prize
being a leg of mutton. One reason was because the grease was
so messy, but the chief reason was that everyone made fun of
those who were trying. No one liked to be laughed at when they
were looking silly. I didn't myself, but I didn't mind that if I
could only win the prize.

There was a big crowd now, not only on the beach but on the
cliff which was quite close, and gave a better view. As soon as
Henry had written my name down, I looked round, a bit afraid
that Dad might be in the crowd and want to stop me because of
my having my best clothes on. And then I got a surprise, for on
the cliff among the other people was a lady and a little girl with
spectacles. It was the wife of Colonel Watson and his daughter.
The colonel wasn't with them though. They wouldn't know me.
They hadn't seen me that day at High Batts station, when I had
seen them. But I thought of Gyp, and how lucky I was that I
had left him at home.

Just then Henry rang his bell and shouted :

" Any more for the greasy pole. We've only got seven entries
for a leg o' mutton prize. Any ladies like to have a go ? "

The crowd laughed at this. No one else asked to have their
names put down, and then Henry shouted :

" Righto. Let's make a start. Come on, Jake. You go first.
And I'll give you a side of bacon as well as the leg o' mutton if
you touch that flag at the top."

I knew that Jake was only trying as a joke. He didn't mind
people laughing at him. Although he was so strong, he was very
fat and heavy. He was in his best clothes. He didn't seem to
mind that. He reached up his hands as high as he could on the

pole and then clasped his thick legs round it and tried to haul
himself up. Because of the soft soap his hands just wouldn't
hold, and when he left go, the stuff was sticking on him, and on
his clothes, and he even had some of it on his face, which he tried
to scrape off with his hands, but only made it worse. It was
just as funny as the flypapers in *Darky Town*.

And the next one to try was Mr. Tims himself. He wasn't
wearing his uniform, but white canvas trousers and a flannel
vest, which the coastguards always wore for doing dirty work.
I thought he was only doing it for fun too. He was not so fat as
Jake anyway, and because Jake had scraped a lot of the soap off the
pole, Mr. Tims did manage to get a little bit higher. He could
grip all right with his legs. It was through not being able to
hold with his hands that he had to give up, and I saw now what
the winner would have to do to get to the top.

Everyone who climbed would take off some of the soap, and
everyone who was a good climber was bound to get a little bit
higher than the one before him. I was glad that I hadn't to try
yet, but I had taken off my jersey to be ready. There were no
other lads on the list, only men, and the next one to try was a
fisherman whose nickname was Dud. He was the bowman of
the lifeboat.

He wasn't doing it for fun. He was a chapel man and never
went into the pubs. He was in rough clothes, and before he tried
he picked up a double handful of wet sand and rubbed it on the
inside of his trousers. He *was* a good climber. The sand helped
him to grip with his legs, and that let him reach his hands up
above where Jake and Mr. Tims had reached, and his feet then
were about a yard from the ground. He couldn't get any farther,
and all he had done when he gave up was to make it a bit easier
for the next man, a young sailor who also rubbed the inside of
his trouser legs with wet sand. But he didn't get much higher
than Dud, and the next two, who were also sailors, only beat
each other by inches.

I'd already got an idea that Henry Newton, because we had
always been such good friends, wanted me to win, and that was
why he had put me last on the list. He gave me a pat on the

shoulders when my turn came. I'd already rubbed sand on the inside of my shorts and bare legs.

There was a bit of laughing as I started. But there was also a bit of cheering and clapping when I climbed up quite easily to where the last sailor had had to let go, where most of the soap had been rubbed off. I clung on with my legs then and reached my hands up to where it was soaped, and although it was so slippery I managed to hold on long enough to let me get another grip with my legs. There was loud cheering then. But when I reached for another hand grip, I started to slip down, and I just couldn't stop myself.

It was Jake's turn again. The crowd roared with laughter when he took a drink from a bottle of beer, then handed the bottle to Mr. Tims. He didn't bother about rubbing sand on his hands or legs. He got hold again, but as soon as he tried to grip with his legs, he just slipped down and he was almost helpless with laughing himself.

When Mr. Tims got hold, Jake put his arms round him, and actually lifted him up against the pole. This wasn't fair of course, but it was only done as a joke. I knew that neither Jake nor Mr. Tims thought they could win for they were far too fat. The ones I was afraid of winning was Dud or the sailors. Dud had rubbed more sand on his hands. He wasn't laughing. He was just thinking of the leg of mutton.

This time he got higher than I had done. He was nearly half-way up to the top when he had to come down. The sailors got higher, but not one of them was as good a climber as Dud. And although I wasn't either, I was lighter than any of them, and I knew that if the others went on rubbing off the soap and getting higher every time I stood a good chance of winning.

The crowd cheered when I had my second try. I did a little better than the first time. I used my body as well as my legs to grip, but I just couldn't hold on hard enough with my hands to get a big pull up. I had to slither down.

Jake and Mr. Tims had now given it up. It was Dud's turn. I was sure that no one in the crowd wanted him to win. They only cheered when he slithered down, although he had got much higher than me and was actually not more than six feet from the flag.

One of the sailors had given up too. The others had their try, and were beaten, but they had got a little higher. It was Dud again and I thought that this time he was going to do it, for he had done a very clever thing. He had filled one of his pockets with sand, and while he hung on with his legs, he took out the sand, and slapped it on the pole above his head, on top of the soap, to give his hands a grip. He was a very strong man, with thick arms. But he was also very heavy. He gripped with his hands and heaved, and he did get another higher grip with his legs. He reached up his hands and they were only a few inches from the flag. One more heave and he would get it. But his legs began to slip. He just couldn't hang on, and down he came to the ground.

It was the sailor's turn next. If the first one didn't get it, the second one would. It looked as though I wouldn't get another chance. But a wonderful thing happened. I didn't know whether Henry had spoken to them or not, but both sailors said they'd had enough. Henry gave me a pat on the back.

" Up you go," he said. " And don't come down again until you've touched that flag."

I did what Dud had done. I filled one of my trouser pockets with wet sand, and plastered more sand on my legs, which were already a bit sore. I started to climb. Even where the soap had been rubbed off the pole was slippery, but the sand helped and up and up I went, with the crowd cheering. I didn't look at them of course. All I looked at was the little flag on the mast top. I got up to where Dud had made his highest leg grip, and his last reach for the flag. It was only about a foot away, but there was soap even by the flag itself, which was tied with a thin piece of string.

If only I could get a hand hold just below it! With one more heave then I was sure that I could grab it. Again I did what Dud had done, took some sand from my pocket, and slapped it on, as high as I could reach, but instead of trying to grip straight away I scraped the sand with the soap sticking to it off the pole, and then put some more sand on. And then I did take a good grip with both hands, let go with my legs, and gripped hard with them again. They were slipping, but I heaved again, reached up one hand and gripped the flag, pulled it loose. Then with everyone cheering like mad and clapping their hands, I let myself slip down to the ground. And Henry gave me the leg of mutton.

It was a good job Mother hadn't seen me then, for Jake, who she thought was one of the most horrible characters in Bramblewick, picked me up with the leg of mutton in my arms, and held me on his shoulders for everyone to see. I could smell the beer in his breath. But I didn't mind. When he set me down even Dud patted me. I felt excited and proud, but more than anything I was pleased I had won such a valuable prize. I knew that Mother would be pleased, seeing how poor we were. It would last for at least a week.

The sports were now over. Everyone was going back to the fair or home to their tea, and I hurried home, not tempted to spend any more money at present. I saw Mrs. Watson and the little girl by the merry-go-round, but I steered clear of them.

I was a little worried about what Mother would say when she saw my trousers and shirt, both thick with soft soap and sand. I held the leg of mutton in front of me when I walked up the stairs. She had heard me coming and was at the stairs top and so was Gyp, very pleased to see me. I could tell though before I got to the stair top that she was in a very happy mood.

She looked in surprise at the leg of mutton, and when I told her what had happened, she hugged me and kissed me, and said how clever I was, and that I mustn't worry about my dirty trousers and shirt for as it was soft soap that was on them, she would only need water to wash them, only I must change into my second best and also have a good wash before tea. She had made some special buns which she knew I would like.

Then she said it was one of the luckiest days we had ever had. The two ladies had come back and they had decided to take two pictures at half-a-guinea each, and as a guinea was a shilling more than a pound she would let me have that shilling to spend at the fair.

Then she asked me if I had seen Dad on the beach. I said I

hadn't. I was sure that if he had seen me climbing the greasy
pole and winning the prize, he would have come up to me. She
said that was rather strange, for he had come in, soon after I
had gone out, and had rushed off as soon as he'd had dinner,
saying he was going to put the finishing touches on the picture he'd
been painting up the road, then go and watch the sports. He
hadn't been home since, and he didn't know about the two pictures
being sold. It would be a nice surprise for him. And so would the
leg of mutton.

While I was changing I looked at the goldfish swimming about
in the jam jar and I thought that as Mother was going to give me
a shilling and I still had sevenpence left I would buy a proper glass
bowl for it, and another fish to keep it company.

We heard Dad coming in and wiping his boots on the mat
at the bottom of the stairs. Mother had put the leg of mutton
on a dish in the middle of the table, and she whispered jokingly :

" Don't tell him, until he sees it for himself. Let it come as
a real surprise."

He came in. He was smiling. He rushed straight to Mother
and gave her a kiss, then he picked me up and danced round the
room shouting " hooray—hooray." Gyp was dancing round too,
barking excitedly.

I thought that Dad had either seen me win the greasy pole
or that someone had told him, yet he hadn't as much as looked
at the leg of mutton itself. He gave Mother another kiss, and then
he said :

" Well, what do you think happened? I can still hardly
believe it myself. It's just like a dream."

Mother was looking very puzzled.

" What has happened ? " she said. " Why don't you tell us ! "

Dad sat down, in his chair, but he got up at once and paced
up and down the room, with Gyp barking at him, as though he
thought that Dad was playing a game with him. And then Dad
picked him up and patted him and said :

" I'll tell you. Only it still seems too good to be true. I was
just waiting for the paint to dry before packing up, when a
gentleman, with a lady and a little girl, came down the road. It

wasn't until they stopped that I realised that it was Colonel Watson and his wife and daughter."

"Well, they admired the painting very much, although the colonel didn't say anything about buying it. He did say though that he would like to see more of my work. I said I would be very pleased indeed to take them all to the studio, but as Mrs. Watson wanted to take the little girl to the fair and the sports, the colonel said he would come by himself and join them later. They had left their motor car on the bank top.

"What a nice man the colonel is! And I could tell as soon as he got inside the studio, that he knows quite a lot about painting himself. He's a very good critic. He didn't hesitate to tell me what he didn't like, or what he liked either. Among other things I showed him the unfinished painting of the wreck, and he said that the lifeboat was out of drawing, although the wreck itself and the sea and sky were very good indeed. But the thing that impressed him most was the portrait of Baden-Powell. He knows the general quite well for he had served with him in India and Afghanistan. They are really friends. Then he asked me if the portrait was for sale, and if so how much. I told him that I'd done it from a cigarette card, more for practice than anything else, but that it had led to my doing one of the vicar's son, and that the vicar had paid me ten pounds for that one. He said well I'll give you ten pounds for Baden-Powell and without hesitation he took out his wallet, and gave me this."

Dad took two pieces of crinkly paper from his pocket and held them out for Mother to see.

"Five pound notes!" Mother said. "How wonderful! And on top of everything else, for I sold two half-guinea sketches to-day, and look on the table. Who do you think won that?"

Dad looked at the leg of mutton.

"Do you mean to say he won the greasy pole! Bravo. I wish I'd been there to see him do that. You must tell me all about it. And you've actually sold two sketches. What a lucky day. But I still haven't told you everything. I said to the colonel that he would make a good subject for a portrait himself, especially in uniform. He laughed at that, but he said he might consider having one done of his little girl sitting on her pony, only I would have to go to his house to do it, for she couldn't ride such a long way. I would have to go to High Batts station, and he would drive me from there in his motor car. He would talk this over with his wife. She's quite a pretty little girl, in spite of her wearing spectacles. I wouldn't paint her with those of course. It's the thin end of the wedge, anyway. Come on, let's have tea, and then we'll shut up the shop and all go down to the fair. I'd like to have a go at the coconuts. We could have a ride on the merry-go-round. And most likely we'll see the colonel."

We started tea. I had never known Dad and Mother so excited and happy and jolly, although I couldn't help thinking that Dad was wrong about the colonel's daughter being pretty.

And then we heard a man's voice in the street outside, where some people were walking up from the dock. He was shouting:

"Has anyone seen Doctor Whittle? He's wanted urgent up at the vicarage. The major has battered Mr. Macdougal half to death. The major's escaped on his hoss. No one knows where he's got to."

26

Dad got up and rushed to go downstairs.

"I must find out what has happened," he said.

Mother looked very frightened. I felt frightened too.

"Please don't be long," she shouted after him. She opened the window, and we both looked out. We saw Mrs. Anderson just fastening her front door. Dad had got a little way down the street. He was talking to Henry Newton who must have been on his way up from the dock when the man who had shouted had hurried down. He and Dad now started towards the dock, which was almost hidden in fog that was swirling up from the sea.

There was no one else in the street. Mrs. Anderson had opened an upstairs window that was almost opposite to ours. She leaned out and spoke to Mother:

"Did you hear what the railway porter said? The major's killed one of his keepers and has escaped. You keep your downstairs door locked. He's a madman. He'll be bent on murdering someone else. I hope they catch him before it gets dark. It's coming on foggy too."

She shut the window again before Mother had time to tell her that the man hadn't said that the major had actually killed the keeper.

I could tell that Mother was trying to be brave. She asked me to get on with my tea, but she didn't have any more herself. I knew she was waiting for Dad's footsteps outside, and him opening the street door, which he had closed but not locked. I could tell that she was pleased that Gyp was in the room with us, for she kept on stroking him. She said to me:

"How clever of you to have won the greasy pole. What a

feast we are going to have. I wonder if it will keep until Sunday, or whether we ought to roast it to-morrow. And isn't it wonderful about Dad selling the portrait of Baden-Powell to Colonel Watson ? It is funny the way things happen. I don't suppose he would have spoken to Dad if he hadn't remembered coming here first with the policeman to see about Gyp, and that wouldn't have happened if you hadn't found Gyp. He is a nice doggie, isn't he. He *has* been missing you all day."

She stroked Gyp again, but Gyp gave a sudden bark as the street door opened again, and Mother jumped. But it was only Dad. He came in, but he didn't sit down. He was looking very worried.

" It's true about the major," he said. " It was Jack Gibson, the railway out-porter, we heard shouting. He'd been sent down by the station master to find Doctor Whittle, and to let the police sergeant know. Luckily the sergeant was in the dock, and some-one said they had seen Doctor Whittle in one of the pubs, and he would soon be found and be on his way to attend to Mr. Macdougal.

" It was Mr. Perkins who had told the station master, because he was the first man he had seen when he had found out what had happened. Mr. Perkins had been off-duty. He had gone to see the vicar to tell him how things were going on, and to take him some plants the major had pulled up. He had left Mr. Macdougal and the major in the garden, and the major then had seemed calm.

" As he came back he actually saw the major on his horse, bareback and without even a bridle galloping across a field on the Thorpe side of the vicarage. He rushed to the vicarage and found Mr. Macdougal lying unconscious in the garden, with blood on his face, and that's all the porter knew."

" How dreadful," Mother said. " But what about the vicar. Was the major riding towards the vicar's house ? "

" I don't suppose so. The major wouldn't know where it is. It looks as though he was just having a ride. He would have to get across the railway line to reach the vicar's house. Anyway he's got to be found. The fair is over until to-morrow. All the stall-holders are packing up. Every man in the place has got to help to look for him and it's not going to be easy with the fog having come down. I had a word with Mr. Beecham. Two of his men will be out on the cliffs on bad weather watch, but he will be joining the search himself with one other man, and I said that I would go with them. I saw Colonel Watson too. He told me that because of the fog, which will be very thick on the moor road, he would be hurrying home, but that he might come for the horse racing to-morrow. I think I'll take my walking stick with me in case we have to go over rough ground."

"I don't think there's any need for you to go at all," Mother said very anxiously. "Surely there are plenty of other men, with the coastguards and fishermen and the police sergeant."

I was thinking that too, for I was very frightened, and I thought that Dad was really frightened himself, especially as he had mentioned the walking stick, which he didn't usually take with him when he went for a walk.

"I've got to," he said. "I'm not going to let anyone in the place think I'm afraid, and anyway I'll be with the coastguards. Mr. Beecham will have his sword stick of course. I don't think you'd better leave the house though. The fair will be on to-morrow. It's a pity this has happened just when we were going out to celebrate but that can't be helped. I must hurry too. Mr. Beecham said he'd be ready in five minutes. He was getting some lanterns ready in case we have to go on searching after dark."

Dad found his stick. It was one he had made himself from a blackthorn, and it had a thick knobbly end. Mother again tried to persuade him not to go as he moved to the stairs, but he said it was no good, he had given his word to Mr. Beecham, and in any case it was his duty to help the vicar, who would be feeling this more than anyone. We followed him downstairs, and Mother gave him a hug as he opened the door and stepped into the street, and I nearly cried I was so frightened and anxious about him.

"Bolt the door," he said. "I'll knock three times when I come back so that you will know it's me."

The fog had got very thick. He was out of sight in it before he got half-way down to the dock. Mother shut the door, locked it and bolted it, then we went upstairs, and she shut the living-room door too although it hadn't a lock or bolt.

Because of the fog it was already becoming quite dark. She lit the lamp, and drew the window curtains.

" Are you sure you don't want any more tea ? "

I wasn't feeling a bit hungry and I said " No thank you." She wasn't either.

She said :

" Well, I think I'll wash up, then we'll sit by the fire and have a sing song. Then I'll have to think about getting supper ready. Dad is bound to be hungry when he gets back, and I hope that won't be long. I expect they'll find the poor major very soon and get him safely back to the vicarage. Poor man. Perhaps all he wanted to do was to have a ride on his horse. . . . Look at your goldfish. I think the jam jar is too small. I think we'd better put it in the washing-up bowl when I've washed up, and keep it there until to-morrow when you can get a proper glass bowl at the fair."

I helped her to wash up, then we put the goldfish in the bowl, Gyp watching me closely, but not making any attempt to catch the fish. I put some breadcrumbs in the bowl. The fish wouldn't touch them though. Mother had already started to sing " Dear Little Buttercup," but when she sat down she started a hymn and I knew she was feeling religious and that she was trying as hard as she could to stop worrying about Dad and the major himself.

Gyp wouldn't rest. He knew there was something wrong. He kept moving about the room, cocking his ears and sniffing. There must have been a steamer out in the bay. Every now and again we could hear it blowing its horn because of the fog, but apart from that and the ticking of the clock on the mantleshelf there was no sound at all whenever Mother stopped singing or talking. There was no wind. The sea must have been almost dead calm. I thought that everyone in the village except those who were out looking for the major must be in their houses with their doors locked for fear he might come and attack them, and I was getting more and more frightened.

I imagined Dad and Mr. Beecham and the other coastguard walking along the fields in the fog, and the major suddenly springing out at them. Madmen were supposed to be stronger than ordinary men. The major must have been strong to have knocked Mr. Macdougal unconscious. Mr. Beecham would have his sword-stick, but before he could use it the major might easily have attacked Dad and killed him. His walking stick wouldn't be much use.

But I also imagined the major coming to our own door, bursting it open, rushing upstairs and attacking us, and both of us gave a jump when Gyp suddenly barked and we heard footsteps coming down the street. Mother got hold of me and held me tight. They got nearer and nearer until they were just opposite our door, but they didn't stop. They went on down the street, and then all was silent again but for the blowing of the steamer's horn.

We sang hymns, and Mother read aloud from the Bible, but she kept to the psalms, and didn't read out the bit about the Gaderine swine again. She left off to start getting supper ready when it got to eight o'clock, which was really my bedtime, only I knew she wouldn't want me to go to bed until Dad came home.

And it had got to nearly nine o'clock when Gyp barked again, and there were foosteps getting nearer and nearer, and this time actually stopping at our door. And then there were three loud raps.

We all rushed down, with Gyp barking, but although there had been three raps, Mother didn't touch the door until she had shouted :

" Who is it ? "

And we heard Dad answer :

" It's me, of course ! "

He came in, and he shut and locked and bolted the door himself.

His boots and clothes were wet and muddy. He looked very tired and worried, and he didn't speak until he was sitting in his chair by the fire and Mother had started to help him off with his boots, although we were both anxious to learn what had happened.

Then he said :

" The major hasn't been found. We had to give up the search. The fog's so thick you can hardly see your hand in front of you. But they've found the major's horse. It was on the railway line about a mile away from the vicarage. One of the farmers found it. It must have leapt the wooden fence. Every field on both sides of the railway has been searched. The vicar himself has been out looking, shouting his son's name, in the fog. He didn't seem a bit afraid for his own safety. When he was told what had happened he gave orders that if anyone did find the major, they had to be gentle with him, no matter what he did."

" The poor vicar ! " Mother said. " Oh, I do feel so sorry for him."

" Yes," Dad said. " I'm sure that everyone does. Even Mr. Beecham said how he admired him, and that he would have gone on looking for the major all night, if he'd thought it was any good. The vicar was persuaded in the end by Doctor Whittle to go back to his house. The sergeant said he would stay there all night and mount guard, but the vicar told him he must do no such thing, that he was going to leave his front door open, and that nothing would please him more than for his son to walk in. He would have lamps alight in every room. But the sergeant and Mr. Perkins are going to keep watch all the same outside the house, and the coastguard and of course Tom Binns. There's no telling where the major is. The horse may have thrown him, and he might be lying unconscious somewhere. He might be wandering about in the fog. Everyone will be out again to look for him at daybreak."

" What about Mr. Macdougal ? "

" It's not serious with him. He'd recovered consciousness when Doctor Whittle got up to the vicarage. It seems that he and the major had just had a fight, with bare fists, and the major had given him a knock out blow on the face. But his nose is broken and he'll have to go to hospital."

I didn't like Mr. Macdougal, and although I was glad to hear he hadn't been killed, I felt a bit pleased that the major had beaten him in a fair fight.

We started supper. Dad was hungry, but Mother wasn't and although I knew she wasn't so frightened, now that Dad was safe home, I could tell that she was still listening for footsteps in the street and thinking the major might have actually got into the village.

When supper was over she said it was getting very late and that I must hurry off to bed. She lit my candle, but she asked Dad if he would take it and go first, and would he make certain that the yard door was bolted. As there was no way into the yard except by this door, unless someone climbed the cliff from the beach, I wasn't afraid of that. But Gyp wanted to go out, and when he had been I was glad when Dad bolted it.

While I was undressing, Mother hummed a hymn. I knelt down and said my prayers. As I didn't know what to say about the major I just said, " God protect everyone on this dark foggy night " which was what I had heard a chapel preacher say once, only I added " especially the vicar."

" I am sure he will protect all of us," Mother said, as I jumped into bed. " I am sure there is nothing to be frightened of. But I'll leave the candle in the washbowl, instead of the night light."

She tucked me in, kissed me good night and went downstairs. As soon as she closed the living-room door I called to Gyp, who had been pretending to be asleep in his box, and he jumped on to the bed. He curled up near my feet so that I could soon feel the warmth of his body. Soon I heard Dad and Mother going to bed, and I was glad their bedroom was so near.

But I didn't feel a bit sleepy. Although I tried to think of all the other things that had happened during the day, like the stalls in the dock, and the goldfish, and the coconut shy and the sports and the greasy pole, and then coming home and hearing Mother's good news, and then Dad's about selling the portrait of Baden-Powell, I couldn't stop thinking about the major, and feeling frightened.

I imagined him having his fight with Mr. Macdougal. As he hadn't been allowed to shave he would now have quite a long beard, and his hair would be long too, and that would have made

him look more terrible when he'd had his brainstorm. I bet
that Mr. Macdougal must have been terrified of him and tried
to run away instead of fighting back. Perhaps he hadn't tried to
fight back, and had just said that to excuse himself for letting
him escape.

Then I remembered the nightmare I'd had about the major
walking into the church and cutting off the vicar's head, and I
thought of what Dad had said about the vicar actually leaving
his front door open, and that nothing would please him more
than having his son walk in, although he must have known that
he would try and murder him.

I wished that I could feel sleepy and stop thinking. I wished
that instead of it being so still and quiet, I could hear the sound
of the sea. I wished that it could be a real storm, with the wind
howling and the big waves crashing on the cliff foot and making
the house tremble, as it had done the night of the wreck, after
the men had been rescued.

I wished that everything could have been different, that the
major instead of being mad, could have been a real hero, so that
his father could have been proud of him, and lived with him
happily at the vicarage for years and years, until at last the vicar
himself died of old age.

I wished that even now some wonderful thing could happen,
as it had done in the miracle of the madmen living among the
tombs. That the major could do something very brave like
rescuing someone from drowning. That another storm could
come on, with a wreck.

I started to imagine this happening, that the lifeboat gun had
been fired, with everyone in the village rushing down to the
dock. The storm was even worse than the one when the ketch
had been wrecked. The waves were enormous, the wind blowing
with terrible force.

The ship was on Cowling Scar, just where Neddy Peacock
had been rescued. The waves were washing over her. The crew
were in the rigging, shouting for help, and praying. The vicar
was among the crowd in the dock. But the tide was up, with the
great waves rushing up the slipway, and although the lifeboat

house doors were open and the coxswain and crew in their life-
boats, the boat wasn't being moved.

The coxswain was looking out to sea, and he shouted :

" It's no use. We can't pull out through seas like them. We'll
all be drowned."

The vicar got hold of him and shouted at him angrily :

" You've got to do it. It's your duty. You're a coward. If
you won't do it then someone else must. I'd take her myself if
I was a younger man. Isn't there some man here who will do it ? "

And then I imagined the major himself, not with a beard or
looking mad, but just as he was in Dad's portrait, young and
strong and brave, coming to the vicar's side and saying, quite
calmly :

" I'll do it. Come on, everyone. Get the boat launched. I'll
be your coxswain."

I imagined the boat being launched, and pulling out through
the waves with the major steering, and encouraging the crew and
then returning with all the men of the ship safe on board, and
the people cheering and the vicar shaking the major's hand and
patting him on the back.

And that was as far as I got with what I was imagining for a
church bell had started to ring, in a very funny way. It wasn't
slow and regular, as it was for a funeral, or quick as the vicar had
rung one bell on Mafeking morning, but quick and then slow, then
quick quick again. Then it stopped, and it was another bell ringing, not so deep but going quicker.

I sat up in bed. Gyp was sitting up too, listening. I could see
his ears twitching. Then I heard Mother's voice from the bedroom, saying anxiously to Dad :

" Whatever has happened ? Can you hear ? The church
bells are ringing."

" Of *course* I can ! " Dad answered. " I'm not deaf."

The bells went on ringing in the same crazy way, first one
bell and than another. There were footsteps in the street, and
voices. I thought I heard Henry Newton shouting to someone :

" Eh—what's happening ? "

But just then Dad said to Mother :

" It must be the major himself. He's found his way into the
church and the belfry. No one in their senses would ring the
bells like that. It can't be anyone else. Well, if it is, they'll
be able to get him now. Mr. Perkins and the sergeant and the
coastguard will be rushing along to the church. I'd better get
up and find out."

" No, no," Mother said. " There'll be plenty of helpers without you. Oh, I do hope there is no struggling or fighting, or
anything like that. The poor, poor man. He must have taken
sanctuary. He must have been wandering about in the fog, cold
and wet, and found the church door open. He may have got over
his brainstorm, and not want to do anyone harm. He may be
ringing the bells because he needs help. I do hope they'll be
kind to him."

The bells stopped ringing. I could hear the steamer blowing
again. I was still feeling frightened, but not so frightened as
I had been before, for if the major was in church there was
no fear of him breaking into our house and attacking us. And
perhaps already Mr. Perkins and the others had caught him.
There were footsteps, and voices in the street again. Gyp barked.

I heard Dad say :

" Well, I must get up and find out what is happening. I'll
just go down to the dock and see Mr. Beecham."

" Then I'll get up too," Mother said. " Put the kettle on so
that you can have some tea before you go. But you mustn't
go farther than the dock."

Mother came upstairs, saw me sitting up wide awake and
said :

" You ought to be asleep. Did Gyp wake you up ? "

" I can't sleep," I said.

She put her arms round me.

" Well, there's no need to be frightened now, for we think
the major has been found. Dad is going out to see. But if you
like you can come down to the kitchen and lie on the sofa till
Dad gets back, and Gyp can come too. I'll make you a nice cup
of cocoa."

We went down to the kitchen. Dad had lit the lamp, and put

some dry sticks on the fire to make it blaze up. But he had got his coat on, and without waiting for his tea he went downstairs. He had his walking stick with him. Mother went with him and locked and bolted the door.

Mother made me sit down in Dad's armchair by the fire, and put a blanket over my shoulders. Gyp of course was on his favourite place on the fireside mat. He wasn't curled up though. He was still on watch.

Mother didn't say anything as she set about making the tea and my cocoa. She was humming a hymn, but I knew she was waiting and listening for Dad's footsteps and his three raps on the door.

The bells hadn't rung again. Now and again we heard footsteps in the street, and Gyp barked, but we didn't hear any loud voices. The steamer went on blowing, so that the fog must have been just as thick as ever. The time was nearly midnight. I had never been up so late as this before.

Mother gave me my cocoa. She poured out a cup of tea for herself and sat down in her own chair, just staring at the fire. It was nice and warm and the cocoa made me feel sleepy. I must have dozed off, and it was Gyp who woke me up and Dad knocking at the street door.

Mother went down to let him in. They both came upstairs. Dad was looking very sad, but not a bit frightened. Mother helped him off with his coat, and he sat down in her chair by the fire. She poured him out a cup of tea, and he took a sip at it before Mother said :

" Is it bad news ? Have they found him ? "

Dad didn't look at Mother when he answered. He was just staring at the fire.

" The major has passed away," he said in a shaky voice.

" How terrible. How terrible. His poor father. What happened ? Does the vicar know ? "

" Yes. I haven't been up there, of course. It was the coast-guard who told us all about it. It was the major who was ringing the bells. Poor fellow. No one will ever know how he found his way into the church or why he went there. His mind was deranged, of course. But I remember Mr. Conyers telling me once then when the major was a young man, and home on leave from the Army, he would sometimes go to bell-ringing practice, and join in.

" They found him lying on the belfry floor," Dad went on, his voice still shaking. " There was Mr. Perkins and the sergeant, the coastguard, Tom Binns, Doctor Whittle and the vicar himself, who had never gone to bed. He was half naked, the coastguard said. His shirt was torn to ribbons, his body covered with scratches. He must have been thrown from his horse. He must have struggled through a barbed wire fence."

" Oh, the poor, poor man. Was he dead ? "

" No. The coastguard said he was still breathing. But he was unconscious, and Doctor Whittle said he'd had a stroke. They got the stretcher from the vestry. The vicar insisted that he should be carried to his own house, and he put his own coat over him.

" When they got there, the vicar said he must be put in his own bed, and they did this, and the vicar himself put the bed clothes over him, and tucked him in just as if he had been a baby. And then the vicar ordered everyone, including Doctor Whittle, out of the room. But Doctor Whittle had felt the major's pulse on their way to the vicar's house. And he told the coastguard as they came away from the house, that his life had gone."

*   *   *   *

Mother wouldn't let me go to the major's funeral, as she thought it might give me bad dreams seeing his coffin being lowered into the grave. She wouldn't have gone herself if she hadn't been so sorry for the vicar, and wanted to show her respect for him. Dad had to go, of course. She said that I had better go for a nice walk with Gyp.

She didn't say where I was to go, or forbid me to watch the procession, so I pretended to set off for a walk up the fields beyond the drying ground, but actually I went up the bank and beyond the railway station, and found a place in a field where I could look through the hedge on to the lane which I knew the

procession would take and see it without being seen myself.
I kept Gyp on his lead.

The major was to be buried in the same grave as his mother,
who had died many years ago. This was at the old church,
which was nearly two miles up the hills from the village and was
only used for funerals, and then only for the relations of people
who had been buried there, for the graveyard was full. I had been
in this graveyard several times. Some of the tombstones were so
old that you could hardly make out what was written on them.
Many of them had the names of sailors and fishermen who had
been drowned in Bramblewick Bay. I had seen the one to the
vicar's wife, which also had on it the name of the son who had
been lost in Australia, although of course his body wasn't there.

The place where I hid was about half-way up the lane to the
church. It was the Saturday of Whitsuntide week. The fog had
gone and the sun was shining. I couldn't see the church itself,
for it was hidden by trees. It had only one bell, in a small tower.
The bell was tolling, very slowly. Dad had told us that the
service was going to be conducted by the vicar's friend, the
Marquis of Normanby, who would be waiting at the church
in his clergyman's robes.

There was a sharp bend in the lane below me. I was standing
up, looking towards this, when I saw Dad and Captain Redman,
and two other men who were church wardens, all dressed in
black, walking slowly round the bend, and close behind them
was Mr. Conyers, and all the members of the choir in their
surplices. I crouched down, holding Gyp very tightly. I still
had a good view through the hedge.

Behind the choir was Mr. Beecham, followed by Mr. Tims
and the other coastguards, all wearing their swords and medals,
as they had done the day the major had come home, when everyone except Mr. Beecham and the major himself had been so
excited and happy, with the band playing, and the children waving
their flags. Mr. Beecham had been cross then. Now he looked
just solemn and sad, and I was sure that he had got over all the
feelings he'd had against the vicar, because of *Darky Town*.

Everyone was walking very, very slowly. No one was talking,

or even whispering. All I could hear was the sound of boots on the hard road, some of them squeaking because they were new, and, not very loud yet, the slow clomping of a horse's hooves.

Behind the coastguards came the coffin itself. It was being carried by six men of the lifeboat crew. They weren't wearing their life jackets, as they had been when they'd hauled the carriage with the vicar and the major in it from the station. They were in their Sunday jerseys and walking boots, with only their red tam o' shanters to show that they were lifeboatmen. The coffin was nearly covered with a big Union Jack, and on top of this were piled wreaths and bunches of red and white roses, and I could smell the scent of the roses as the coffin passed close to where I was hidden.

Then, behind the coffin, came Tom Binns, holding the halter rope of the major's charger. The charger's coat was very glossy. The leather and metal parts of the bridle and saddle were beautifully polished. Fixed in the stirrups were the major's riding boots, with silvery spurs on them. They were upside down, to show that they were empty and their owner dead. And the charger itself, which was limping a bit, seemed to be bowing its head, and its big brown eyes looked sad, as though it knew that it would never carry its master again.

Then came the vicar, by himself. He was wearing his long fur-collared coat, and he was bareheaded. He had his silk hat in one hand, and in the other was a big bunch of red roses. He was holding himself straight, walking steadily, looking ahead. There weren't any tears in his eyes. He didn't look really sad : only stern and brave and proud.

Following him were the Shepherds. They were just in their Sunday clothes, without their sashes or crooks or gloves. Doctor Whittle, who looked quite sober, was walking with the chief Shepherd. There were sailors and fishermen and farmers and shopkeepers, for all the shops were closed because of the funeral. Henry Newton was there, and Mr. Birch from the gas-works, and Ikey's Uncle Jake and even Neddy Peacock, with all the coal dust washed from his face, and wearing collar and tie.

Then came Miss Lawson, with the biggest girls from her school, each one carrying a bunch of flowers, and behind them, still coming round the bend in the lane, were more people, mostly women, but certainly more than there had been in the procession from the station to the vicarage the day the major had come home, Wesleyans, as well as church people.

I saw Mother among them walking close to Ikey's mother. Mother looked terribly sad, and as she got nearer to me I crouched and didn't look again until I knew that she had got well past me. I was scared too that Gyp would scent her and bark so I held my hand over his mouth.

At last came the end of the procession. The lane was empty. But I waited, listening to the tolling of the bell, and then I heard the sound of singing. The head of the procession must have reached the gateway into the churchyard. The Marquis would be standing at the church door to lead the way in, as I had once seen the vicar waiting at the new church door to begin a funeral service. It was the choir that was singing as the coffin was being carried inside.

The singing was sad and gloomy. I thought how different everything was to the day the major had come home. Although I would have liked to have seen the Marquis, I was glad that I wasn't going into the church, and that I wasn't going to see the coffin being lowered into the grave. It was sadder and gloomier even than the Queen's memorial service had been, although that was the day when I had first found Gyp.

I stood up, and I turned, and looked down away from the church, towards the bay and the sea. The tide was half-way down, just as it had been then. The sea wasn't really rough, yet when the bell and the singing stopped, I could just hear the sound of the waves on the scar ends. I gave Gyp a hug, and I took off his lead, and with him barking excitedly, I ran down the field. There would be time for a walk along the beach and games with Gyp, before Dad and Mother came home.

27

It was a Saturday in September that Tom Binns brought a message for Dad that the vicar wished to see him at the vicarage where he was now living again.

The summer holidays were over. All the visitors had gone. The salmon cobles and pleasure boats had been launched up the cliff. The fishermen had started long-lining for cod.

It had been a good season for salmon. The weather had been calm most of the time, and none of the fishermen had lost any nets as sometimes happened when sudden storms came on. It must have made Neddy Peacock feel vexed to see boxes of salmon and salmon trout going up to the station on Knagg's cart, almost every weekday, with not a fish from him, for he hadn't been able to find a boat cheap enough to take the place of the one that had been smashed up.

He had been crab and lobster-hunting every low spring tide. He couldn't make more than a few pence this way even when he had a good catch. With the sea being so calm he hadn't been able to get much driftwood either. He looked more grumpy than even when you saw him in his warehouse or carrying bags to his customers who of course didn't need so much coal in summertime. Yet every one knew he had plenty of money, far more than all the fishermen had together.

We weren't so poor now as we had been. Lots of lucky things had happened since Whit Monday when I had won the greasy pole, and Dad had sold the portrait of Baden-Powell, and the major had died. It had been the best season for business since we had come to Bramblewick especially during August. One week Mother had taken nearly ten pounds in the shop. The favourite subject for visitors was the view from the beach showing the coastguard station and slipway, and the cottages on the north cliff, and the bay and Low Batts in the distance.

Dad had painted this so many times that he said he could do it blindfold, and that he was sick of it. He called this, and all the other half-guinea water colours he painted for the shop, pot-boilers, and said that apart from the money they were really a waste of time. If ever he became famous and rich as an artist, it would be with his portrait painting.

Colonel Watson had invited Dad to go and see him one day. I'd felt vexed about this, for although I was sure the colonel would have liked me to go too, Dad said that he must go by himself, as he was sure that it was a business engagement. He had just taken a sketch book with him.

He couldn't stop talking when he got back. The colonel had met him at High Batts station in his motor car, and had driven him to the house. Dad must have forgotten that I'd had a ride in the motor car, the way he described everything about it. He said he had been a little bit nervous at first, but had soon got used to it, and that it was a wonderful sensation. If ever we became really rich he would certainly get a motor car.

He had guessed of course that the colonel had asked him to come to discuss doing a portrait of Penelope. Her mother had dressed her up in her riding clothes with a velvet riding cap, and she had sat on her pony, just to see how she would look. Dad had told the colonel and Mrs. Watson that he thought it was going to make a charming subject, and although he had never painted a pony before, he was sure that he could do it with about half a dozen sittings. He had made a quick sketch, showing the pony's head and shoulders and the girl in outline, and they had been very pleased with it.

They hadn't discussed the money side, but it had been practically fixed that Dad would do the picture. As Penelope was going to stay with some relations in Paris for all the summer holidays he wouldn't start it until the autumn. The colonel had given him a nice tea and driven him back to the station, so Dad had had two trips in the car, while I'd only had one. I don't know how many times he said that Penelope was pretty, which she wasn't.

But Mother, although she said she would never believe that motor cars were safe and that she would never want to ride in one, was pleased about Dad having fixed up to do the portrait. She said that we were now almost all right for the winter so far as money went, and that if the picture was done and paid for before Christmas, we might just have enough to take us to Liverpool for the Christmas holiday. We would have to stay some of the time with Aunt Annie, but have at least a week with Aunt Harriet, and that meant we might go and see a Gilbert and Sullivan opera, if there was one showing at the time.

We would be able to see the docks, and go on the overhead railway and visit the museum and the art gallery, and go into the big shops, one of which was so big that you could get lost in it, and also go in the ferry steamer to New Brighton.

Except for having to stay with Aunt Annie I was very excited about this. The only thing that worried me was Gyp. It would be dangerous taking him to a place as big as Liverpool, with all the traffic. I was certain that Aunt Annie wouldn't like him either.

Dad said that if we went away Gyp could go and stay with Colonel Watson. I thought this just silly, for he would escape at the first chance and run as fast as he could for Bramblewick, and it would be awful if he got to our house and there was no one in.

I had been in the country getting brambles for Mother the day the vicar's message came for Dad. Gyp had been with me of course and had nearly caught a rabbit, which had got into its hole just in time. I had picked enough brambles to make some jam as well as pies, and Mother wasn't a bit vexed that I was late for tea.

She told me about Tom Binns coming, and that Dad had hurried off as soon as he had got himself tidy. He had been gone about an hour. She had no idea as to what the vicar wanted to see him about. The vicar had only been back at the vicarage a week. The house had been done up. All the barbed wire had been taken away from the garden walls. Tom Binns had had two men to help him clear the garden too, filling up the holes the major had dug looking for diamonds and replacing the rose bushes, although it would be next year before they bloomed again.

As soon as Dad came in, we could both tell that something exciting had happened.

He was just like he had been when he'd had the good news about selling the picture of Baden-Powell. He kept on walking up and down the room, saying :

" I can't believe it. I just can't believe it ! "

Then at last he sat down, and he said :

" The vicar has actually agreed to my painting his portrait. And not only that—he has promised to ask the Marquis, next time he sees him, if he will let me do a portrait of him, and give me sittings. The vicar will give me sittings himself."

" How wonderful ! " Mother said excitedly. " Is that why he asked you to go and see him ? "

" No," Dad answered. " It was another matter, and very very sad. He was sitting in the library, and when I went in I couldn't help thinking of the last time I had seen him there, when he was looking forward so much to his son's home-coming. He had the photographs of his two sons still on the table. But I didn't see my portrait of the major. And it was that he'd wanted to see me about. He wasn't in any way upset. He just told me that the portrait had been accidentally damaged, and that he wondered if I could do another one, exactly like it."

" Poor man," Mother said sadly. " I hope you told him you could."

" Of course. And I also said that I wouldn't want any money for it either. It would be a pleasure for me to do it."

" I'm glad you said that. And what did he say ? "

" He said he wouldn't dream of letting me do it for nothing. Actually I think it must have been the major himself who smashed the first one up. Anyway I had the courage then to ask the vicar about his own portrait, for I was thinking then more than ever what a splendid subject he would make. In spite of all he has gone through he looked so noble and proud. He just said yes, and that was when I asked him about the Marquis."

There were tears in Mother's eyes.

" What a good man he is. What a good man. I'm so glad that he is back at the vicarage. That he will have his garden, full of roses again, and at least a portrait of his son to remember him by. You must make it the best portrait you have ever painted. But it's good news for us too."

Mother gave Dad a kiss, and then she hugged me, and started singing " Dear Little Buttercup." I knew what she was thinking about of course, and though I was still a bit worried about taking Gyp to Liverpool, I thought that if I never let him off his lead it would be all right.

THE END